DESTINED FOR MURDER

A NOVEL

BY DAVID MENON

SHADOW PUBLISHING.

Copyright 2022. David Menon. All rights reserved. This is a work of fiction. Any resemblance of any character to any real person, living or dead, is purely coincidental.

David was born of an English mother and an Indian father, neither of whom brought him up. He spent his childhood in Derby but has lived all over the UK and for several very happy years he lived in Paris. He's currently based in St Annes, Lancashire. He loves to travel, he loves Indian food closely followed by French, he's into politics and current affairs and all the arts of books, films, TV, theatre, and music. He's a devoted fan of Stevie Nicks who he calls 'the voice of my interior world'. He likes a gin and tonic in the evening followed by a glass or three of red wine with his dinner. Well, that doesn't make him a bad person.

And he once made a cheese sandwich for the actress Julia Roberts.

David has a YouTube channel on which he's progressively posting videos to do with his life and his books. You can subscribe to it at 'David Menon Books'.

You can also go to David's Facebook page 'David Menon Writer' to find out a little more about all his crime fiction work. He also likes to take his imagination to the other side of the mirror and write books about the contemporary drama of love and family life. Find out more about these titles at another Facebook page titled 'Silver Springs Publishing'. He's also on Twitter as 'David Menon Writer' and Instagram as 'theenglishvisitor', where he's also planning to post photos and videos. You'll also find him on Linkedin.

And you can also go to any Amazon site around the world to find out about any of David's books and that's where you'll be able to buy them too!

This is for anyone who's ever lived on Ramsay Street ... I'm going to miss you.

PROLOGUE

Terry Patterson saw everything.

Nobody cared that he saw everything because nobody cared about Terry Patterson now that he lived on struggle street. Drunks in suits cared enough to kick him where it hurts when they stepped over him. They cared enough to shout out their alcohol inspired accusations at him. They cared enough to spit on him. But that's the extent to which the care he received would go. Then of course there was the Christian do good brigade. The women who never wore make-up and the men who'd never been kissed. They thought that their mission was to bring what they saw as all the lost souls like Terry off the streets and into the loving arms of Jesus. But Terry couldn't accept that Jesus could possibly love the likes of him and that meant that some of the Christian do good brigade would deny him the offer of tea and a mattress in a church hall. Their offer of help depended entirely on him agreeing with their perspective on life. That was the condition they attached to the fulfilling of their Christian duty. And if he couldn't accept that Jesus could love an absolute failure like him then they left him there and moved on to the next one.

But Terry saw everything.

He shuddered when he thought of how he'd got into this

mess. He'd been downwardly mobile since the bank had taken his flat back off him. During a period of eighteen months when he'd got seriously behind in his mortgage payments, he'd come up with three different plans to pay off what he owed them, and he'd failed on each one of them. The bank had just got mightily pissed off in the end. He'd tried to rent a flat, but his credit rating was so bad that no letting agency would touch him with the proverbial bargepole and even private landlords hadn't appeared too keen to do business with him. He'd put that down to the fact that he'd never had the money for a bond or to pay a week or a month's rent in advance. And that tended to put the kibosh on things. He'd once had a large circle of friends, but their numbers had depleted as his life had descended into the nothing that it was now. Even those he'd known for centuries had suddenly lost touch with apparent ease, and that had really hurt.

He'd had a beautiful flat in the centre of Kingsbrook. Two bedrooms. He'd modernised and decorated it to his particular taste and filled it with things he'd collected on his travels that had taken him all over the world. It had broken his heart when he'd had to sell everything before he'd had to vacate the premises. But at least it had given him some cash flow which had meant that he'd been able to stay in a budget style hotel for the first month or so of being homeless. But then the cash had flowed away. He'd had a good job for several years before he lost it. He'd earned good money. But he'd never been sensible with it. He'd tended to use it to fund temporary pleasures instead of investing in his long- term future. Tomorrow was always something to be dealt with after he'd had a good night out tonight. And he was still too young to access his superannuation. Besides, he hadn't retired.

His parents had long since passed to the other side.

He had family, lots of them. He had three brothers and two sisters. But none of them had been able to clean up their spare room to give him sanctuary even though it had been Terry who'd nursed both of their parents in the final years of their lives. It had fallen on him because he was the only one who wasn't married with a family of his own. He'd done it without question. He'd done it because he'd loved his parents. He hadn't done it with the expectation that he'd get 'paid back' when he needed something. But it did disappoint him that his brothers and sisters seemed to have such short memories when it came to what he'd done for the family. Nothing must interfere with their routines. Nothing must interfere with doing the weekly trip to the supermarket on a Friday even if it was to reach out to their homeless brother.

He'd seen one of his grown-up nieces getting on a train to the city the other day. He didn't go up and speak to her. He was embarrassed about his appearance. He waved though as the train pulled out of the station and disappeared down the track. It made him wonder what she was going to the city for. She'd been on her own and was dressed in a very business-like style, so he'd assumed she was travelling for work. He'd forgotten what she did.

It was his sixtieth birthday today.

He remembered that much about his miserable existence.

But it didn't matter as he sat up on his makeshift bed outside the train station. It was rush hour. People rushing home to Lasagne whilst watching Home and Away or the footy. He started begging people as they ran up and down. He might make enough for a cup of tea. And perhaps even a sandwich. Or a can of lager to feed the stereotypical image of those who refused to give money to beggars. It might also make him feel better for five minutes. Alcohol had long lost its ability to affect his mood for any real length of time.

He was invisible to the world.

But he did see everything.

Including murder.

1.

Never mind how many of them had come after him. Whether it was one or twenty it didn't really make much difference. He would have to fight for his survival no matter how many of them there were. Ethan had been terrified that this would happen. He'd tried to play the game. He'd tried to lie low. Keep his head down. Watch what he said and who he said it to. He hadn't wanted any connections to be made. He hadn't left any opening in the things he'd said that someone's imagination could climb into and draw the right conclusions.

But someone was there now. Someone was in this house and was intent on doing him harm. Otherwise, why would they be there? And why would he have heard them creeping about? Why hadn't they just knocked on the front door like a normal person? Why hadn't they responded when he'd called out? Why had he left that back door open? Because it was bloody hot. The middle of summer. That's why he'd left it open. But in doing so he'd left himself open to whatever their intentions might be. He'd been careless. Whoever was there hadn't come to grab a beer and have a catch up. They'd come here to kill him. They'd come here to take him out.

They'd come to stop him talking about what he knew.

What he'd seen evidence of.

What he'd seen that had taken him to the edge and back again.

He was aware of the increasing pace of his breathing. How could he not be? It was starting to feel tight in his chest. He could feel the sweat begin to pour out of the unseen crevices of his skin. He could feel his legs begin to shake involuntarily. He wanted to piss. He wanted to piss himself. But he wouldn't give them the satisfaction of seeing that. They would consider it a triumph. They would rejoice in striking that kind of fear in him. They would see it as a battle won inside the greater war.

It was silent in the house. No breeze blowing through the open windows. He should never have left those windows open. What was he thinking? All he could hear was the sound of passing traffic. Neighbours coming home or going out. Kids thinking it was all just one big playground. Exhausted parents looking on to make sure the kids didn't come to any harm whilst all the time going back in their minds to a time before they'd had them. Exhausted parents who were too tired for sex and had put that side of their relationship on hold until the kids were older and wouldn't be so immediately dependent.

He wondered if the day would ever come when he'd see it all too.

Why should he not just because of what others were so intent on hiding?

Why should he conform to their twisted logic that was drenched in evil?

He stood there waiting. He had his back to the wall just beside the door that led into the living room from the hallway. He could hear him. It must be a him. It was never a girl. This kind of industry was one of the last bastions of sexism. A girl could never be someone who might be required to kill. He could hear him breathing. He could hear him take each step. He could almost hear him wondering where the enemy was. Was he waiting to ambush him? Was he waiting to make an example of him?

Then Ethan saw it.

He saw the end of the gun start to appear and progress slowly through the doorway. He then saw the fingers of the hand that was holding it. The hand was firm. It was steady. A steady hand at the end of an outstretched arm that was pointing straight ahead. The other hand was clasped around the wrist of the gun holding hand. Whoever that hand belonged to wanted to know if his prey was there and waiting to trap him.

Ethan decided to take his chance.

He reached out and used his fist against the gun holding hand. The gun dropped to the floor. With the force that came from the element of surprise, he smashed his intended assailant's right elbow against the frame of the doorway and pushed the lower arm backwards so that his elbow snapped. He saw the excruciating pain burst out on the man's face. He dropped to the floor and then Ethan stamped on the man's broken elbow. The agony inspired screams he gave out were deafening as he writhed about.

'Fucking bastard!' the man managed to throw out between gasps of agony.

The man passed into unconsciousness and Ethan took that as his opportunity to pick up the gun that the man had dropped and run outside. He saw two other men come chasing after him, also with guns in their hand, and he managed to run through the garden of the house on the other side of the road and out onto the road behind it. He flagged down a passing car and when they slowed down to avoid knocking him right over, he jumped into the back and shouted at them to drive on.

The man was driving. The woman was sitting in the front passenger seat. The man put his foot down but both he and the woman looked shocked and bewildered. A stranger with a gun in his hand had just jumped into the car they'd been paying for these past three years. They'd just dropped her mother off. They wanted to catch the Channel 7 news. Or the Channel 9 news if it was their favourite presenter. Then they'd open a bottle of wine and make dinner. What the Hell was all this about?

He hadn't taken early retirement for stuff like this to happen.

2.

Fawcett Drive was shaped like a 'U' and connected at both ends to the main highway heading north out of Kingsbrook. Detective Sergeant Jason Farrell of the NSW police was accompanied by one of his two usual sidekicks, Detective Senior Constable Zoe Dawkins and she was driving. She pulled up a couple of properties short of where the crime scene was located. There was quite a crowd gathering outside number 17 which was where they were heading. It looked like the usual mixture of sticky beaks from the neighbourhood mixed with a growing number of members of the press, including Ellis Stratton who Farrell immediately recognized as being from the Kingsbrook Courier. He didn't blame the local people for wanting to know what was going on. A murder had taken place within their community, and they wanted to know what it was all about. Should they feel safe in their beds tonight? It was the fervent nature of the press that got to him at times but there was no meat for these crocs to chew on yet. The area seemed pretty ordinary. Immaculately kept gardens. Fences that were mostly painted white. They'd passed a playing field surrounded by overhanging giants of trees just before turning into Fawcett Drive and that had been straight after they'd gone past a row of shops that included a milk bar, a McDonalds, and the constituency office of the local representative to the NSW state legislature, Andrew Phillips who was from the Liberals. No doubt there would be a dry cleaner's and a florist in there somewhere but at this moment, Farrell had no inclination to confirm that.

Farrell and Dawkins made their way through the gathering

audience and successfully avoided all the questions. It wasn't time to get into all that yet. Not until much more was known about what might've gone on here. The house was, like all the others around it, all on a single level and surrounded by a veranda that was two steps up. This was where they were joined by the third member of their threesome, Detective Constable Ryan Markovic. He'd already been there for over an hour doing all the preliminary work on this brand- new investigation. It was always the junior officer who formed the advanced detective party. Farrell had never seen himself as any kind of traditionalist, but this particular workplace custom seemed to work and however innovative he liked to be he also believed that if something isn't broken then don't waste time trying to fix it. He and Dawkins donned all the protective blue nylon covers for all their clothes, including their shoes, so as not to contaminate the crime scene. Markovic had been in them since he arrived.

'So, what's been going on here then, Ryan?' Farrell asked once they were all 'dressed up' and ready to proceed. He looked around for the forensics investigator, Dean Robson, but he was nowhere to be seen at that precise moment even though Farrell knew that he must be around somewhere.

'I'll warn you both' Markovic cautioned with a nod towards the inside. 'It's not pretty'.

Markovic had really impressed Farrell when he'd worked up from uniformed Constable on the first case Farrell had worked on after he'd arrived at the Kingsbrook cop shop, and that's why he'd fought like Hell for Markovic to be given the opportunity to permanently fill the space in the investigative team that Kingsbrook had sorely needed. He'd had to fight the NSW force hierarchy, not to mention upsetting the police federation that represents police officer's interests, because it meant that Markovic would have to jump a couple of stages in the promotion process to take the role, but nobody else at Kingsbrook had wanted the job and couldn't care less about the leaps over them that Markovic would be making. There was a part of Farrell that hadn't liked that obvious complacency in the uniformed ranks at the station at which he was commander. He'd seen complacency lead other officers into some horribly bad decision making or indeed, to no decision at all. He wasn't going to let that happen here and would keep an eye out for it. But just in terms of Markovic, and the potential he'd seen in him, which was subsequently backed up by the evidence of his performance, Farrell had allowed the complacency of others to lead to him getting his way in the end. Markovic would still have to attend a course at the police academy in the city, but Farrell was putting that off for as long as possible. And he knew that Markovic himself wasn't looking forward to going on it. He was more of a practical hands-on kind of learner rather than a classroom textbook devotee.

Markovic led Farrell and Dawkins into the living room of the house. There was blood and the stench of death everywhere. Two people, a man and a woman, had been tied to two dining chairs that had been placed back- to- back in the middle of the floor. The hands and feet of both of them had been bound together using thick black tape with their hands resting on their laps. It looked like the tape had also been used to gag them with. Rope had been wrapped around each of them and then extended to bind the two chairs together. Whoever had done it all had done a pretty thorough job, Farrell thought. They'd been shot in the head, and it looked like it had been done at pretty close range. They looked like they were in their mid to late fifties and Farrell assumed they were a couple from all the pictures of them he could see around the room. There were also pictures of what looked like their grown- up children and their partners, and of a little boy about three or four who Farrell took to be their grandson. Happy family shots. Barbecues. Sitting on beaches. If Farrell wasn't mistaken there was more than one that looked like they'd been taken in and around the town of Echuca on the NSW/Victoria border.

His parents had taken the family there a lot when him and his sisters were kids and he'd been there a few times with his own daughter Sapphire too. There was also one where the couple were either side of the little bloke who looked like their grandson, holding his hands as they lifted him up in the air. They were all laughing, and it looked like he was loving it.

'You weren't joking when you said it wasn't a pretty sight, Ryan' Farrell commented. 'Do we have any ID for the victims?'

'Yes, boss' Markovic began in a solemn voice. 'Mr. Glen and Mrs. Rosemary Hathaway. They've been married for thirty-five years. They have two grown up children, Scott, and Lena. Both are married and live here in Kingsbrook, Scott has one son, but Lena doesn't have any children. It was Scott Hathaway who found them. He's sitting outside on the back veranda, but I don't think he's in any fit state to be interviewed just yet, boss. He's in deep shock. His wife Joanna arrived a few minutes ago and is with him'.

'Well, whoever did this made quite a mess,' Dawkins said. She'd flinched when she'd first seen the victims. It was pretty hard core. She'd never get used to seeing people who'd been victims of utter savagery and she was glad about that. She wouldn't want to get too hardened by the job and what it brought her into contact with.

'Too right there, Zoe' Farrell said, looking around. 'This was a room where happy family memories were made. Now it's been turned into an execution chamber, and nobody would ever remember the happy times anymore'.

'And you say it was their son Scott who called this in after he'd found them, Ryan?' Dawkins asked of her best mate Ryan. She and her boyfriend Sadiq had been over at the home of Ryan and his husband Max, a local schoolteacher, at the weekend. They'd all got pretty wasted, mainly on wine, which was particularly funny where Sadiq was concerned because he didn't drink much so when he did go for gold, he ended up being pretty hilarious with the state he got into.

'Yes' Markovic answered. He sometimes only had to look at Zoe and they'd both burst into giggles. But they were very professional at work. At least they always tried to be. It didn't always work. 'He'd dropped in on them for a cuppa like sons do'.

'Was there any sign of a break-in?'

'No. No sign of a break-in at all. We've found what looked like his wallet and her purse on their bedside tables and it doesn't look like either of them have been touched. The bank and credit cards are still there, and cash is in each of them which, when combined, adds up to about a hundred and ten dollars. Apart from this room the rest of the house is tidy, boss. It certainly doesn't look like anyone has gone through the place. It doesn't look like anyone has been looking for anything. Everything looks like it's where it should be'.

'So, it doesn't look like a robbery at all then' Farrell ruminated aloud.

'Then what were the murderers after?' Dawkins wondered. 'A late middle- aged couple in the burbs. What the Hell could the motive have been to create this horror show?'

'I've ran them both through the system' Markovic said. 'They're both absolutely clean. Nothing on either of them'.

'Let's go through and speak to Scott Hathaway' Farrell said who then stepped forward to lead the way. 'I agree with you Ryan that this is probably not the best time to interview him as such but at least we can make contact'.

Dawkins and Markovic followed Farrell through to the back where Scott Hathaway was leaning into the arms of his wife Joanna who was holding him tight. It was a sight that was familiar to all three of them when rellies were trying to come to terms with what had happened to their loved ones. Scott Hathaway looked pretty smart. Expensive looking suit, same with the shirt. He'd loosened his tie and unfasted the top two buttons. Highly polished shoes that also looked like they'd set him back a bit. He must've come straight from work. Farrell wondered what he did. The BMW parked outside was his too apparently. His wife had caught Farrell's eye too and not just because of the cut above casual clothes she was decked out in.

'Mr. Hathaway?' Farrell ventured cautiously. He then introduced himself, Dawkins, and Markovic before explaining that they would be the team who would be investigating the murder of Hathaway's parents. 'I'm so sorry for your loss, Mr. Hathaway'.

Hathaway took a few moments to compose himself before answering. 'I don't understand' he said, his face reflecting how utterly broken he was feeling inside. Broken. Bewildered. Completely unable to take in what he'd seen. He'd lost all focus. His mum and dad. His dear mum and dad. They'd been such good parents to him and his sister and yet they'd met such a horrific end. How could that be right? They'd never done any harm to anybody. 'My mum and dad were beautiful people. I just don't understand how something like this could've happened. I don't understand why'.

'We're at a total loss, detective' Joanna Hathaway said in a faltering voice as she held on to her husband. 'My husband is right. My parents-in-law were beautiful people. You have to find who did this. I know you must get people saying that to you all the time, but you really have got to find out who murdered my in-laws'.

'We will certainly do our best, Mrs. Hathaway' Farrell responded in a quiet but determined voice. 'Mr. Hathaway, we understand you have a sister. Have you spoken to her?'

'I have' Joanna Hathaway told them. 'Lena and her husband are on a kind of adventure holiday up in the Northern Territory, looking at wildlife and whatnot. That's very much their thing. I managed to get through to her on the phone and as you can imagine, she was distraught when I gave her the news although I didn't go into all the details. I just said they'd been found dead, and it looked suspicious. I didn't want her to know anymore until she got home. They're flying back from Darwin as we speak. They were lucky that it's a day when Qantas have a direct flight to Sydney. They just made it, otherwise they'd have had to change planes at either Brisbane or Melbourne. Their car is at the airport, so they'll drive straight back here'.

'Okay' Farrell said who then began to phrase the routine question he always had to ask in these situations. Routine but it always made him feel like a complete drongo. 'I appreciate how difficult it is, but Mr. Hathaway, can you think of anyone who would want to do this to your parents?'

'No!' Hathaway emphasized. He stared blankly at Farrell as if he'd just dropped from Mars or something. 'I can't understand it. My parents didn't have enemies. They were just an ordinary couple who loved each other and loved their family. I don't know how we're going to tell our son that he won't be seeing his beloved Grandma and Grandpa again. It's going to break his little heart'. He buried his face in his wife's shoulder and she wrapped her hands in a caress around the back of his head.

'My brother is looking after our son Barney at the moment' Joanna Hathaway said. 'He'll probably stay with him tonight and we'll pick him up in the morning'.

'Okay' Farrell said. 'We'll leave you for now, but naturally we'll stay in touch and if you can think of anything, however insignificant you think it might be, then please tell us. In the meantime, we'll be working as hard as we can to get to the bottom of what happened here. I promise you that'.

'Thank you, detective' Joanna Hathaway said who looked like she was pleading with Farrell, Dawkins and Markovic to just leave them alone. They would talk to them. But not now.

The three detectives walked back into the house where the teams were continuing to work away. Farrell couldn't help thinking that, despite the obvious affection they were showing for each other, there was something strangely amiss about the young Hathaway couple. Was the affection genuine or just put on for the crowds? Farrell couldn't put his finger on it, but he suspected something. He mentioned it to Dawkins and Markovic who both said that they'd had the same feeling. That there was some kind of chill in the displays of affection. If there was something to be discovered about them then it would flag up in the investigation.

'What's the story so far with the neighbours, Ryan?' Farrell then asked.

'The neighbours on one side, number 19, are a Mr. and Mrs. Murphy, both similar age to the Hathaway's and like them, both retired, and were both at home but didn't hear any disturbance of any kind and certainly no raised voices or cries for help' Markovic explained.

'Seriously?' Dawkins exclaimed who was also wondering how the killers managed to come and go without being noticed. 'That just doesn't make sense. The neighbours must've heard or seen something that they can tell us about?'.

'The curtains were drawn' Markovic said. 'No surprise there. The killers wouldn't have wanted an audience but it's not unusual anyway when the sun is beaming straight into your living room'.

'What about the neighbours on the other side, Ryan?' Farrell asked.

'They are a Mr. Alexander and a Mrs. Olga Chernenko, both originally from the Ukraine but both with permanent residency here in Australia now'.

'I'll bet they're relieved about that given what's happening in their home country right now,' said Dawkins. 'I saw it on the news last night. It's terrible what's happening over there'.

'It certainly is' Markovic agreed. 'Anyway, according to the Murphy's they're an absolutely delightful couple in their thirties, both working full-time, and they're in Adelaide right now attending the wedding of two other Ukrainian immigrants. They're not due back until the day after tomorrow but I'll get it all checked out by then'.

The forensics investigator, Dean Robson, walked over to where Farrell, Dawkins, and Markovic were standing whilst they went through their deliberations. Robson's team were all over the site with their cameras and recording with their tablet computers.

'What have you got to tell us, Dean?' Farrell asked.

Robson used one of the paper towels that his mother had given him that morning to wipe his forehead free of the sweat that came with taking his more than ample frame around. He'd actually put on more weight recently, but he was reacting with his usual blind eye approach by doing absolutely nothing about it and claiming that he was more than content with his life as a thirty-two- year- old man who still lives at home with his mother and has never had sex. His job gave him a reason to communicate with people. Otherwise, he rarely initiated conversation with anyone.

'This to me looks like a contract hit, detective' Dean asserted. 'They were professionals who knew exactly what they were doing'

'I agree, Dean' Farrell said. He'd been thinking along the same lines. 'And they must've used a silencer on the gun'.

'We'll keep on going through the place as diligently as we can' Robson went on. 'And there's not a whole lot to go on so far. But we'll keep on trying, and we'll get the bodies down to the lab for the autopsy which we'll be doing later'.

'Okay, thanks Dean' said Farrell who watched Robson walk away and couldn't help amusing himself by thinking that if Robson's backside was one of the local houses, he'd struggle to get a mortgage on it. He shared his joke with Dawkins and Markovic, both of whom had to stop themselves from bursting out laughing. Nothing like a bit of humour when you're in a room with two people who've had their heads blown off.

3.

The Kingsbrook cop shop had been almost completely transformed in recent months. An upstairs had now been created covering half the length of the entire building and making use of some of the cavernous space provided by the absurdly high ceiling. Farrell had sometimes wondered if the original intention had been to create a ground and first floor inside, but that for some reason they'd altered the plans. Maybe they'd run out of money? But whatever, he was happy with the new geography of the building. The first floor included the investigative team office which included a team briefing area, plus interview rooms and a private office for Farrell. Not that he used it much. He was rarely seen sitting in there and was more often than not in the main investigations team office with whoever else was there. Dawkins, Markovic, or both. It was just after nine on the morning after the bodies of Glen and Rosemary Hathaway had been found. Kingsbrook was nervous. Cold blooded murder in the suburbs tended to do that to a small town.

It was halfway through the morning when Farrell came into the office. He was a late show because he'd attended the autopsy of the two bodies that they'd found at 17, Fawcett Drive. It had confirmed what they already knew in that the victims had been shot in the head at close range and would've died instantly. There was no trace of any tranquilising drugs in their bloodstreams which had led Robson to conclude that they must've been fairly obedient as they were being led to their deaths.

Or had been made to be obedient.

'They were probably too terrified to do anything other than what they were told' Farrell began as the three of them sat around the table where they held their meetings during cases. He'd already stuck pictures of Glen and Rosemary Hathaway on the white board at the far end of the long rectangular table that dominated the room. 'That's why there was no sign of a struggle'.

The team were joined by uniformed Senior Sergeant Joel Stringer who believed that an incident on the afternoon of the murders and in the same vicinity was connected to them. He stuck a map on the white board of the area he wanted them to focus on.

'Boss' Stringer began after Farrell had sat down. He placed his fingertip on the relevant parts of the map that he wanted the detectives to focus on. 'Gun shots were heard coming from a house here at 47, Park Street yesterday afternoon. A man was then seen running across the street and into the garden of number 38 on the other side. He was carrying a gun of some kind and he was being pursued by at least one other gunman. He fired into the space behind him at least twice according to the residents and the gunfire was returned. He ran through to the house that backed onto number 38 which brought him into the garden of 27, Mountain View Road. A man called Nick Silverman lives there but was at work at the time that all of this was going on. But his neighbour, Kirsty Walker, at number 25, was at home and saw the man run out into the road in front of an oncoming car which had to break sharply to avoid knocking him down. He jumped into the back of the car which then sped off. It was being driven by a late middle- aged couple'.

'The Hathaway's'.

'It seems likely, boss since the car in question was identified as a red Toyota Camry and I understand that's the make of car that was registered to the Hathaway's?'

'Yes, I can confirm that' said Markovic. 'It has to be them, boss'.

'And boss, if I could also add' Stringer went on. 'Kirsty Walker gave us an impression of the man who she saw jump into the car that is pretty much a match for the photograph from the driver's license of the man who was being pursued'. He put the photograph and the artist's impression of the man seen by Kirsty Walker side by side on the white board. 'We retrieved the license and other personal belongings from the house at 47, Park Street'.

'There's definitely a likeness' said Dawkins.

'I agree'. said Farrell. 'So, who is this man who lives at 47, Park Street, Joel, and what do we know about him?'

'His name is Ethan Morgan, boss' said Stringer. 'We know about him, and he's registered in the system, because of three speeding tickets that almost cost him his license. He has no other criminal record but interestingly, he'd been working for Barnett Holdings for the previous five years since he left university, in their company accounts section. He was fired from his job because he supposedly broke company confidentiality rules, but Barnett Holdings have not revealed how he allegedly did that. And he was taking them to court over his dismissal, but he suddenly dropped the case without warning and apparently without giving a reason, and it was after that he tried to break into the house'.

'Interestingly though, boss' said Dawkins, raising her eyes from the computer screen she'd been looking at. 'Guess who the director of human resources at Barnett Holdings is?'

'Anthony Albanese?'

'Even better. It's Scott Hathaway. The son of our two victims'.

'Really? Then he would know all about Ethan Morgan's strife with Barnett Holdings'.

'Well as head of human resources, how could he not know?'

'Well, we'll certainly have to question him about it'.

'And it was the disturbance that was reported at Morgan's house yesterday afternoon that caused him to run, boss' Markovic added.

'But were the Hathaway's in their car in the nearby street purposely to give this Morgan guy an escape or were they commandeered by him on the spot?' Dawkins wondered. 'And who were the intruders at Morgan's house that made him run and who then pursued him? Were they something to do with Barnett Holdings and if so, did Scott Hathaway know about them?'

'I agree that we need to make a couple of stretches here if we're going to try and see if it all makes something of a complete picture' said Farrell who didn't think they were quite at that point yet. 'Joel, the occupants of the house where Morgan and his pursuers ran through the grounds? Have they been able to give any descriptions on whoever they may have seen?'

'No, boss. It all happened before they even noticed and when they heard the gun shots they got down and laid themselves low. The only description we've got is that of the man getting into the car that stopped and which looks like it was Ethan Morgan'.

'And I suspect that Ethan Morgan has gone to ground?'

'Yes, boss' Markovic confirmed. 'Nobody has seen him'.

'We need to search his house' said Farrell who was beginning to feel like they might just be getting some kind of hold on what might be going on here. There was still a long way to go yet though. 'I'll get Dean Robson and his team to do a DNA sweep too. We'll issue a warrant for Morgan's arrest. He is now our prime suspect for the murders of Glen and Rosemary Hathaway. I also suspect he might be able to tell us who his two pursuers were and why they were after him. Did anybody see what happened to Morgan or anyone else involved in his pursuit, Joel?'

'Not from what we've gathered so far but we're keeping a

presence down there, boss' said Stringer. 'But I think it would be useful for the uniformed team on the ground to take a picture of Morgan and ask people directly if they've seen him or if they know him'.

'Agreed, Joel, and thanks again.' said Farrell. 'Stay with us whilst we look at what else we've got on all of this'.

The room was small, but it suited them. Previously, it wasn't always easy conducting murder investigations downstairs when they were positioned behind the main desk where people came to report that their cat had gone missing. It also created more space on the ground floor for the uniformed cops to spread out a bit, so everyone was a winner.

'Now, forensics have just about completed their sweep of the Hathaway house and they've found five sets of DNA inside' said Farrell. 'Presumably two of them will belong to the Hathaway's themselves but they're going to run them all through the system later today. I suspect that one of them will be that of Ethan Morgan'.

'Boss, I've also asked Dean if he and his team would check for DNA in the Hathaway's car too' said Markovic.

'That was a good call, Ryan.' said Farrell. 'Considering we're now more or less certain it was their car that picked Morgan up'.

'Well boss, I checked the red Toyota Camry when I first got to the house and the front end was warm, suggesting that it hadn't been long since it was used. This could be confirmed just by what we know about Ethan Morgan running from his pursuers and apparently getting a lift from the Hathaway's, but it's also borne out by what I've found out about Rosemary Hathaway's mother. She lives in an assisted living gated community for the retired with thirty houses, each with only one bedroom. It's called Eden House and the residents are kept an eye on by a team of staff and there's a community hall where they hold functions and classes and stuff to keep the oldies occupied and I suppose try and prolong the onset of dementia. You get the idea'.

Farrell laughed. 'Sounds like I should get my own olds moved in there.'

'Where are they this week, boss?' Dawkins asked. She knew how notorious Farrell's parents were for not growing old gracefully. Well fair play to them Dawkins thought. They should keep it going as long as they can, and she also knew that Farrell thought that too.

'They're being a bit boring this week really, Zoe' Farrell answered. 'Just a bit of mountain climbing near Christchurch over in New Zealand'.

Dawkins smiled. 'Nothing too strenuous then?'

'No. Piece of bloody cake. It is for them anyway. They're fitter than I am. So, Ryan, Rosemary Hathaway's mother lives in this Eden House?'

'That's right, boss, and the manager confirmed to me that both Glen and Rosemary Hathaway visited Rosemary's mother, Patricia Green, earlier yesterday afternoon and that they were in their car'.

'I presume Patricia Green has been told about what's happened?' Dawkins asked.

'Yes, she has' said Markovic. 'No surprise but she's apparently in pieces. But what is of primary relevance to our investigation is that all visitors are timed in and out of Eden House because they have to pass through the gates in both directions. They confirm that the Hathaway's drove out through the gate at approximately 1510 yesterday afternoon. Now, Scott Hathaway says he found his parents just before five yesterday afternoon and his call to us came through at two minutes past five. Which means that these murders took place within a slightly less than two- hour timeframe'.

'Then the killers must've been organised' Dawkins said. 'And they must've been certain that the Hathaway's were their target'.

'And boss' Stringer began. 'All of this makes the connection with Ethan Morgan even more believable. Eden House is at the bottom of Mountain View Road and the Hathaway's were heading up Mountain View Road away from Eden House when they picked Ethan Morgan up'.

'Well then all of these dots are starting to be joined up'. said Dawkins.

'We'll issue the warrant' Farrell said. 'And in the meantime, we also need to talk to the daughter. And talk again to the son too. This was in no way some random attack. It was too vicious and too precise for that and besides, nothing went missing. They went to the Hathaway's because of what they thought they could tell them. They weren't interested in making a few bucks from what they could find. And we need to find out who was connected with who. Was Morgan working with whoever else was in the Hathaway's house? Were they the same ones who'd been chasing him?'

'And still it comes back to what would a couple like the Hathaway's know that would get them murdered?' Dawkins said. 'They hardly seem like gang material'.

'Well let's hope that Ethan Morgan can fill in the gaps for us'

'Or could it be a case of mistaken identity?' Dawkins suggested. 'Could there be another couple of the same age in Kingsbrook who are getting away with it tonight? I mean, although it seems unfathomable that the Hathaway's were involved in anything they shouldn't, we also know that not all of our oldies are upright citizens, no matter how respectable they might seem on the outside'.

Farrell smiled. 'I certainly get that, Zoe. Anything significant from canvassing the neighbourhood around the Hathaway's house yet, Ryan?'

'Not yet, boss' said Markovic. 'But we have got more on the Hathaway's themselves. Both were retired. Rosemary used to work at the Riverside High School as an administrator. Glen

Hathaway on the other hand worked for the Kingsbrook Courier. Not as a journo. He was production manager who made sure each edition got out and was distributed on time. He'd been there his entire married life and both he and Rosemary retired about nine months ago'.

Farrell inwardly groaned at the thought of a connection with the Kingsbrook Courier and this murder, however tenuous or remote that link might at first appear to be. The Courier had been part of the first investigation Farrell had been involved with after he'd been transferred to Kingsbrook almost a year ago. It had turned into an extremely messy and pretty nasty situation involving police involvement in historic child sex abuse in the town. And although Farrell had won plaudits for sticking his neck out and exposing the bastards, by the same token he was also sure that some in the force would probably not spit on him if he was on fire. Dobbing on your colleagues was not done even if they had been sexually abusing children.

'What we also now know is that the Hathaway's didn't own their house, boss' Markovic went on.

'Then who did?'

'Barnett Holdings'.

Farrell pulled a face. He hadn't heard of Barnett Holdings until he was told that Ethan Morgan had worked for them but left under something of a cloud. Dawkins decided to fill in the gaps that had obviously appeared in the boss's thinking.

'Boss, the Barnett family live in the house on Stony Hill that overlooks the whole town from the west' Dawkins explained. She knew the boss would probably not know about the Barnett's because he was from the city. But they were very much part of Kingsbrook life. 'It's the one you can't help but see when you look up in that direction'.

'Yea, I know which one you mean' Farrell concurred. 'It is pretty impressive'.

'It does kind of dominate the town, a bit like the parliament in Canberra which I'm sure they modelled it on knowing them'.

'How do you mean?'

'Boss, the family arrived here from the UK straight after the second world war and are believed to be related to or are members of the British aristocracy. Nobody knows for sure. They keep their lives very private and have never really involved themselves in the community. Same as nobody knows why they came out here, but they must've brought a lot of cash with them because they now own about ten percent of all residential properties in Kingsbrook and have a portfolio that includes ownership of many more across the rest of New South Wales and into Victoria. They're one of the wealthiest families in the whole country actually'.

'And nobody knows much about them even in this day and age of social media and the internet and all that?' Farrell questioned. 'Seriously?'

'They're good at covering their tracks, boss' Dawkins confirmed. 'Always have been and they're second generation in Australia now'.

'Third, actually' Markovic corrected.

'I must've missed that email' Dawkins quipped and exchanged a friendly wink with Markovic. 'There are all kinds of stories obviously. From the unbelievable to the downright bizarre. Some say they were extremely wealthy criminals who'd used their connections in the high end of British society to escape charges of some kind, and some say they were aliens who jumped out of a spacecraft, and they couldn't get home for some reason. There was an actual UFO sighting in Kingsbrook in early 1946 which fits with when they arrived here, so all the crazies put the two things together'.

Farrell laughed. 'Well alien or not let's make a point of going to see them. There might be something they can tell us.

I mean, how long had the Hathaway's been renting off them? Presumably all the time they'd lived there?'.

'Exactly that, boss' Markovic confirmed. 'Thirty-one years'

'Okay, well look' Farrell continued. 'I need to go and talk to the press and tell them about Ethan Morgan and the warrant that will be out for his arrest and why. After that there are several people now that we need to go and talk to, and we can't do much more than that until we track down and arrest Ethan Morgan and get those DNA results so we can see what they tell us'

As the meeting dispersed with Dawkins and Markovic heading for their desks to get organised for the rest of the day, Farrell asked Senior Sergeant Stringer to hold back for a moment.

'How's it going at the coal face, Senior Sergeant?'

'Well apart from the day- to- day flow of criminal activity I've got a couple of open cases, boss' Stringer answered with a slightly amused look on his face. 'But nothing I need to worry you about at this stage and certainly nothing that hints at being tied to this murder investigation'.

'And what's going on with you, Joel?'

Stringer shrugged his shoulders. 'You know me, boss'.

'Yes. And that's why I asked'.

4.

The thing that Oliver Townsend hated about taking the flight from London to Australia was that if you pick one that leaves London in the evening then, with the time change, you'll land in the lucky country early on the morning of the day after tomorrow. But you're not able to check into your hotel until the afternoon so you have to face filling several hours when all you want to do is curl up somewhere and have a little snooze.

But Oliver would have to concede that landing at just after five in the morning is also pretty cool in some ways. It means you can watch the sun coming up. It means you can walk through the international arrivals' terminal at Sydney airport and it's as if another light goes on with each of your steps or another shop opens or McDonald's opens and beckons you in a loud enticing voice and suddenly all you want is a sausage and egg McMuffin with cheese even though you've been stuffed to the limit on the twenty-odd hour flight from the other side of the world. He grinned as he thought of his mate Toby who wouldn't be seen dead in McDonald's because he saw it as 'food for common people'. Toby was the biggest snob and yet was proud to vote Labour. A good friend but a total hypocrite. But as Oliver succumbed and tucked in to his McMuffin, with coffee and a side of hash browns, he was loving every mouthful and outside it did feel like the city was coming alive even though jet lag was making him feel like death.

He caught the airport train through to Circular Quay in the city. He only had a smallish case which was on wheels. He liked to travel light. He only brought the minimum of the clothes he thought he might need on his trip, and he especially only brought the minimum of underpants. He'd much rather buy underpants whilst he was away than have a bag of dirty ones that he'd worn, sitting in his case. He did indulge in an over the shoulder bag but that was to carry the necessary personal bits and pieces like his laptop, his tablet computer onto which he'd downloaded heaps of music and books, his passport, tickets, and a notebook and pen that he often found useful. He liked his technology, but he still preferred to keep an old-fashioned paper diary that he bought from the Cancer Research Trust in memory of his dear old mum. It had been three years since the breast cancer had claimed her as a victim. He still missed her. Like mad at times. They'd been close. His dad had recently met a woman called Annette with whom it looked like things might be getting serious. He was pleased for his dad who hadn't wanted to know about meeting another woman for the first couple of years he'd been a widower. The grief over losing Oliver's mum had ripped through him like the sharpest knife. But in these past few weeks he'd been out with a couple of ladies that people had set him up with. Annette was the first one who seemed to have started to matter to him. Like cooking Sunday lunch together matter. Like going shopping together matter. Like staying over matter. Like planning a weekend away together matter. Like watching telly holding hands on the sofa matter. With a bottle of wine. Oliver knew his mum wouldn't have wanted his dad to spend the rest of his life on his own. He was only fifty-eight and hopefully had years ahead of him. And neither Oliver nor his sister Phoebe would want his dad to spend those years being lonely. He still liked to go to the pub for a beer with Oliver though. Usually once a week or so. And Oliver hoped that would always be the case because he and his dad really were best mates.

He went down the escalator at Circular Quay station and walked to the front of the main drag in front where all the green and yellow ferry boats depart from. It was well into commuting time and the boats coming into Circular Quay were packed out with folks heading for work in the CBD and other parts of

Sydney's inner city. The boats going out to places like, amongst others, Manly, Mosman, and Parramatta, were almost empty in comparison. It was just the way it was at this time of the day. He stood there and watched it all happen with the opera house to his right and the magnificently imposing harbour bridge up to the left. It was warm but it was also rather cloudy. The blue sky wasn't much in evidence yet although he could see it trying to show itself in one or two places. He loved the view. As he stood there admiring it, he was reminded of the first time he'd seen it over ten years ago, when he'd come down to Australia as part of the travelling that he'd done during his gap year between school and university. It had taken his breath away then. And it still did now. He lived in Windsor back in the UK and had a view of the Castle from his back garden making him a near neighbour of Her Majesty herself. It was all very nice, but he preferred the view in front of him right at this moment. Besides, he thought the monarchy was a very tired old concept in this day and age and totally drowning in misplaced sentimental bollocks. If he was an Australian, he'd vote for it to become a republic next time they have a referendum. Mind you, he'd voted to 'remain' in the UK's referendum on membership of the European Union. So, he didn't have a great track record of being on the winning side when it came to referendums.

With his brain as scrambled as it was from the jet lag, he turned and walked into the City Extra café where he could sit at one of the outside tables and have the same view he'd just been enjoying. The café was built underneath the elevated track of the train line that had just brought him from the airport. He ordered some raisin toast and a flat white. He looked at his watch and couldn't believe that it was still only ten past eight. Then he decided to quit being so tight with himself. He wasn't rich. He'd been through medical school and was now practising as a GP back in Windsor so he was on a pretty reasonable salary which meant he could indulge himself now and then. So he decided that once he was done here at City Extra, he was going to walk round to his hotel up in the Rocks. He could almost see it from where he was sitting. He'd go up and see if he could check-in this morning by paying for an extra night. Hang the expense.

He'd been to Sydney several times. He'd come to spend two or three weeks in Australia every year. He considered himself lucky that he was able to do that. And when he was in Sydney he always stayed at the Mercantile. It was an Irish pub with rooms on the main George Street in the Rocks and a two- minute walk up from Circular Quay. He much preferred its very local informal style to some big swanky place that was part of an international chain. Again, he thought about his mate Toby who vehemently asserted that he simply couldn't stay in anything less than a five-star hotel. More pretentious bollocks from Toby but he did have a good side to him, and he had given Oliver a lift to Heathrow to catch the flight down here. But Oliver would much rather stay in a hotel that was locally owned and run rather than some giant edifice to worldwide corporatism that had no distinguishing local features and, once you were inside, you may as well be anywhere in the world.

The last time he'd stayed at the Mercantile it had been St Patrick's night and with it being an Irish pub it had been absolutely packed to the rafters. They'd had a three- piece band playing Irish folk songs and the atmosphere had been tremendous. Oliver still didn't know how he'd got back to his room that night or if he'd been alone when he did. The next morning he'd woken up, alone, with the absolute hangover from Hell and had not got around to doing anything he'd planned to do that day. A great night though.

As it happened the girl on duty that morning recognised Oliver from his last visit and, after a yarn with the manager, she only charged him fifty percent of the extra night's rate and checked him in to the first room that morning that had been cleaned and serviced. It was basic but it had a lovely big bed, clean toilet and bathroom, a fridge, a TV. What more did he want? And it was at the front of the building, so he had a view of the Opera house on the other side of the Quay, although slightly obscured by the building on the other side of the street. He looked to the right and could just about make out the Zia Pina pizzeria further down the street. That's where he'd go for dinner tonight. It was a small Italian where he'd always found the food and the service to be excellent. He'd probably have one of their Aussie pizzas with a topping of egg, bacon, and sausage. Maybe some squid to start. He really liked it in there with its red check tablecloths and bare brick walls. The atmosphere was always good.

Yes, he'd eat at the Zia Pina tonight.

Nothing wild on this trip though.

He'd need all his wits about him for the business he had to do.

He'd need all his wits about him for when he got to Kingsbrook.

5.

Farrell's mood wasn't lifted at all as Dawkins drove them to the offices of the Kingsbrook Courier. He'd met the current editor Ralph Mancini half a dozen times since he'd taken over and didn't like him. He didn't like him at all. A feeling that had been further entrenched in Farrell's psyche when Mancini had tried coming on to Farrell's daughter Sapphire in the pub one night. And right in front of Farrell for fuck's sake! Sapphire had been alright about it. She'd actually laughed it all off. But it had taken Farrell all he had not to deck the dirty bastard. He was a thousand years older than Sapphire for one thing and indeed, that should've been enough for him not to see a girl in her late teens as some kind of potential sexual conquest. Especially when she was the daughter of the town's chief police officer. He'd had some bloody nerve. Farrell and his daughter were close. They always had been.

'I'm no big fan of this Mancini character, Zoe'.

'Because of him coming on to Sapphire in Ned's Place that night? You've got every reason for him not to be at the top of your Christmas card list, boss. I was there that night and I wanted to put the bastard out too'.

'She's a grown woman but she's still my little girl' Farrell admitted with a grin.

'You're her dad and you'll always be protective of her, boss. Even when she's married and has got kids of her own, you'll still feel it'.

Farrell could feel himself blushing. 'You're probably right, Zoe'.

'Isn't she supposed to start university soon?'

'Don't' Farrell said. 'She's talking about putting it off again because of her relationship with Dylan. I mean, he's a great young man and all that and very dedicated to building his internet business which is already making him heaps of cash apparently. But I want Sapphire to have her own career, Zoe and make her own heaps of cash. You know?'

'I do'.

'I don't want her to play second fiddle to some man's career'.

'I get that, boss. Really, I do'.

'Look, I shouldn't ask' Farrell began after he'd decided to make reference to the fact that his daughter Sapphire worked as a waitress at the café that Dawkins' boyfriend ran. 'But do you know if she's been talking to Sadiq at work about it?'

'He hasn't said, boss'.

'It would put you in a difficult position if he had though and I understand that. I shouldn't have asked you. I just don't know what to do for the best, Zoe. I can't insist that she goes a certain way because I don't have the right to do that. I've never agreed with parents dictating to their kids about what they should do with their life. But especially with a daughter I wanted her to believe that she can achieve just as much as any boy could. You know? She's clever. She's intelligent. There must be heaps of opportunities out there for her. I don't want her to give up on going to look for them'.

'I can appreciate how hard it is to let go, boss. I really can'.

'You'll find out yourself one day when you have kids of your own'.

'I'll have to ring you up for advice'.

'You do that. And Zoe, thanks for listening to me going on'.

'Anytime, sir. I'll always be ready to listen'.

'You're a good mate, Zoe'.

'It works both ways, boss'.

'Especially when I'm buying in the pub, right?'

'That's when you're everybody's best mate, boss'.

Dawkins always enjoyed her drinking sessions with her workmates, usually Farrell, and Markovic, but often also including one or two of the uniformed station bound officers too. Senior Sergeant Stringer was nearly always part of the group if he'd finished for the day. It was always in Ned's Place which was the pub just around the corner from the Kingsbrook cop shop and nobody ever got totally wasted. And nobody had enough class to get what Aussie rockers INXS had once called getting 'elegantly wasted'. Most people had two, sometimes three at the most, before they all went home. It was just a way of taking the pressure off the day and 'bonding' as a team. But the thing was that her boyfriend Sadiq had been dropping hints lately that he'd love it if she just came straight home to him at the end of the working day. He wanted them to start thinking about marriage and babies. And it wasn't that she was against that. Sadiq would make a great husband and a great dad. She wasn't even put off by the potential difficulties of marrying the culture of a Palestinian refugee with her own Aboriginal culture. Indeed, that would be something that she would celebrate. She embraced diversity as being such a positive thing. She'd come from the most marginalized section of Australian society. Her people were at the bottom of the social heap and Sadiq understood that, coming as he did from a homeland that had been occupied for decades by a foreign power that had done the same to his people. She'd fought her way into the place she'd found in contemporary Australian life, a place that had eluded too many of her fellow Aboriginals and she wanted to hold onto that for as long as she could. She knew that Sadiq would prefer her to be a stay-at-home Mum, but she earned more as a police officer than he did from running the café. He owned the lease but not the building and had to really watch his profit margins. He loved his work. But Dawkins loved hers too.

'I wonder why the Hathaway's rented their house for all these years?' Farrell ruminated.

'Not everybody craves the responsibilities of a mortgage, boss. I mean, the thought of it hanging round your neck for the next twenty years is too much for some and they prefer the freedom of being able to come and go'.

'What are you and Sadiq going to do? Carry on renting?'

'Not sure yet' Dawkins admitted. 'Neither his family nor mine are in any position to help really. On his side there's only his mum anyway'.

'What happened to his dad, Zoe?'

Dawkins paused to take a deep breath before answering. 'The occupying Israelis built one of their illegal settlements on the West Bank, close to where his family lived. But it meant that the journey to school for some of the Palestinian kids would then take two hours whereas before it only took twenty minutes. And I'm talking each way'.

'You're joking?'

'I'm not. You see, it meant that the kids had to go through various Israeli check points that they hadn't had to before.'

'How could any of that be right?'

'It's only right in the book of the Israelis and every American President. Anyway, it led to protests on the streets by the local Palestinian population. His father was part of it. None of them were armed but the Israelis opened fire, and several were killed, including Sadiq's father'.

'I'm so sorry, Zoe'.

'No Israeli soldier was ever charged with anything but there is no justice for the Palestinians'.

'And the world doesn't seem to do anything to help them'.

'Nothing at all. Because Palestinians don't matter. Israelis do but Palestinians just don't. That's why when Israel launches attacks on Palestinians the world says that Israel has a right to defend itself. But when Palestinians fire rockets into Israel they're called terrorists. Even though the Palestinians are being illegally occupied by Israel. And what gets to me, what really gets to me boss, is that Sadiq is such a good man that he hasn't let his bitterness cloud him to the fact that there are two sides here. He supports the right of Israel to exist. He just wishes that Israel and every American President would also support the right for the Palestinians to have their own viable state too'.

'He's a good man, Zoe'.

'He is and he's not the only one, boss. But it suits the approach taken by Israel and every American President to ignore Palestinians like Sadiq and concentrate solely on those who advocate violence to achieve their legitimate aims. It's the same as some white Australians who concentrate their view of Aborigines as drunks and wife beaters and ignore positive contributors to greater Australian society like me'.

'I've been so bloody lucky compared to some others, Zoe' Farrell said. He had been lucky. He knew that. He knew that growing up white in Australia meant that he got first choice at the table. It had to change though. It really had to. And he was doing his best in his own little piece of this big world to make that change happen. 'I'm your average white guy who grew up in the burbs within a loving family and was given a fair go at everything'

'But at least you recognize that, boss. A lot of people who've had your upbringing wouldn't. They wouldn't see that others have to fight their way to that fair go simply because of the colour of their skin and their cultural background. You should be proud of yourself'.

When they got to the premises of the Kingsbrook Courier it all seemed very different from the last time they were there when Gina Carter was editor. Farrell had never thought that Gina was a bad person. She was just a tart with a heart who'd got herself in too deep with a romantic situation that she ultimately had no control over. She'd just wanted to be loved and to matter to someone. There was no law against that. It's what everybody wanted even if they didn't admit it. And Gina was the kind of person who would never have admitted to it.

'Do you want me to do the interview with Mancini, boss?' Dawkins asked with a knowing smirk as they walked through the reception area of the Kingsbrook Courier building.

'No, you're okay, thanks Zoe' Farrell answered, smiling. 'I can play nicely with Mancini'.

Mancini looked serious and was serious when it came to the business of the newspaper. His clothes were neat and had been carefully pressed. His tie was just the right length for the bottom tip to be just crossing the line of his trouser belt. His black leather shoes were polished enough to the extent that you could probably see your face in them. His wedding ring was glaring at Farrell. He clearly didn't take his vows seriously but then Farrell couldn't throw stones from his own glass house on that one. But then again, Farrell hadn't been unfaithful to his wife until after he'd found out that she'd been unfaithful to him, not that he thought that was any excuse really, but it was a form of mitigation. And to be fair, he knew nothing of Mancini's home situation other than he was married. But he had come on to Farrell's daughter so that's what made him a total slime bucket.

'Now the last time you two came to see the editor of this newspaper, she ended up being forced to watch her lover being murdered' Mancini said with a half- smile. 'I hope you haven't brought the same omens with you today'. He sat down at his desk and asked Farrell and Dawkins to do the same on the other side facing him. 'But ignore my feeble attempts at humour. I presume you're here about Glen Hathaway?' He shook his head. 'I can't believe what's happened to him and Rosemary. Even a hardened old hack like me is struggling with it. We all are'.

'Did you know him well, Ralph?' Farrell asked.

'I did actually' Mancini answered, looking almost surprised at the question. 'He retired barely three months after I took up the reins here but yes, I got to know him pretty well and we still met up for a beer now and then, usually along with a couple of the other retired or senior members of staff. He reminded me a lot of my dad who I lost to cancer a couple of years ago. I really am pretty shocked and saddened by it all. Rosemary was a lovely woman. I know that people always talk glowingly about people when they die and overlook the truth that they were an absolute arsehole when they were alive, but it's true in Glen's case. He was a good one. He really was. Never had a bad word to say about anybody which is what makes what happened so unfathomable'.

'When did you last speak to him?'

'About a week ago. We'd arranged to meet up, but I'd had to cancel because I had to attend a meeting in the city with the new owners of the paper that came about at the last minute. We'd made a new arrangement for this coming Thursday'.

'Ralph, is there anything you can tell us that might help the investigation?'

'Absolutely not. As a newspaper we are of course covering the story and conducting our own investigations. I knew Glen Hathaway. And I want justice for him and Rosemary as much as you do, detective. That's why the picture you've released of Ethan Morgan will be going on the front page of our next edition. We can support each other's efforts here, detective. I'll certainly be doing that from our side'.

'Did you cover the dismissal of Ethan Morgan by Barnett Holdings?'

'We did a short piece on it, but the fact was that Morgan wouldn't talk to us about it'.

'Do you know if he was talking to another paper?'

'I don't think so' Mancini mused. 'He seemed to be scared of his own shadow when our reporter went to see him and got nothing that we didn't already know, all of which is in the public eye. I doubt he'd have had the nerve to talk to one of the big boys'

Kingsbrook cop sergeant Mary Chung had been at her usual place all morning sitting at the desk just inside the front door which was the first contact anybody coming into the station had with any police officer. Farrell had asked her gently on occasions not to be quite as disparagingly strict and hard faced with everyone who came in. Some were victims and needed reassurance and sympathy. His talks with her had worked. She had been adopting a demonstrably softer tone with some people, like the old lady who came in and was distraught after some little shit of a youth had snatched her purse as she came out of the local Coles supermarket.

'I always count my cash after I come out of a shop' the lady had appealed in a fragile voice after Chung had sat her down and was holding her hand. 'I like to reassure myself of what I've got to spend and what I need to save some for. I'm the same when I take some money out of the bank machine on the wall. But this young boy snatched the lot this morning. A hundred dollars it was. He'd taken it and was well away before I really knew what had happened. It made me almost glad that my Harold passed away last year. He'd have gone for the little bugger but that would've probably ended up killing him. As it was, he spent months dying of the cancer that had taken him. It had started in his stomach and spread to his prostate. We'd been married forty-five years. Four kids. A dozen grandkids. A couple of great grandkids too now'.

Chung had hugged the lady almost to within a breath of her dear life and made her at least three cups of tea. She'd even organised a collection amongst the station staff to replace the hundred dollars that had been snatched from the lady. It had ended up amounting to almost 150 dollars in the end. Chung had arranged for two officers to drive the lady home and introduced them to her as 'two of our most handsome fellas in uniform for you'. At least the lady had gone home with a smile on her face as she walked along to the police car in the middle of the 'two most handsome fellas in uniform' who'd each linked arms with her. So Mary Chung had worked out the occasions when it was appropriate to apply soft power. It scored points for the reputation of the police as well as being the decent human thing to do. It does sometimes help to show that human beings inhabit police uniforms.

But one thing that hadn't changed about Chung was that on some days she would bring in enough home cooked food to feed the entire NSW force, let along just the Kingsbrook cop shop. It was all cooked by her husband who sold it in the family convenience store a couple of kilometres outside of the town centre. Today Chung had brought in her husband's Szechuan prawns and egg friend rice, a particular favourite of the squad and it was warming up nicely on the plug-in hot plate in the cop shop rest room that people used to warm food up on. Chung kept the door of the rest room open so she could keep an eye on it before it was time to invite everyone who was there to come and get theirs.

The enticing aromas were satisfying the senses of Senior Sergeant Joel Stringer no end, especially as he'd only popped in to work after a few hours' sleep following a night shift. He was looking forward to grabbing a bowlful of Mr Chung's delicious tucker but in the meantime, because the three detectives were all out interviewing people, he was handed the DNA results from the crime scene at 17, Fawcett Drive. As expected, one set each belonged to Glen and Rosemary Hathaway. A further two didn't have a match on the database.

And the final one belonged to Ethan Morgan.

6.

As he was driving to the home of the Hathaway's daughter and son-in-law, Markovic stole a moment or two to think about his husband Max. It was Max's birthday in a few days and this year Markovic wanted to do something special for him. The poor bugger had been working so bloody hard in his job as a local schoolteacher, trying to inspire the kids to think about pursuing a worthwhile future for themselves. It could be a bloody thankless task. He tried to concentrate hardest on those from less advantaged backgrounds who got little or no encouragement in their education at home. And he did get through to some. He got them to believe in themselves and to believe that they were just as worthy as anybody else of getting somewhere in life. But others were more difficult to reach. The ones who were only interested in going for what seemed like the easiest option. He never gave up on them though. He saw it as one of his duties as a teacher to find the self-belief in his students and bring it out fully into their consciousness. Markovic was so incredibly proud of the approach that Max took to his job, and he wanted to spoil him a bit on his birthday. He had thought about booking a room in some fancy hotel in the city and then taking him for dinner at one of the seafood restaurants in Watsons Bay. They both loved their seafood. But in the end, he'd decided on the idea of going up to Palm Beach, at the very top of Sydney's northern beaches, staying at their friends Rudi and Avalon's b and b and having dinner at the local Barrenjoey restaurant. They loved it at Palm Beach. They loved the food at the Barrenjoey, and it was always good to see Rudi and Avalon. But they were also saving up for holidays in Europe next year. They planned to do London, Paris, and a week on a beach in Spain. So, he knew that Max wouldn't want Markovic to splash out too much. He'd booked some leave to coincide with Max's birthday which conveniently fell in the week of the school holidays, and he made a mental note to ring Rudi and Avalon later and see when they could fit them in. Then he'd book a table at the Barrenjoey asking for the outside lower terrace that overlooked the bay. Yea. That's what he'd do. Then the next morning they could take a long walk along the beach and have a swim before heading home. Sweet.

With his plans for Max's birthday now decided upon he returned his thoughts to the case they were working on. The background checks that had been done on the Hathaway family had come up with a big fat zero. Markovic had agreed with Farrell that they needed to involve the Melbourne police in looking into their chief suspect Ethan Morgan. He was from down there and his parents would need talking to as part of the overall investigation into tracking him down. There was a good chance that he might make contact with them.

Markovic was also beginning to think that the attack on the Hathaway's might've been down to them somehow getting caught up in the wrong place at the wrong time with the wrong people. They could've been complete strangers to Ethan Morgan. But if that was the case then where did he go? Had he been forced to go with whoever had killed the Hathaway's? And if so, then why? None of it made any sense but then Dawkins is always saying to him that it's not their job as police officers to make sense of anything. They had to get the facts and use them as the law required. He knew what she meant although he didn't altogether agree. He thought it was more complicated than that. And to try and make sure of everything, Farrell had ordered that this house, and the one belonging to Scott Hathaway, must be kept under surveillance.

'Can I get you some tea or coffee, Ryan?' asked Lena's husband Gareth in the kitchen of his house. Markovic was standing in there with him, and they'd already agreed to use first names.

Markovic thought it made things just that little bit easier in these situations. It tended to remove the communication barriers that often become apparent. They were waiting for Lena to come downstairs. She'd apparently been having a lie down. Markovic heard the toilet flush upstairs. She must be on her way.

'I'll have coffee, please Gareth' Markovic answered, smiling his gratitude. 'Just with milk, no sugar, thanks. I guess you've taken time off work to be with Lena?'

'Yes' Gareth answered as he moved around the kitchen gathering three large cups for the coffee and looking like he hadn't slept much over the last day or so. He was in a plain dark blue t-shirt and jeans. Green eyes, golden blond hair combed back and sort of parted on the left, a square jaw, a dimple in his chin. He had several bracelets on his left wrist made of various materials, leather, some kind of thread, a silver metal one. On his right wrist was a chunky type of big silver watch. He was tall and slim with a broad slightly athletic frame. Markovic thought he probably went to the gym but to exercise as opposed to pump. His posture made clear that he was carrying no excess fat anywhere. He was straight up and down. No kinks or curves. A good-looking man with a beautiful wife. Markovic hadn't actually met Lena yet, but he'd seen the pictures with his detective's eye after he'd entered the house. Lena and Gareth Sampson were one of those couples who make everybody sick because they're both deadly good looking. They were selfish in that they shouldn't have married each other. They each should've married an ugly person who would feel a whole lot better having one of them on their arm. And they'll certainly make beautiful babies.

'I expect your employers were understanding?'

'Well, I already had a few days of my holiday leave left, so did Lena. We weren't due to be back from the Northern Territory until the weekend. But yes, the company I work for have been very understanding about beyond that and said I can take as much time as I need'.

'Where do you work, Gareth?'

'I work for a marketing firm in the city' Gareth answered. 'I manage several accounts here and in New Zealand. I'm about to take one on in China too. The firm is expanding overseas, and this particular contract will mean me making two or three trips a year to Shanghai'.

'So, you commute every day into the city? On the train?'

'Yea' Gareth said, rubbing the back of his neck. 'It can be a bit of a drag at times to be honest. I don't mind the journey as such, and I love living out here because it's kind of in the country but isn't if you see what I mean. But all of us who catch the 7.58 from Kingsbrook every morning, have kind of got to know each other a bit, and we tend to have a bit of a yarn on the way. And that's fine if you're feeling up for it but sometimes you just want to tell people to shut the fuck up with their totally meaningless shit whilst you catch a bit of shut eye.'

Markovic smiled. 'I can well imagine. Sometimes basic politeness is a little overrated. I take it Lena doesn't commute?'

'No. She's secretary to one of the doctors, Dr Khaled, a cardiologist at Kingsbrook General. He's a really good boss too. Him and his wife came to see Lena this morning to see how she was and if there was anything they could do'.

'That is good' Markovic agreed. 'And how is she?'

'Well … it's bad enough dealing with the fact that your parents have been murdered. But what makes it even worse is that we'd just found out before we went on holidays that Lena is pregnant with our first child'.

'Oh God, Gareth, I'm so sorry'.

'We want to celebrate and look forward to us becoming a family' Gareth went on. 'But it's all been shattered, and I just don't know how we're going to put it all back together. I'm absolutely rapt at becoming a dad but how can I even think about showing that with all this going on now'.

'Did her parents know?'

'No' Gareth answered as he shook his head. His voice began to tremble. 'We were going to tell them when we got back. Same with my parents but they now do know of course. My parents and my in-laws were good friends and met up socially at least once a week. They've been completely thrown by all this too'.

Lena then stepped into the kitchen and immediately fell into the arms of her husband. Gareth ran his hands across her back and through her long hair. He was desperate to take her indescribable pain away but having to settle for knowing that he can't. But they would get through this. He would be the strength his wife needed to get them through it. He loved the bones of his wife and he'd be everything she needed.

'Darling, this is Ryan of the Kingsbrook police' Gareth introduced. 'He's one of the detectives who are working on your mum and dad's case'.

Lena managed a half-smile when she introduced herself to Markovic and then Gareth led them all through to the living room area of the large open plan ground floor of the house. It was all very modern with its exposed brickwork and giant TV screen on one wall. A total contrast to the Hathaway's place. Markovic liked it. It suited his taste, but it would never suit his husband Max. Markovic embraced Japanese style minimalism, but Max preferred a more cluttered look. They'd had their only real arguments over how they would decorate their house. They'd eventually arrived at a compromise, but it had been pretty hard fought. Lena then asked Markovic to confirm that an arrest warrant had been issued for Ethan Morgan in connection with her parents' murder.

'Yes'. said Markovic. 'At this time, he's our suspect but I should caution it is only early days in the investigation'.

'So, you haven't been able to apprehend him yet?'

'No but the warrant has gone nationwide, and we don't know if he's actually left the Kingsbrook area at this stage'.

'Then what can you tell me, Ryan?' Lena pursued in a slightly raised, irritated voice. 'What can you tell me in the way of getting justice for whoever did this evil thing to my parents? Just what can you tell me?'

Gareth rubbed her shoulders. 'Lena darling, we've got to let the police do their job'.

'Gareth, they were shot in their heads!' Lena reminded her husband emphatically. As if he'd forget the details. 'My Mum and Dad who our baby will never meet. I'm so sorry if I'm just a little bit impatient for answers'

'Lena' said Markovic. His heart went out to her. He understood exactly why she was coming across the way she was. He really did. He'd seen it all before. Her beautiful face was etched in anguish. Her soul had been shattered at the same time as she was beginning to carry a new life inside her that she'd created with the love between herself and Gareth. He got it. He really got it and if she wanted to take her frustrations out on him then she could. His back was broad. 'I understand your frustrations, I really do. And I would love to be able to give you the kind of news you're desperate for right now, but I can't. We can't put anything in a time frame at this stage and I'm sure you appreciate me being candid with you rather than offering you false promises'

Lena's shoulders sank. This police detective was sitting there in front of her representing officialdom and yet she could tell that he was trying to put a very human face on it. On what he had to do and where he had to take her. He had to take her to somewhere that couldn't provide the truth that she needed and may never be able to. Her brother Scott had identified the bodies of their Mum and Dad. The whole process had been a thousand times worse for him because of that. Because of how they must've looked which was so unrecognisable to the man and woman that she and Scott had known as their parents. She couldn't even bare to picture it and she knew that it had destroyed the ground from underneath poor Scott. And with all of that considered she knew that she should give this detective something in the way of generosity. She would have to try. If anything, she would have to try so that he could get on with doing his job. After all, it was only the police who could provide the answers that would lead to justice for her Mum and Dad.

'I understand' Lena said. 'I'm just struggling'.

'I know'.

'You say there was no sign of a forced entry into my parents' house?'

'That's right'.

'Which means what?'

'That the killers were either let in willingly or they threatened your parents into letting them in'.

'Oh God' Lena gasped.

'Lena, you've seen a picture of Ethan Morgan. Do you recognise him at all?'

Lena shook her head vigorously. 'No, absolutely not. We've never seen or heard of him before'.

'Neither of us' Gareth added. 'We don't recognise or know anything about him'.

'And now we have the fact that this Ethan Morgan or some other random stranger or strangers somehow got into my parents' house and murdered them on some otherwise normal afternoon. It's hard. It's bloody hard to get my head around'.

'Lena, is there anybody you can think of who could've done this to your parents?'

'Ryan, I've wracked my brain and just can't think of any

reason why someone would want to murder my Mum and Dad' Lena started. She pushed her hair back behind her ears with her fingertips. Her eyes were swollen from all the tears. 'I spoke to one of them at least once a day. So did my brother. We were all very close. If they'd been involved in anything they shouldn't have been then my brother and I would've known'.

'They wouldn't have been able to hide anything from you?'

'No' Lena insisted. 'You read about it happening, but you never imagine for one second that your own family could be destroyed by it'.

'Read about what, Lena?'

'Family secrets. Disgusting and vile family secrets held by one half of the family that the other half only learn about when something devastating happens. But it doesn't happen to families like ours. Not to families like ours'.

'When was the last time you saw your Mum and Dad?'

'It was about ten days ago before we went on holidays' Lena answered with a brief but loving look at her husband. 'Gareth told you I'm pregnant?'

'Yes' Markovic said. 'Congratulations'.

'Thanks, but it doesn't feel much like that given the circumstances' said Lena in a somewhat morbid voice. She patted her stomach lightly as if to reassure her baby that it's mama was still there. 'But I suppose it's a sign that life goes on despite what's happened'. She let her head fall on Gareth's shoulders. He caressed the side of her face with his hand.

'If you can hold on to that belief then it will no doubt help you in what are going to be very difficult days ahead' Markovic warned. 'I presume Barnett holdings will want to take possession of your parents' house back?'

'Yes' Lena said. 'Although they've not exactly been very sensitive about it'.

'They said that they'd give us two weeks after the funerals to clear all my in-laws stuff out of the house and then they'd want to take possession back immediately' Gareth explained. 'Like Lena said, not exactly sensitive'.

'It doesn't sound like it, no' Markovic agreed. 'What was their relationship like with Barnett Holdings?'

'Well, my parents have been loyal and trustworthy tenants for over thirty years' Lena pointed out. 'My brother and I grew up in that house. We have so many memories there and as far as I know the relationship was good. More than good. That's why their insensitivity is so bloody annoying'.

'Do you know why your parents didn't buy their own place?'

'That didn't have much money when they first got married and then when they did, they just thought what's the point? They liked the house and where it was. A good school nearby for me and my brother too'.

'So, the family were very settled?'

'Very' Lena confirmed. 'And the house felt like ours even though it wasn't'.

'It was home'.

'Exactly' Lena went on before her demeanour changed and she started to cry. 'They would've lived out their retirement there. They would've drunk wine on the back veranda and had the grandkids for sleepovers. They already idolised my nephew Barney'.

'And so does his Aunt Lena' Gareth reminded her gently.

'Well,' Lena said as she wiped her face with her hands. 'It's an aunt's privilege. And he'll be a great little playmate for our one'

'My older brother has got two kids who their uncle Ryan idolises but me and my younger brother don't have any kids yet' Markovic told them. He and his husband Max had talked about adopting and definitely wanted to do that, but they hadn't made any firm plans so far. 'But we're both hoping that we'll become parents sometime in the future'.

'Well, we weren't planning it or not planning it' Lena said. 'But we're more than happy anyway'. She turned and kissed her husband. He was still holding on to her as if she'd fall apart if he let go.

Markovic decided that his time would be better spent chasing up the gathering of information relating to the case rather than try and talk to two people who were still profoundly shocked at what had happened. He thanked them for the coffee and assured them that the investigative team would remain in constant touch and keep them updated on how things go.

'And we'll keep you informed in the search for Ethan Morgan' Markovic assured. 'But remember, he may not be the killer. But if he wasn't, he may be able to tell us who the killers were'.

Gareth then saw him to the door.

'Ryan, do you know when we'll be to have the bodies?' Gareth asked after he'd opened the door and Markovic had stepped outside. 'Lena and her brother Scott are anxious to make all the necessary funeral arrangements'.

'It's impossible to say at this time, Gareth, I'm sorry. They probably won't be able to be released until we've completed our investigations. That's not unusual in cases like these'.

'Cases like murder you mean?'

'Exactly. I'm sorry I can't be more precise'.

'Well, I understand but I don't think that either Lena or Scott will understand for long though. I just wanted to make you aware'.

'Okay' said Markovic. 'And listen, be careful of approaches made to you by the media. Let me know if you get into any difficulties with them'.

7.

Senior Sergeant Joel Stringer was used to treading a thin line between being professional and reckless. The reckless part usually came about because he was a married man with four children who couldn't keep it in his pants. He usually managed to wrap it all up in a box and file it away without anyone being any the wiser. He never hid the fact that he was married with four kids from any of the other women he slept with. He never failed to impress upon them that he was a married man with four kids who would never leave his wife and family. And he always tried to keep it all separate from his work as a police officer. Most of the time he succeeded although he had almost come a cropper once just after Farrell had taken over at Kingsbrook and was on his first murder investigation. It was only because Farrell was a fair-minded bloke who saw the bigger picture of stuff that Stringer had got away without losing his job or worse, being charged with something that would lead to him losing everything else too. He really had been that close, and he'd never forget it. He'd never forget the faith and trust that Farrell had placed in him. It had saved his career and every other part of his life.

And he knew that the boss wouldn't rescue him twice.

Her legs were wrapped around the small of his back after he'd entered her and was thrusting away with his hands linked with hers and their arms outstretched to either side. She was always careful not to dig her nails into his back because marks like that would arouse potentially devasting consequences at home if his wife saw them. He leaned down and kissed her neck, tenderly and yet conveying all the lust he was already leaving her in no doubt that he felt for her. She lifted her chin and started gasping even louder than before as she felt him coming up to the finish line. She was wet. She always was with him. Her vagina tightened around his dick and then he was emptying himself into her.

They hadn't used any protection.

They never did.

He trusted her use of the pill to stop him from having a kid whose life he would never be a part of.

'That was beautiful, babe' Tracey breathed after he'd come out of her and turned over onto his back. She turned too and snuggled up to him. She rested her hand in the middle of his chest rug and her nipples were still hard from the sensation of him fucking her and they felt good against his skin. She knew that he liked the feel of them too.

'There'll come a day when I can't even manage to pleasure myself so I'm making the most of it whilst I can' Stringer admitted. It was more than half true. He loved sex. He loved his wife Amy, but he craved variety in the bedroom. He knew that most would label him a bastard for thinking like that, but he couldn't really give a fuck about what other people might think. The only feelings he cared about were those of his wife. His sharpest critics would probably be the ones who hadn't had a fuck since Bob Hawke was PM. Jealousy always provoked the most ardent criticism. People reach a point where they condemn what others can get but they can't.

And yet he knew he shouldn't be playing around with Tracey. She was a desperate girl. Desperate for a normal relationship within a normal life. Desperate for what he couldn't give her. Not that she ever cried on his shoulder or any shit like that. She only ever showed him a bloody good time, but he was wise enough to read between the lines of some of the things she said. When she let her guard down slightly. She'd lost both her parents when she was in her twenties. She's in her late thirties now. She had no siblings. Her extended family were mostly in Sydney, but she didn't seem to have much in the way of contact with them except for a Christmas card. She worked in Ned's Place for the company more than anything. That's where he'd met her. She was behind the bar one night and there was an instant attraction that was mutual. It was her first night of working there. She'd fallen out with the owner of another pub in Kingsbrook and left there when she'd found the job at Ned's Place. He'd managed to flirt and make all the necessary moves without anyone noticing. He'd got quite good at it. He'd had a lot of practice.

'Are you on shift tonight, darling?' Tracey asked.

Stringer sighed. 'Yep. We're still short so I'm having to do some filling in'.

'Can't Farrell do something to fill the gaps?'

'To be fair it's not his fault. He can only go as far as head office budgets allow'.

'I could never do your job. I'd be scared the whole time'.

Stringer held her tight and kissed her head. 'Well, I can't say that I'm never scared'.

'What's the latest on the Hathaway couple?'

'Now you know I can't discuss cases with even naughty girls like you'.

Tracey laughed. 'I thought my charms might lead you to tell me stuff that would put me in the know and therefore the envy of everyone down at the pub'.

'Nice try'.

The sound of a baby starting to cry after he wakes up and wants to see a familiar face came through from the second bedroom next door and permeated their post-coital atmosphere like the firing of a missile from an Australian Navy ship.

At least that was how it sounded to Tracey.

This was one of those times when she wished that desperation didn't lead to her being so accommodating of those who she gave everything to, but who could give her next to nothing in return. Except for a great fuck that is.

'Sorry' Stringer said as he sat up and swung his feet out from under the sheets and placed them firmly on the floor. 'Duty calls.'

Tracey watched as Stringer put his pants back on and got back into his jeans, t-shirt, socks and trainers. He looked good in his casual garb. He looked bloody good in his police uniform. He didn't look good to her as he was obviously preparing to leave. Once he looked respectable again, he went through to the second bedroom in Tracey's house where he'd left his six-month old son, Elliott, who'd been fast asleep at the time, and was the fourth child of Stringer and his wife Amy. The other three were at school and care of all four of their children was split between Stringer and his wife and the two sets of grandparents. Amy had gone back to work in the human resources office of a local engineering company, and this afternoon childcare responsibilities were with Stringer. And he knew that little Elliott would be asleep in the afternoon which is why he'd agreed to coming over to Tracey's house.

'I need to get on anyway' Stringer said as he walked back into Tracey's bedroom with a newly pacified Elliott in his arms. He was with his daddy now. The world was okay even though he didn't know what the world was yet. But it was okay anyway. 'I've got to pick the other kids up from school'.

Tracey got out of bed and put on her silk robe. Only mistresses have silk robes. Wives don't. Only mistresses believe in the power of sex to make you and your man feel on top of the world. Wives think of sex as a means of conceiving the kid they were desperate for or that new dining room furniture they'd seen in some shop.

And they say that prostitutes are immoral? Seriously? Oh but of course she forgot. If you wear a wedding ring it lets you off from behaving like a prostitute inside a marriage when you want something for the house, whilst ignoring your husband's need for sex when there isn't anything you want for the house. Tracey would love to be a wife. But she'd be a very different one from those who are married to the men she sleeps with.

Stringer threw the bag of stuff that all parents of little babies carry with them these days over his shoulder. He kissed Tracey on the cheek and was then out of the door and on his way back to what observers would call his normal family life.

She didn't know when she'd see him again. She'd see him in the pub when he was in there and she was behind the bar, but she didn't know when he'd come round to 'see' her. It would be whenever he could get away and that meant not making any specific arrangements. She just had to wait for his call.

But not for the first time in her life, Tracey's soul began to cry because she wasn't the woman that 'her' man was going home to.

When the family came together for dinner which was on all the nights that Stringer didn't have to be on duty, Stringer loved the feeling he got from them all sitting there. His older two, Bryce aged 12, and Kerri-Anne aged 10 were both now starting to get opinions about things that they'd seen on the nightly news or about which they'd heard Stringer and his wife Amy talk about. Bryce especially was beginning to pick up on the world around him and beyond. He had quite a serious head on his shoulders except when it came to rugby which he was totally crazy about. Kerri-Anne wasn't really into sports but then she wasn't really girly either. She was a bit of a tom boy and Stringer had the feeling that he'd grow closest to her as she grew up. Then there was Madeline who was five and still full of fun and who they thought would be their youngest before nature had intervened and decided to give them little Elliott before it was all too late. Elliott was in his highchair but took a place round the table between his mum and his dad who each took it in turns to feed him his dinner. Stringer's wife Amy had made one of his favourite dishes of hers. Lamb chops that she'd fried and served with baked pumpkin, and potatoes that she'd partly boiled before taking them off the heat. Then she'd chopped them up and mixed them with chopped onions and bacon and then frying it all in a little oil for a few minutes. It was a family favourite, and they were all tucking in enthusiastically, except for Elliott who was eating from his own menu that was more appropriate for a six-month old little person. Stringer was relieved that he was able to place the different parts of his life into compartments that he was determined would never threaten each other. What he'd been up to with Tracey that very afternoon was in one compartment. Being with his wife and family now was in another compartment which was at the top of his emotions. He considered himself lucky. And he hoped that his luck would never run out.

Detective Sergeant Zoe Dawkins shocked herself when she realised that she was feeling rather broody. She was watching Scott and Joanna Hathaway's little four-year-old son Barney splashing about in the pool they had in their back garden. His parents were sat there in chairs at the poolside, both in a t-shirt and shorts, and Dawkins had noticed that Joanna had been pretty thorough in covering her young son in sun protection lotion. It was a bloody hot day with clear blue skies and that was good in one way. But as a parent you had to make sure that your little one didn't fall victim to the nastier side of the good weather. Neither Joanna nor Scott were fussing over Barney in that very paranoid or controlling way that some really fuss pot parents do. They were just looking after him and making sure he was okay. That's the kind of parent that Zoe herself thought she would be. She'd never want to smother her kids and as the thoughts processed through her mind it made her wonder if she and her partner Sadiq should think about starting a family. She knew that he was more than keen and perhaps she was getting to the table quicker than she'd thought. And little Barney here was as cute as bloody Christmas with a highly inspiring smile none of which helped.

'Scott, did your Mum or Dad ever mention the name of Ethan Morgan?'

'No' he replied and rather more impatiently than Dawkins would've liked. It even provoked a look of mild disdain from his wife. 'But he's the guy you've issued the arrest warrant for, right?'

'Yes'.

'So, you must think he did it?'

'He's our only suspect at the moment and we want to question him' Dawkins went on. 'That doesn't necessarily mean he actually committed the murders'

Dawkins wondered why Scott Hathaway was suddenly looking a little uncomfortable.

'But your boss Farrell told me when he called that Morgan forced my parents to give him a lift and his DNA was all over the back seat of their car and in the house'.

'And so is the DNA of two others in your parents' house that so far remain unidentified'.

'So why are you sitting there asking me stupid as fuck questions that you already know the answer to when the killers of my parents are still out there?' Scott raged.

'Scott, that's enough' Joanna chided. She'd gone as red as a tomato. 'Losing it with the detective isn't going to get justice for your parents any quicker'.

'No, but it makes me feel better for just one nano second of the fucking day' Scott shot back at his wife in an evidently faltering voice.

'It's okay, Joanna.' said Dawkins.

'No, it's not okay, Detective'.

'Zoe'.

'Zoe'.

Scott closed his hands together and raised them up to rest under his chin. He stared at the grass that his chair was resting on. Then his eyes looked up and he watched his little bloke playing. This house. This bloody lovely house and all the things in it had been on shaky ground lately. Just like his marriage had been too. He was so bloody glad of Joanna now though. She and Barney were getting him through it all.

'You see, the problem we have Scott' Dawkins began. 'Is that we can find no reason why anyone would want to do this terrible thing to your parents. We're going deep into everything associated with them. Deeper. And nothing is coming back'.

'That's because there isn't anything' Scott retorted. 'We keep telling you that over and over again. The very idea that my Mum and Dad could be involved in anything they shouldn't is ludicrous. Bloody ludicrous'

'And that's why we're putting everything into finding Ethan Morgan' Dawkins stated.

Scott stood up. 'I'm sorry but I can't deal with this anymore right now. I keep seeing my Mum and Dad when I found them. I can't get the image out of my head'.

'That's understandable,' said Dawkins. 'But you're sure you didn't see anybody else?'

'Yes, I'm sure'.

'Nobody driving away as you were approaching the house?'

'No! I didn't see anybody, and the door was shut like it always is and I used my key to unlock it like I'd done a million times before'.

Dawkins then stood up and their faces were level. 'I understand you've given an interview to the Kingsbrook

Courier?'

'And that's why you're really here' he charged with words delivered through clenched teeth. 'To see if I've told them anything I haven't told you'.

'All I'd need to do to find that out is to contact them, Scott'.

'The last time I looked we lived in a free country and if I want to talk to the press then I will'.

He was beginning to seriously piss Dawkins off now. She'd tried the whole empathy and understanding thing and all he'd done was throw it back in her face. So, fuck him. If he wanted to push it, then she'd push it back.

'But the Kingswood Courier are not going to be able to find your parents' killer or killers. We are. The police. So, can I please suggest that you place your primary trust in us? I think you might find that it will ultimately prove to be beneficial to what both you and the police want to achieve here'.

'Whatever' said Scott dismissively before turning and starting to walk back into the house.

'Scott, do you know Ethan Morgan?'

'No' Scott answered as he carried on walking.

'You didn't recognise him from his picture?'

Scott paused but didn't turn round. 'You already know that I said that I didn't'.

'Then how can you say you don't know him when he was recently fired from his job at Barnett Holdings and was taking the company to court over that dismissal which was for allegedly breaking company confidentiality rules'.

Scott stopped and this time did turn round to look at her.

'But then he suddenly dropped the case'.

'I don't know anything about that' said Scott, quietly but with a firmness in his voice.

'But how could that be, Scott? You're head of human resources at Barnett Holdings. How could you have not known about it?'

'I was not aware of it, and I won't repeat myself again'.

Dawkins stared into his eyes. She knew a downright liar when she saw one. 'Well, it will be part of our investigation but if you can remember anything that differs from the account you've already given us about the Morgan court case then it would be in your best interests to tell us'.

Scott turned and paced swiftly back into the house. In a second or two he was out of sight.

'Are you accusing my husband of lying?' asked Scott's wife Joanna. 'You can't be that heartless to ignore the fact that he's still in shock after discovering his parents?'

'I'm not accusing him of anything' Dawkins replied, ignoring Joanna's little dig about being heartless. It wasn't worth responding to. 'It's just that the story he's told us doesn't make any sense. Can you shed any light, Joanna?'

'No' Joanna replied swiftly and without any trace of the warmth with which she'd spoken to her earlier. 'And I think you'd better go'.

Little Barney then climbed out of the pool and Joanna picked him up even though he was soaking wet. He gave her a big kiss.

Dawkins then gave Barney a surreptitious little wave and left them.

8.

Farrell woke up and had the taste for fried eggs on toast for brekky. He showered and got himself dressed and ready for work, but he was dispensing with wearing a tie today. Even though it was the tail end of summer there was something of a heatwave going on which had sent temperatures into the early forties in the last few days. It had been bloody hot. The trash bins at the cop shop were full of empty bottles of water whilst the fridge in the staff rest room was stacked with full ones. The situation had led to the disgust of one of the uniformed constables who was something of a greenie and had chastised everyone for adding to the growing environmental fuck-up with all these plastic bottles when there was water in the taps that was good enough. Farrell could see his point, but it wasn't always easy to find a tap to put your mouth under when you were out chasing villains. The man's heart was in the right place though. Farrell would give him that.

He opened his own fridge door and discovered that they had no eggs. He could've sworn that they did have some. But that meant that his immediate catering plans were in absolute tatters. He chided himself. Very first world problem which meant that it wasn't really a problem at all.

'Morning, dad!' Sapphire greeted as she breezed into the kitchen and gave her dad a kiss on the cheek.

'Morning, darling' he greeted back. 'Listen, next time one of us goes shopping we need eggs. I'll put them on the list'.

They had a small white board in the kitchen that was hung onto one of the two upright storage cupboard doors. Much like the bigger one Farrell had in the team briefing office down at the cop shop. The storage cupboards were set against the wall, one at either end, with the sink, dishwasher, chest height oven and tall fridge between them. The hot plate, working surfaces, and drawers with cutlery, pots and pans, were all on an 'island' in the middle and beyond that was the dining table with six chairs. The washing machine along with iron and board were in a small room to the side. The kitchen and dining area were on the first floor of the house and a floor to ceiling window gave a view of the bush that started just beyond. Farrell loved that view. He loved starting out at it with his first coffee of the day. Daydreaming. Wondering if he still had a marriage left in more than name only.

'Were you looking for eggs for your brekky, dad?'

'Yea. I was going to have them on toast'.

'Well why don't you give me a lift to work, and I'll fix you some there?'

'That'd be great, love, thanks'

'No worries, dad. Lucky for you that I'm on the early brekky shift. So, are you ready now?'

They set off in Farrell's car and he asked Sapphire if she'd heard anything from her mother. His wife called their daughter far more than she called her husband. Not that Farrell got jealous about it. That wouldn't be right. But he sometimes relied on Sapphire to keep him up-to-date with what her mother was doing and where she was doing it. His wife was a make-up artist on film and TV sets and her work took her all over the place. The only thing was that she'd seemingly grown increasingly reluctant to find her way home between assignments. It wasn't new. It had been going on for years. Farrell had virtually brought Sapphire up as a single parent. And neither he nor his wife had faced up to the inevitable.

'She's in Adelaide working on a thing for British TV starring the lovely Jaime Dornan' Sapphire told him with a warm rush going through her voice. 'He's an Irish actor and boy is he hot'.

Farrell smiled. He'd never heard of this Jaime Dornan which was no surprise because he really wasn't up on celebrity related stuff. 'I thought your heart belonged to Dylan?'

'My heart does belong to Dylan, dad. But I'm not dead and I still notice other guys who I think are good looking. Like Jaime Dornan who apparently is happily married and has three kids which makes him even more attractive'.

'Is he back from that trade fair thing in Melbourne?'

'He's back tomorrow' she enthused as she rubbed her hands together with joy. 'I can't wait'.

Farrell laughed. 'I'll bet you can't' Then his voice changed. 'Is your mum planning on coming to see us sometime before the next millennium?'

'I don't know, dad. She hasn't said'.

Sapphire knew that it broke her dad's heart the way mum was so indifferent towards him. She didn't know what had actually gone wrong between them, but she saw more of her mum when she visited her at the flat her mum had rented in the city. She hadn't told her dad about that little development yet. He still thought her mum stayed with Sapphire's maternal grandparents when she was 'too exhausted' to make the journey to Kingsbrook between jobs. Sapphire found it a heavy burden to be stuck in the middle of them though. She adored her dad and would acknowledge that her mum could be bloody selfish in the extreme. But she was still her mum. And she loved her. Even though she could strangle her at times.

'Well next time you speak to her tell her my phone number hasn't changed'.

She placed her hand on her dad's shoulder. He was a tough old cop who'd dealt with all kinds of things that she could never imagine. But he was still her dad. And she hated seeing him hurt the way he did over her mum. Neither of them had been saints. But at least her dad seemed to be prepared to put up a fight to save whatever they had. Her mum didn't seem to be.

'Dad, why don't you and mum sort things out once and for all? Surely, you'd both be better off cleaning the slate and moving on with your lives?'

'Because I still love her, Saffie. I still love her and that's why I just can't give up. That may make me sound like a complete idiot when both your mum and I are leading separate lives essentially'.

Sapphire rubbed her dad's shoulder and smiled resignedly at him. 'You'll always have me, dad. No matter what'.

He briefly touched her hand. 'I know sweetheart. And you'll always be the very best thing your mum and me ever did'.

When they got into town, Farrell drove up the main street and turned right at the clock tower. He then turned right again into one of the nose-in spaces which was right outside the Oasis café where Sapphire worked. Her boss Sadiq with his short jet black hair, dark eyes and gym built muscles was a good looking young guy and also the partner of Detective Senior Constable Zoe Dawkins. He and Farrell always had a good old yarn about this and that. They got on well. He gave Farrell a table close to the main bar counter. Sapphire took over as his waitress.

After his food arrived, Sadiq carried on serving customers and he was also putting up large printouts of the star of David all over the place along with a banner carrying a slogan that Farrell took to be in Hebrew. Farrell was intrigued and between mouthfuls he asked Sadiq what it was all about. He answered in his usual English spoken with an Arabic accent, but which had now taken on a strong Australian twang.

'It is the start of the Jewish festival of Passover tomorrow' Sadiq told him. 'I have a lot of Jewish customers and you'll notice on the menu that there are several Kosher items. I just like to show that I'm grateful for them coming in here and spending their dollars. And that I'm not a bitter man, you know. My people have suffered immeasurably at the hands of the Israeli state, and my own family have been torn apart as I know Zoe told you, but that doesn't give me the right to be against every Jewish person. That would be wrong and stupid. It wouldn't be making any kind of progress. I want my people to have their own state but not at the expense of the state of Israel. We both have a just cause and we should live alongside one another but without one being more powerful than the other. That's all I want. And you know, it's absolutely crazy to think that migrating to the other side of the world has meant that I can now have Jewish friends. Absolutely crazy. It could never have happened back home. The Israelis who populate the illegal settlements on our land justify their actions by telling the world that we're all terrorists. They want us to hate them. But I won't. I just won't. I'm not going to fill my heart with hatred just because it suits their position'.

Farrell watched Sadiq go about his business whilst he processed all of what he'd just said. And he came to the conclusion, and not for the first time, that Sadiq really was a man amongst men. He was sure that Sadiq's murdered father was looking down on him and was justifiably proud of his son.

The final forensics report had been delivered and it supported everything that it had been in the autopsy and in the initial report following the sweep of the Hathaway's house. Fingerprints belonging to Ethan Morgan were found all over the Hathaway's living room where they'd died, but the two mystery guests had been careful to minimise what they left behind of themselves.

'The mark of professionals' said Farrell whilst he sat with Dawkins and Markovic in the team room and repeated what they already knew. 'We're not dealing with your average crim here'.

They had definitely been done over. Bruises on both of

their bodies were identified as the result of high impact blows. It looked like they'd been subjected to some pretty extreme violence before being put out of their misery.

'So did the killers think that the Hathaway's had information that they needed but that they wouldn't pass on for some reason?' Dawkins wondered.

'Or were they genuinely in the dark about what the killers were looking for?' Markovic added.

'Boss, what are we going to do about Scott Hathaway?' Dawkins asked. 'There's something amiss there. Whether it goes as far as knowledge of his parent's killers or not is another thing, but there's something there he isn't telling us. It's like when we first met them and we all thought something wasn't right about Scott and his wife Joanna'.

'I'm planning on bringing him in for questioning, Zoe' Farrell responded. 'And I agree that from what you said about the way he was with you yesterday that there's something he's hiding. I wanted to let him stew for a bit before we sweep in. I've got uniform keeping tabs on him so that he doesn't slip away. We'll bring him in under caution this arvo'.

The canvassing of the neighbourhood around the home of the Hathaway's had brought frustratingly little in the way of tangible results. Farrell was looking over the latest information passed to the detective team by their uniformed colleagues, and it was almost laughable. One woman said she had seen a man speed off in his car from outside the house, but her husband said that she was on tablets due to the onset of dementia and couldn't really be trusted. Then another woman said she thought she'd heard a car speeding off, but her four-year-old son was throwing up at the time, so her attention had been somewhat distracted. It almost made him want to lose the will to live. These murders took place in the late afternoon when people would be walking their kids home from school, coming home after finishing their early shifts, and the retired or those on days off might be in their gardens enjoying the sunshine. Then there was the pair of old ducks who were two women in their seventies and who'd 'shared a house together for the last forty years because neither of whom had ever met their Mr Right. They'd been watching re-runs of 'Sons and Daughters' on one of the cable channels on that particular afternoon because they 'absolutely loved' the character of 'Pat the rat' and missed her from today's TV screens. Farrell thought they were probably a lesbian couple who'd got together at a time when people didn't admit to being in a lesbian relationship and have maintained their open secret even in these more enlightened times.

The breakthrough came with Bob and Janice Cartwright who lived two doors down from the where the Hathaway's had lived. Farrell went to see them with Markovic, and they were immediately reminded of the story of the Cartwrights. With Bob's retirement package from the national electricity supply company that he'd been with for the last forty years, they'd decided to buy themselves a caravan with which they were going to 'tour around the great land of Australia' whilst they were still young enough to have the energy to deal with such a trek. It was the second marriage for both of them. It had been less than a year since they'd tied the knot. They both had children and grandchildren that they were 'blending' together and the previous spouses of both of them had also remarried so there was no bitterness coming from anywhere to spoil the party. Late on the afternoon that the Hathaway's were found murdered they'd left for a short practice run to the Blue Mountains.

'We're still getting over the bloody shock,' said Bob. He and Janice were sitting on one couch in their lounge and Farrell and Markovic were sitting on the other.

'We were friends with Glen and Rosemary' Janice added. 'And for something like this to happen in our neighbourhood is pretty frightening. Bob was saying that he couldn't even remember the last time there was even a burglary on this street. Isn't that right, Bob?'

Bob nodded his head. 'It's always been pretty safe around here'.

'But I feel that now we're going to have to think more carefully about our security' Janice went on.

'We're pretty certain this was a targeted attack, Janice,' said Farrell. 'It wasn't random'.

Markovic noticed how Bob sat further forward on the couch than his wife, presumably to try and hide the extent of his pot belly. Janice was still slim and trim making Markovic wonder how on earth they managed to have sex. That's if sex was part of the deal between them. From the looks of things Bob would split Janice in two or perhaps she always goes on top. But then again would a couple like Bob and Janice know what it meant by the woman going on top? They'd both probably always done it in exactly the same way as when they were married to their first spouses, and since the two of them had been together they'd continued the same tradition. Still, they had their caravan and their trip around the country to look forward to. He hoped the caravan had its own dunny. They didn't want to be stopping in the middle of the outback to bend down and do one in case a bloody great snake went up their arse. But good on them for giving love a second chance. It made him think of his friend Rodger who was sixty, gay, and had always been single. He'd reluctantly decided to accept that it wasn't going to happen now. Sixty in gay years is about 293 and Markovic would acknowledge that the gay scene is very youth and body orientated. Single gay men of sixty were rarely interested in each other. They tended to look for much younger men who liked to date older men because they had daddy issues to work out. Whereas women of a similar age didn't really care if the man they met had a pot belly the size of Tasmania. As long as they weren't desperately ugly and were good company, had a solid private pension plan, a top of the range car, and held doors open for ladies to pass through first, they tended to go for it. Markovic and his husband Max felt so lucky to have found each other in their mid- twenties. They'd met after they'd each been dumped by their previous boyfriends but had clicked straight away and couldn't see past each other now. Markovic's friend Rodger said that it was so obvious that their union was meant to be and that because he'd never clicked with anyone it obviously meant that for him it just wasn't meant to be. And he just had to take it on the chin whilst watching couples all around him being happy together. That's just the way life is for some people. They have to be content with so little.

'But the fact that you don't think it was random almost makes it worse,' said Bob. 'To think that some gang or other would burst into our previously safe and secure neighbourhood because they were after two of the nicest people that we'd ever met is even more frightening in a way'.

'I just can't fathom it' said a suddenly tearful Janice who then linked hands with her husband. 'When I first moved in with Bob, Rosemary took me under her wing a bit and she became one of my best friends. I used to sit with her on their back veranda many an afternoon whilst we put the world to right over a cuppa or two. I'm going to really miss her'.

'And neither of us can even begin to believe that they were involved in anything that would lead to them being killed like that,' said Bob.

'Everybody we've spoken to tells us that, Bob'.

'What did you both actually see happening the afternoon before last?' Markovic asked. He thought he'd try and move things on otherwise they'd be there all bloody day. The tone of the boss's voice in his last line to Bob Cartwright had carried what Markovic had grown to identify as his slight impatience.

'I was just putting the second suitcase into the back of the car' Bob started.

'We like to put them on the back seat instead of the boot so we can see them and keep an eye' Janice offered.

Two suitcases for just a two- night trip away, thought Farrell.

A little bit excessive. They probably had to pay for excess baggage whenever they went anywhere by plane.

'It was quiet as usual round and about' Bob went on. 'Nothing much happening'.

'Nothing much does at that time' Janice chimed. 'It isn't quite time for people to be coming home from work'.

For fuck's sake, thought Farrell. 'So, what caught your attention?'

'A car came speeding down the road from the direction of the Hathaway's' Bob revealed. 'It was a black Lexus and it looked pretty spanking new. There was one guy driving but what really struck me was that there were two men on the back seat who looked like they were fighting'. He made an attempt at impersonating two much fitter men at odds. 'Just like that. Fists going all over the bloody place. One of them was that Ethan Morgan you're looking for. I know it was him because for a split second he looked straight at me, and then I recognised him from the picture you put out'.

'It was definitely him?'

'It was definitely Ethan Morgan and after the car passed his head went down. So, I presume that means the other fella won whatever fight was going on between them'.

'Did you get a look at the license plate of the Lexus?' asked Markovic who'd been writing everything else down.

'No mate, sorry,' said Bob. 'It all happened way too fast. But it was definitely Ethan Morgan. I can tell you that much'.

9.

Oliver Townsend woke up in his room at the Mercantile in Sydney and looked at the bedside clock. It was just coming up to 8 A.M and he'd slept for about six hours which wasn't bad for his second night of body clock adjustment. He didn't feel too bad at all. No mashed feeling in his head or of his legs being heavier than normal as he stepped around his room. It all added up to him feeling like it was going to be a good day. He had a shower and got dressed before packing his things together. When he'd finished, he paused and flicked through the breakfast TV shows for a minute or two to catch up on what was going on. He'd missed the main news coverage but was able to catch snatches of an interview with an actor who was leaving the soap opera 'Home and Away' after several years of playing one of the show's most popular characters, an interview with Australian born Nicole Kidman who was promoting her latest Netflix TV drama set in early 20th century Sydney, and an interview with the CEO of the Australian airline Qantas on returning the company back to some kind of normal following the global pandemic that had wreaked havoc on the world's airline industry. He caught it all before the hunger pangs started to show him who was boss. He went downstairs with his stuff and checked out of the Mercantile. He then walked the two or three minutes down to Circular Quay where he bought that day's copy of 'The Australian' from the newsagent before heading into the City Extra restaurant where he ordered scrambled eggs on raisin toast and a flat white. He sat there drinking the very welcome coffee whilst waiting for his food to arrive. The place was pretty busy with all the brekky trade so he knew it may take a little while. His waitress was called Louise and she was from Glasgow. She was a pretty girl and one of the many young Brits who were working down in Oz. They often travelled around the country and stayed wherever they could find a job, but Louise said she'd found herself a big Aussie boy called Clayton who was a chef in one of the many other restaurants in the city and with whom it was all getting pretty serious in the romance department. She'd moved in with him and was staying put in Sydney. She hadn't dared tell her mum and dad back in Scotland that because of Clayton she might decide not to return. She'd really miss them, but they could always come down and visit. And Clayton had already said that he'd prefer her to stay out here rather than him move with her back to Scotland. He was from a big family who were all fanatical about their Aussie rules footy and he didn't want to leave them. Besides, it was too bloody cold in Scotland. Louise said she had to agree. She loved the Australian climate even during the winter months. Oliver said that it sounded like she'd already made up her mind to stay in Australia with Clayton. She smiled coyly and agreed. She was well and truly in love and was prepared to stay on the other side of the world for it.

Oliver had often thought about moving to Australia himself. Then when his mum got sick, he just didn't think about it again for a while. Something about Australia had always found something in his senses that made him feel like the country was pulling him towards it like a magnet. Right from when he was a little boy and had first learned how to read an atlas. He'd identified Australia. He'd pointed to it.

And making this trip was part of the result of finding out why.

With the ferry boats coming in and out just a few metres away and the metro trains running through Circular Quay Station, which was directly above the café, Oliver flicked through the pages of his newspaper and came across an article detailing the murder of Glen and Rosemary Hathaway in Kingsbrook. It immediately pulled him in which wasn't surprising considering he was heading for Kingsbrook. The police were hunting a man called Ethan Morgan whose picture was included in the piece and two mystery men who they were eager to talk to in connection with the murders that had severely shaken the otherwise fairly quiet sort of town.

He sat back and reflected whilst catching the sun that was beaming down from above the Sydney Opera House that was over to the right.

He'd be arriving in Kingsbrook at a time when there were at least three potential killers on the loose.

An hour on the train from Sydney's central station to Kingsbrook and a little bit of jet lag was starting to kick in. It hadn't all flushed out of his system just yet.

The journey had gone through never ending suburbs which eventually did give way to small, detached towns. But with the amount of building that he could see going on they wouldn't remain detached for very much longer. He got off the train at Kingsbrook and slid his ticket through the machine at the gate of the two track, two platform station that was at one end of the town's main street. Oliver went straight to the mobile café he spotted that was parked just outside the station. Oliver looked at the menu of basic food and drink items but opted only for a large black coffee from the man who was serving. It was just before midday and although the smell of chips and burgers was very enticing, he decided it was too early for lunch. He'd wait for an hour or so before he went looking for a feed. He did buy a coffee and a sandwich for a middle- aged looking man who was clearly sleeping rough. He'd made himself up a bed just a few metres away from where the catering van was parked. He took the coffee and the sandwich to the man who thanked him for them. He then took his own coffee and perched himself on one of the long seats on the other side of the van. A little while sitting in the midday sun whilst his coffee kicked in would be enough for now.

He'd already downloaded a map of the centre of Kingsbrook, and he took it out of his shoulder carrying bag to look at and try and get his bearings. It wasn't difficult. Kingsbrook wasn't exactly the same size as Sydney and he could see that the hotel at which he'd booked a room for half a dozen nights, the Clarendon, was just up to the west of the town centre. It was really heating up and he didn't feel like walking even though it didn't seem that far. So, he went up to one of the taxis that were parked just up to the left and first of all apologised for the shortness of the trip before saying where it was that he wanted to go. The driver just smiled and said 'No worries, mate. Jump in'.

The Clarendon was set in its own grounds and the driveway to the main entrance meant that it was about a hundred metres back from the road. The taxi dropped him off and he went into reception where the walls were decorated with large paintings of what Oliver took to be the surrounding countryside. Several two-seat black leather couches were arranged around low tables before the desk stretched across in front of him. Behind that were a pair of glass doors leading to the swimming pool that had several sunbeds around it but only a couple of them were occupied. To the left of the desk was a lounge bar and to the right was the hotel restaurant. Shooting upwards on either side were the rooms meaning that the whole complex was in a kind of U shape. They were clearly coming to the end of the housekeeping of the rooms for that morning. Oliver could see the trollies at this end of the corridors on either side. And they didn't look like they'd only just started being used.

'Welcome to the Clarendon' greeted the ever so smiley receptionist. She was in her uniform of black collarless jacket, black skirt, and white shirt with a large collar that was outside the jacket. The name on her badge said 'Katrina' and she had shoulder length blond hair and a very affecting smile. And she was directing it straight at him. He felt almost dazzled like he'd just swapped a country town in New South Wales for somewhere in southern California. The Americanisation of the western world had even reached places like Kingsbrook. She checked his ID with his passport and as soon as she saw he was a doctor she asked if she should address him as Dr Townsend. He smiled, shook his head and said that Oliver would be absolutely fine.

Katrina was flirting away with him quite unashamedly as she set forth to avail him of all the town's attractions. She also told him that his room was ready and had indeed been one of the first to be serviced that morning. She said that the restaurant only served breakfast, which was included in his rate, but that there were several restaurants within walking distance and several more a short taxi ride away. That suited Oliver. He didn't mind having breakfast in whatever hotel he was staying in. Maybe lunch if he was pushed for time. But he detested the very idea of having dinner in a hotel. Except if it was in the Raffles hotel in Singapore where he'd taken the Indian buffet a couple of times when he'd stopped over on the way to Australia. That was pretty special. But otherwise, he liked to get out into a place and discover its restaurants when it came to having dinner. And she gave him quite a list of restaurants in the town offering Malaysian, Vietnamese, Chinese, Japanese, Indian, Lebanese, and pubs offering Aussie style pub grub. It didn't sound like he'd be short of anywhere to go whilst he was there.

But then again, he didn't know how long it would take to conduct the business he'd come down for.

He didn't tell this Katrina that though.

She told him the bar was open basically all day and only closed when the last guest retired to their room.

'And the hotel is full tonight' Katrina went on with her smile widening with each syllable of every word. 'So, it'll probably be quite lively in there, particularly early on'.

'Then I'll probably set aside some time to check it out' said Oliver, beaming back at her. He couldn't help it. There was no concierge in the hotel, so he stepped back and grabbed the pull-up handle of his case in one hand and his key to room number 7 in the other. He threw his personal bag over his right shoulder. 'Thanks, Katrina'.

'Oh, you're so welcome Oliver' Katrina gushed. 'Just call down to me if you need anything. I'll be here until three and then it'll be Nathan for the rest of the day. I'll be back in the morning'.

He waved at her before disappearing down the corridor to room 7, smiling to himself. Some people really are shameless. Albeit in an amusing way.

During the afternoon he had a wander around town and bought some of what he'd call essential items for having in your hotel room like a bottle of wine for when he fancied a tipple, some snacks, and some biscuits. He also grabbed a light lunch of a Greek salad wrap before going back to the hotel and doing some final research whilst lounging by the hotel pool.

That evening he took one of Katrina's recommendations and had dinner at a Malaysian restaurant where he gorged himself on a beef rendang curry with rice. It was bloody lovely. He got back to the hotel just after nine-thirty and saw that there were a few revellers in the bar. So, he went in and ordered a glass of Australian shiraz. The barman was called Nathan and he was doubling up as the hotel receptionist. It was obviously what they had to do on the late shift. He was a youngish guy who nevertheless seemed to be working pretty efficiently. He must have a strong work ethic. He was tall and very slim. It must be from all that running around.

'So, you're the English hunk of spunk who checked in today'.

Oliver turned his head and saw a woman heading over to him with a glass of red in her hand. From the glazed look in her eyes and the way she was so carefully placing one foot in front of the other, it wasn't the first one she'd had that evening. She was wearing a sleeveless white top that was so low cut it made Oliver feel like she'd stepped into his doctor's consulting room back home for an examination. She had a wide belt on that was also white and a mightily short skirt with thin horizontal blue and white stripes on it. High heeled slingbacks were on her feet. Her blond hair was shoulder length and in masses of curls. It also wasn't natural. Oliver could see her black roots. Her fingernails were too perfectly shaped not to be false and were painted in black.

'Well, I'm Oliver Townsend, yes' Oliver answered, smiling and extending a hand. 'I don't know about anything else'.

'Oh, I certainly do from where I'm standing'. She locked eyes with him and after taking his hand she held it in the air between them. 'A doctor's hands. Firm when they need to be but enquiring and gentle otherwise'.

Oliver laughed. 'Who writes your script?'

'Nobody, darling. I'm Polly Henshaw. I own this hotel'.

She instructed as opposed to asking Nathan behind the bar to turn Oliver's order for a glass of shiraz into one for a whole bottle. Before Oliver had time to protest the bottle was in her hand with two fresh glasses and she was leading him by the arm to a table in the corner with a couple of chairs. She sat down and crossed her legs over. She was careful in the way she moved herself. Only he could see that she wasn't wearing any underwear but everyone in the bar was able to witness her obvious desire to claim his butt for the night. He'd dressed fairly casually for the evening. A dark green linen shirt with rolled up sleeves and a pair of light blue jeans with soft casual shoes in a kind of light brown suede effect material.

'Are you married, Oliver?' she asked in an increasingly shaky voice.

'No, Polly' he answered. She'd been pouring herself the lion's share of the wine. It was a shame because it was a pretty nice one. He'd had two glasses with his dinner, but he was nowhere near as affected as she was. He reckoned there must be quite a story behind the owner of a hotel like this getting wasted and hitting on one of the guests so publicly. What with this and the way Katrina had been with him when he checked-in, he wondered if all the female staff were on heat in this place.

'Well now there's something interesting'.

'Is it?'

'I'm married' she stated through clenched teeth. 'But there are ... issues, shall we say? Yes, issues in my marriage to Andrew. He's a truckie. That's Aussie slang for a long- distance truck driver. He's on a run to Mildura at the moment. He won't be back until tomorrow. He's my bit of rough but I get lonely because he's away so much. I get really lonely'. She ran her hand up his arm and held it by his elbow. 'Aren't you lonely out here on the other side of the world? We could be lonely together and that would cancel it out for both of us'

Oliver managed to look at his watch. 'Is that the time? Sorry, but I said I'd video call my dad back in the UK. It's mid- morning back there so it's a perfect time'. This was true. He wasn't lying. He had arranged to video call his dad.

'I lost my parents years ago' said Polly in a kind of emotional voice that matched the anguished look on her face. But then a second later her face was covered in the most affected of smiles. 'In a roundabout way that's how I came to be able to buy this place'.

'Have you eaten anything tonight, Polly?'

'Oh, don't give me those doctor's eyes of disapproval' she charged. 'You can't bloody help yourselves even when you're not on bloody duty. Well, if it is any of your business, which it isn't, then no I haven't eaten anything tonight because I'm just not hungry'.

She was wasted now though. She could barely keep her eyes

open. It made it look like Oliver was so incredibly boring he'd made her doze off. Nathan the barman passed by whilst clearing some tables and Oliver whispered to him that somebody should look after Polly. She was so far gone she didn't even notice them exchanging. Nathan said he would look after her with a knowing and weary look on his face. Oliver took that to mean that Nathan had rescued his boss many times before. He quietly confessed that he had to put her to bed sometimes. Oliver thought that went way beyond the call of duty and he wondered how she could run a business if she got into that state on a regular basis? How could she look for the respect of her staff? Especially Nathan when he had to put her to bed. How could she put on him like that? And he'd bet she didn't pay him more than she could get away with.

'Look, I've decided you're no fun at all' she suddenly threw out. 'So off you go and speak to your daddy. What the hell are you doing in bloody Kingsbrook anyway?'

'If I told you that, Polly, I'd have to kill you'.

10.

Harry and Lincoln were both ten years old and lived next door to each other. They were in the same class at school. And they were mates. They loved to use the area around their homes as a place to explore and discover. Not that there was anything left for them to discover. They'd covered all the bush on both sides of the river that flowed two hundred metres down the hill from their houses. They'd only ever been scared once when they'd seen a brown snake in the shrub. They'd managed to step back and been far enough away to avoid it and let it get on with its business. Which it did. It had slithered away. It was the only time they'd ever seen a dangerous snake in the vicinity. They knew they had to be careful of them though and kept their eyes wide open. Today they were accompanied on their expedition as usual by Harry's family dog Rex. Rex was a golden retriever who was as old as Harry himself and who loved being part of the gang with his two small human mates. He never wandered far from their side. He stayed close so he could protect them if they got into any trouble. Although if any brown snake did come along, he would get up close and snarl at it without realising just how much danger he would be in. Dogs had never heard of Steve Irwin. Or that British guy David Attenborough. Rex stayed close to his fellow gang members with his tail wagging and his tongue hanging out of his open mouth.

When they got down to the banks of the river where it flowed through their neighbourhood, Lincoln looked out and saw something that made him stop and take notice. It looked like a body. It must've been washed up. It was barely out of the water. It looked like a dead body. He froze. He'd never seen a dead body before. Neither had Harry who also froze when he caught up with his mate. Rex was fearless and ambled up to the body sniffing all around it. The body was face down and the hands and feet had both been tied. It was also topless. They stepped forward but didn't want to touch anything. It looked gross. And it stank. It looked like a grown-up. They were glad they couldn't see its face.

Because even fearless explorers with a golden retriever for protection can get scared when they're only ten and they find a dead body just a couple of minutes away from home.

Farrell went through the necessary procedure to indicate that this interview with Scott Marshall Hathaway was being recorded, and introducing himself with Detective Senior Constable Zoe Dawkins, and that Scott had declined his right to have a lawyer present, even though Scott was being interviewed under caution and he understood that to mean that he didn't have to answer any questions but that anything he did say may be taken down and used in evidence against him. They were sitting in one of the three interview rooms in the upstairs 'detectives' area at the Kingsbrook cop shop. Farrell had to loosen his tie. It was hot up there.

'You're sure about not having a lawyer present, Scott?' Farrell wanted to confirm. They were now in possession of documents obtained under warrant from Barnett Holdings showing that Scott Hathaway had been directly involved in the situation of Ethan Morgan going from model employee with a bright future ahead of him at the company to somebody who they treated as some sort of enemy. He was looking forward to hearing whatever Scott had to say about it. Farrell suspected that Scott would probably surround the whole thing in complete bullshit.

Scott bristled. 'You're implying that I might need one'. He was sitting up in his chair with his hands placed just above his knees. He was a tall man and his uncrossed long legs extended right underneath the desk.

'I'm not implying anything, Scott. You've made that leap yourself. Is it your guilty conscience peeping through there?'

'I don't have a guilty conscience' Scott said, testily.

'I think you do, Scott'.

'You've got a nerve putting me through this so soon after I found my murdered parents'

'You misled us, Scott'.

'You're a heartless bastard. I still haven't slept properly since I found them. I still can't get the image out of my head'.

'I'm sure it isn't easy'.

'Then what the fuck am I doing here?' Scott raged. 'You should be out there looking for their killers. You should be out there looking for Ethan Morgan!'

'Calm down, Scott'.

'Don't you fucking tell me to calm down!'

'Why did you lie to my colleague detective Dawkins here?'

Scott found it difficult not to look up at Dawkins before he replied. 'I didn't lie to her'.

Farrell sucked in air through his teeth. This man sitting in front of him was really starting to test his patience. He took a sideways glance at Dawkins. She looked like she was ready to lose it with Hathaway too.

'Ethan Morgan was about to take your employer, Barnett Holdings, to court for unfair dismissal. You are head of human resources for the company and yet you claim to have never heard of Ethan Morgan. You're a liar, Scott'.

Scott looked up at Farrell and narrowed his eyes. 'No comment'.

'But why did you lie to us, Scott? Surely you knew how easy

it would be for us to check it all out? And we have checked it all out. You met with Morgan on three separate occasions and then he dropped his case against Barnett Holdings. Was that down to you, Scott? Did you persuade him that it wasn't in his best interests to pursue the case because Barnett Holdings could afford much better lawyers than he could?'

'No comment'.

'What had Ethan Morgan discovered about Barnett Holdings which made them turn against him?'

'No comment'.

'Should we ask them for comment seeing as you've decided to act like you've lost your tongue? Would what they tell us implicate you in something, Scott? Would it link you in some way to the murder of your parents?'

Scott was furious at what Farrell was suggesting. He slammed his fist on the table and was trying to control his breathing.

'Well, it would seem I've struck a nerve with that question' Farrell chided.

'I had nothing to do with their murder!' Scott insisted. 'The very idea that you might think that makes me feel sick to my stomach'.

'Then who did?' Farrell charged. He saw a flicker of something in Scott's eyes indicating that he knew something of relevance. But he seemed determined to keep his mouth shut. 'You're up to your neck in something. Something that I'm guessing led to the murder of your parents. You need to talk to us, Scott. You need to tell us why you've lied to us about Ethan Morgan. Because we just don't believe you didn't know him or anything about him. It's absurd. So, tell us the truth, Scott. Tell us the truth and absolve yourself of whatever is weighing on your mind because I can tell there's clearly something'.

'You know nothing'.

'Then enlighten me. Tell me why you're so scared'.

'No comment'.

'Who were the two strangers who were chasing after Morgan on the afternoon he leapt into your parents' car?'

'How should I know?'

'Because you're involved with them in some way'.

'I told you I'm not involved with them!'

'But you know who they are'.

'I don't know who they are'.

'But let's say you know of them' Farrell pursued, encouraged by how uncomfortable Hathaway was starting to look. If he could only break down the door to the truth that he was hiding. 'Can you at least give us any names?'

'No'.

Farrell sat back. 'Well, you see, we only have your word for it that it was you who actually found your parents dead' He hunched his shoulders. 'Just your word'.

'What are trying to put into this?'

'That we only have your word and that means that you could've been there when your parents were murdered'.

'You're bloody sick'.

'The two strangers who were seen driving off at speed with Ethan Morgan in the back of their car might've purposely done that whilst leaving you in the house to say you'd found your parents and throw us off the scent. Send us down a blind alley that would waste our time. It could've been a way of trying to exonerate you all from culpability'.

Scott shook his head vigorously. 'No, no, no' he insisted.

'That's why we've now instigated a thorough search of your parents' house and all the grounds around it' Farrell told him.

'You can't be serious'

'Oh, I very much am being serious, Scott. I want justice for your mum and dad. So, the instructions to the search team, is to keep an eye out for a murder weapon. A murder weapon that you could've easily discarded in the time between the other two took Ethan Morgan away and when you called in to say you'd found them. See where I'm going with this, Scott? Most of the time murderers are often found to have been close in some way to their victims'.

Scott leaned forward and put his head in his hands.

'Come on, Scott' Farrell urged as he leaned forward before carrying on. 'Our job is to get to the bottom of what happened to your mum and dad and put whoever was responsible for their murder behind bars facing justice. Now that can't be less important than whatever it is you're hiding here. Are you protecting somebody? Because that's what it's starting to look like. Are you really protecting somebody who is more important than your mum and dad?'

Scott looked up and paused. 'Ask my wife'.

Farrell hadn't been expecting that. 'Your wife? What's she got to do with anything?'

'Ask her' said Scott in a quiet, solemn voice. 'Just ask her and she'll give you the answers you need'.

The location of the crime scene was more than familiar territory to Detective Markovic. He grew up in the neighbourhood and used to hang out in the bush and by the river with his mates when he was a kid. His folks still lived in the same house nearby, but he wouldn't have time to call on them now. The identity of the dead body that had been found by the two little blokes and their dog had just shifted the case they were investigating into top gear.

'No debate necessary on the identity then' Farrell remarked after he and Detective Dawkins had joined Markovic at the scene. The body had been placed on its back on top of a body bag ready to be fully inserted before being transported to the forensics lab. 'That's Ethan Morgan alright'.

'And it's a wonder he is still recognisable' said Dawkins who'd bent down so she could view the body closer. 'He was certainly put through it'.

Morgan's face looked like it had been beaten quite heavily and there were bruises all over his exposed torso.

'Somebody was pretty intent on getting something out of him' said Markovic.

'But did they succeed and what are they doing with whatever he told them' Farrell wondered. 'Planning yet another murder? And what might it have to do with Joanna Hathaway?'.

'Yes, that was a turn up, I must say, boss' said Dawkins. She'd kept quiet during the interview that she and Farrell had done with Scott Hathaway just as they'd planned but was as shocked as the boss when Scott had said that it was his wife they needed to speak to. He'd then proceeded to tell them that his wife Joanna had been having an affair with Ethan Morgan. 'And it does make the happy, close, loving family thing about the Hathaway's seem like a bit of a façade'.

'That façade is slipping bit by bit' Farrell agreed. 'I know what you mean, Zoe although my instincts still tell me that the Hathaway olds weren't involved in anything, but we'll see. My mind is still open'.

'My instincts have always told me that no family can be that perfect, boss' Dawkins added. She was there present in the moment like she should be, but her mind had been distracted a little since she'd received a call from her boyfriend Sadiq telling her that a note had been pushed under the door of his café 'the Oasis' with just one word written on it in capital letters. 'TERRORIST'. And he told her it wasn't the first one. He'd received a couple of them over the previous ten days or so and they were starting to unnerve him. Senior Sergeant Joel Stringer was on to it, but she was still planning to have a word with Farrell about it later. Not that she didn't trust Stringer to do his job. Far from it. She just wanted to let Farrell know of the situation. He might be able to offer some insights from his time in the city when he and his colleagues had to work hard to reassure the Muslim community of their safety following Islamic terrorist attacks. Not that Sadiq was a practising Muslim anymore. He was as lapsed from the religion he'd been brought up in as any Catholic who now embraced divorce, a woman's right to an abortion, and equal marriage. But all the ignorant bastards out there who believed that every Aborigine man was a drunk and a wife beater, were also the kind who believed that every Muslim in today's world was a terrorist. She hoped to whoever God was that this wasn't the start of some kind of sustained campaign against Sadiq. He really didn't deserve that.

Farrell smiled. 'We've been police officers for too long, Zoe'.

'I think we've still got a few years left in us yet, boss'.

Farrell was treated to that giant of a smile that Zoe had that lit up a room. He thought that Sadiq was a very lucky man to be on the receiving end of that on a regular basis. He did think that Zoe was an attractive girl with her silky black hair. There was an attraction. He'd admit that. But only to himself. He'd never do anything about it. He'd swore never to have another relationship with someone he worked with. Been there done that and got the kick in the gut for it. Besides, he'd never do that to Sadiq. He was one of life's good guys.

'Well, when you two have finished with your little mutual appreciation society thing that you've got going on here' said Markovic.

'Ah, are you feeling left out, Ryan?' Farrell in a mock voice of pity.

'Well, yes, but I'm a big boy and I'll get over it'. He was going to make another joke relating them to remarks once made by Princess Diana about there being three people in this marriage but instead, he decided to put his serious policeman's hat back on. 'It's a shame about our friend here. I'm sure he could've told us a lot'

'He obviously got himself into something that he couldn't find out his way out of,' said Farrell who then looked up and saw the forensic officer, Dean Robson, approaching. Although considering the steadily increasing size of him, it was more of a waddle rather than a walk. Farrell wondered if the guy had ever learned that healthy and eating can go in the same sentence. 'Dean?'

'Detective Farrell' Dean began in his usual way of only being able to address one person at a time, so it was as if Dawkins and Markovic weren't there. 'The lesson to be learned here is that if you're going to dispose of a dead body in a river then it has to be weighed down with something pretty heavy. Otherwise, it will float to the top like this one did. Throw a body into the sea and the current takes care of it even if it doesn't sink, which it usually does'

'Well, all of that is very interesting and worthy of note, Dean' said Farrell with a withered look at Dawkins and Markovic who looked like they'd lost the will to live. 'But in terms of our investigation?'

'I'd say he's been dead for only three or four hours,' Robson went on. 'And I think he was already dead when he was thrown into the river. If they'd thrown him in when he was still alive then he probably could've at least tried to break free unless he was unconscious or just physically weak after the beating he'd taken. And there's no sign of him struggling. But it looks obvious that he was physically tortured during his final hours of life. He was put through it. There are plenty of marks and bruises to suggest that'.

'What about the cause of death, Rob?'

'Hard to say at this stage. I can't really give any more judgements until I get him to the lab'.

'Okay, Rob, thanks and if you could try and expedite things for us, I'd be grateful, mate' said Farrell who watched momentarily as Robson got back to doing what he did best. Investigating death. He probably found the dead easier to communicate with than the living. 'Ryan, did we hear back yet from the boys and girls down in Melbourne who were checking out Morgan's parents?'

'It's just a parent, boss' said Markovic. 'His Mum. His dad died a few years back and he had no siblings'.

'His poor Mum,' said Dawkins. 'She'll be all alone now as well as having to live with the fact of how her son died. Some people really do get more than their fair share'.

'You can say that again, Zoe,' said Farrell.

'His mum also said, boss' Markovic went on. 'That Morgan last visited her about six weeks ago but kept in touch by phone and he'd been telling her that everything was good. She didn't even know that Morgan had lost his job and had been fighting the company over it'.

'He probably didn't want to worry her,' said Dawkins.

'According to his friends and colleagues he had a pretty active social life here in Kingsbrook, boss' Markovic added.

'Girlfriend? Boyfriend?'

'Apparently neither at the moment' Markovic continued. 'And it was the girls he was into. He'd not long ago split up with someone called Martha Stone who was a senior account manager at Barnett's'.

'Was?'

'She resigned around about the same time that Morgan lost his job at Barnett's, boss'.

'Did she now?'

'She apparently went back to the city and is now working for an insurance company there'.

'She probably just wanted to get away after the breakup with Morgan' Dawkins offered. 'Especially if she found out about Morgan's affair with Joanna Hathaway'.

'That would make sense, Zo,' said Farrell. 'Look Ryan, I know you're in the process of checking Morgan's phone records, but get hold of Martha Stone's number and see if there was any communication between them in these past few weeks'

'I'm on to it, boss'.

'And let's find out exactly where she works and talk to her'.

'I will, boss but here's the thing that I think is also worth noting. All the friends and colleagues at Barnett's we spoke to wanted to do it away from the Barnett Holdings headquarters building and were all anxious that their managers didn't know that they were talking to us'.

'What are they all scared of?' thought Dawkins. 'What are Barnett Holdings trying to keep quiet about to the extent that it's led to three murders. And that's only so far'.

11.

Joanna Hathaway decided that it would be better for her to come down to the cop shop to be interviewed rather than have them interview her at home. She just couldn't answer their questions whilst her husband Scott was there, and she didn't want to put their little son Barney through any difficult situations that wouldn't exactly show his mummy and daddy in a good light. He'd seen enough of that lately. If they interviewed her at home, it would turn into a circus. Scott would not be able to help himself. They'd already lost it with each other three times. And on each of those occasions little Barney had become very distressed. She didn't want to put him through that again. It wouldn't be fair.

Detective Dawkins took her through the same procedure as Farrell had done with Joanna's husband Scott and she also agreed not to have a lawyer present. Farrell also thought it would be more productive if they didn't tell her about the death of Ethan Morgan until she'd spilled whatever beans she had. If she knew something about Morgan that would implicate him in some way, then she might decide it wasn't worth telling now he was dead. It was slightly twisted logic, but Dawkins agreed that it made some kind of sense because whatever could implicate Morgan might also implicate someone else who was still in the land of the living.

'Well first of all, Joanna, thank you for coming in to talk to us' Dawkins began with Farrell sitting alongside her. She noticed that Joanna responded with a barely managed half-smile. 'Now can you start by telling us how you know Ethan Morgan?'

Joanna had her head pointing slightly down. Her eyes were

staring at the floor. Her hands were cupped together on her lap. She was wearing jeans and her legs and knees were firmly together. She was also wearing a large white collarless shirt with the sleeves partly rolled up. Her make-up looked like it had been modestly applied and she was wearing dark red lipstick. Fingernails had all been painted in the same dark shade of red.

'After I had my beautiful boy Barney, I suffered a lot with post- natal depression' Joanna revealed. 'It was pretty intense'.

'Like a lot of women,' said Dawkins. 'My own sister suffered from it too after the birth of both of her two kids'.

'There's still not much in the way of help for women with the condition even in these supposedly more modern times where there's expected to be more understanding for everything women have to go through. I went to see the doctor but even though she was a woman and I therefore expected her to be sympathetic, she didn't really do that much. It's true what they say that some of the greatest enemies of women are other women. They behave no differently to men in that sense. Anyway, she just fobbed me off with tranquilisers and told me to come back in two months if I wasn't feeling any better. She said I had to give them about a month to kick in and then another month in which to assess how effective they'd been. I didn't go back. They did do me some good, but I was afraid of what she might do. That she'd try and say that I was going mad or something and have me sent to some kind of institution. It was irrational I know but you are when you're depressed. At least I was'

'And how did your husband Scott support you through all of this?' asked Dawkins. She wasn't entirely sure where this was all going but she was beginning to get a vague idea.

Joanna let her head fall back and laughed. 'Support? He doesn't know the meaning of the word. Not to me, his wife. Not to me, his wife who'd just given him his son and needed help. Oh no, I had to be the perfect wife and mother just like his own mother had been. I've been living in the shadow of saint Rosemary since the day we got married. I never stood a chance to match up. I'm sorry to speak badly of the woman after what's happened but the Hathaway family was only a happy one if everybody conformed. If everybody did whatever Glen and Rosemary said. You weren't allowed to have an independent mind or even less an independent voice. Scott based everything about our marriage on what he'd observed of his parents. Rosemary had a word with me about my post- natal depression. She said it was a woman's job to work her way through it and that I shouldn't bother her precious Scott with it because he had important work to do. She was a real throwback to the fifties believe me'.

'It sounds like it' Dawkins agreed. She felt a lot of sympathy for Joanna. Her depression must've been bad enough, but she must've felt so alone within this Woman's Weekly family otherwise known as the Hathaway's. But when was she going to get to Ethan Morgan?

'My work as a mother came a very distant second to Scott's career' Joanna went on. 'And don't get me wrong. I wanted him to get on. He was my husband and I loved him, and I wanted him to achieve the best he could. But I lost count of the number of times I picked up a pillow from our bed and slammed it against the wall out of sheer frustration for the fact that I just wasn't being listened to. I didn't have my own parents to turn to because they both died a few years ago. My brother Peter would often take my son Barney when he could see the going was getting tough for me. Peter is a godsend. He works from home as a copywriter so he can be flexible with his working hours. That's how he was able to help me. I couldn't have got through without him and his girlfriend Maria. They've been so good to me. Scott wouldn't notice the daily struggles I had when Barney was tiny, and I was going through it. But Peter and Maria did. Peter has never really taken to Scott. They get on. But only to a point. Peter gave me away when Scott and I got married. But he wouldn't ring

Scott up and ask him to meet him for a beer or anything. He also never bought the whole perfect image of the Hathaway's. He's much wiser at reading people than I am'

'So how does Ethan Morgan come into the picture, Joanna?'

'Scott took me to a dinner held by Barnett Holdings a year ago and Ethan was there. We caught each other's eye straight away. Scott is a handsome man and I've never lost my attraction for him. But Ethan is danger. He's sex. He really is a rip your clothes off and get down to business rather than curl up on the couch with a glass of wine and watch TV kind of guy, you know. I was suffering with the depression and the attention I got from him lifted me in a way that would never come into Scott's head. Scott told me months later that he hadn't even noticed me and Ethan giving each other attention on that night. Anyway, for once in my life I decided not to do the sensible thing and I started an affair with Ethan. And he's a bloody good root. Any woman who's been with him will tell you that, I'm sure. He's by far and away the best I've ever had'. She'd often compared the sex she got with Scott with the sex she got with Ethan since they started their affair. Scott wasn't a bad lover. But he was functionary rather than imaginative and the way they did it would probably never change for the rest of their married life. But with Ethan she got an orgasm just from the licking out he gave her, never mind the fuck during which he made her feel bloody fantastic. 'But Ethan had a girlfriend, Martha and she was a kind of safety net. Although he put it about and chased excitement outside of their relationship, he said he did love her and had no plans to finish with her. So, I've always known our liaison was only temporary. But we carried on in our happily careless way for months. But then something happened with Ethan at work. He wouldn't tell me what, but he said he'd found something out that would have massive consequences if it got out'.

'About Barnett Holdings?'

'Yes. And I honestly don't know what because he told me he

wouldn't tell me in order to protect me. The information he'd got hold of was that lethal. The next thing I knew was that Ethan had been fired and that Scott was the one who'd done it. I lost it when Scott came home that night and demanded to know why he'd fired Ethan. I then confessed to my affair with Scott and told him the reasons why I'd got into it. He was furious. But surprisingly he was forgiving. We're struggling through our relationship at the moment, but he says he wants to make it better. He wouldn't have been able to resist the opportunity for me to humiliate myself tough by coming down here and admitting to my affair with a now wanted man'.

'When was the last time you saw Ethan?'

'About a week ago,' said Joanna. 'It was Scott who told Ethan's girlfriend Martha about my affair with him. It was out of real spite. The gutless wonder. Anyway, Martha left Ethan and went back to the city. But when I saw him a week ago, he was agitated, distracted. It was almost as if he was afraid of his own shadow. I asked him if somebody was after him in some way, but he said no. I didn't believe him. I had yet another fight with Scott and he said he didn't know why Ethan would be so nervous, but he did say the company was preparing a way out of the lawsuit Ethan was bringing against them for unfair dismissal'.

'Do you know how or if any of this could be related to Scott's parents?'

'I honestly have no idea because I don't know what it's all about' Joanna pleaded. 'And I know he's your chief suspect, but Ethan could never have murdered them. No way. He's not a killer. He's really not a killer. Especially in the horrific way it happened to them. I knew they were only happy in a very Stepford Wives kind of way, but they didn't deserve that. Since you made Ethan a wanted man, I've called him, and I've been round to see him. But he hasn't answered my calls, which is very unusual, and when I went round to his place he wasn't there. I'm getting worried to be honest. I can't help thinking he's got himself into some really deep trouble'.

Dawkins and Farrell exchanged looks with each other and then Dawkins lowered her voice as she said 'Joanna, I'm sorry to have to tell you that Ethan's body has been found this morning'.

'You mean he's dead?'

'Yes. And it looks very much like he's been murdered'.

Joanna started crying which turned into heart wrenching weeps. Dawkins went round and pulled up a chair next to her. She put her arms around her tried to comfort her as best she could.

'I realise this must come as a terrible shock, Joanna,' said Dawkins.

'You don't understand' she cried. 'Ethan wanted me to leave Scott and run away with him. And Barney too. He wanted us to start a new life somewhere else, maybe overseas. He said that he'd received some money from Barnett's to keep quiet and saw it as a sign that we should use it to be together and be happy'.

'But you didn't share that view'.

'I didn't know if I did or not' Joanna insisted. 'That's why I was taking my time to try and work out my feelings. Ethan was asking a lot. He wanted me to leave my husband and to take a child away from his father just to run off God knows where. I was confused. My feelings were confused. I was keeping him waiting. If I'd been able to make up my stupid mind earlier, then maybe this wouldn't have happened'.

Uniformed Sergeant Mary Chung came up and stayed in the interview room with Joanna whilst she tried to compose herself enough before she went home. Farrell and Dawkins went back into the detectives' squad room where Markovic was hard at it sitting at his desk and staring intently at something on his computer screen.

'Well now,' said Dawkins. 'The Ice Queen really is melting

these days'

'You mean Mary?' Farrell questioned with a grin.

'You'd never have got her to comfort someone like Joanna Hathaway a few months ago. It must be your influence, boss'.

'Then I shall gladly take the credit, Zoe. Now what did you think about Joanna?'

'I think she's genuine, boss' Dawkins replied. 'She's got a realistic picture of the family she's married into. A bit like Megan Markle who's seen her husband's family for what they really are. But I digress, she gets what sounds like a pretty heavy dose of post-natal, her husband seems indifferent, she meets a guy who treats her like a woman again and not just a mother, but he gets himself into strife where both he and her husband work and before long he ends up dead on a riverbank'.

'Yes, I agree. I think she's genuine too. And at least we know now why Ethan Morgan stayed around. He was waiting. They'd given him money and he wanted to use it to take his girl away from another man'.

'Boss, I've got something here' Markovic announced. Farrell and Dawkins went over and stood behind him. They leaned down and tried to see on the screen what he was so excited about.

'What is it, Ryan?' Farrell asked.

'Boss, this is Ethan Moran's latest bank statement. A payment of two hundred thousand dollars was transferred into his account on Tuesday of last week'.

'Does it say where it came from?'

'It was some kind of offshore account in Vanuatu, boss and no name or title is attached so I'll have to do a search with the federal agencies. But last Tuesday was the day that Ethan Morgan dropped his case against Barnett Holdings'.

'The pay- off that Joanna Hathaway spoke about,' said

Dawkins.

'It would seem like it' said Markovic.

Dawkins cuddled up to her boyfriend Sadiq in bed that night and luxuriated in the feel of his strong arms around her. She'd been thinking a lot about Joanna Hathaway. She'd been absolutely devastated when Dawkins told her that her lover Ethan Morgan had been murdered. During their conversation that preceded it she had confirmed that her husband Scott had lied about not knowing Morgan which made Dawkins wonder what else he'd lied to the police about, and that the image that the Hathaway family gave off to the outside world of happiness to the point of nausea was dependent on whether or not you did as the Hathaway seniors thought you should. Or shouldn't.

'You didn't get any more notes pushed under the door today then?' Dawkins wanted to confirm after Sadiq had received the ones with 'TERRORIST' written on them over the last few days.

'No' Sadiq answered. 'But I've another little problem to deal with'.

'Which is?'

'The kosher catering company that supply me with all my kosher food has gone bankrupt'.

'Shit'.

'Exactly. I've only got enough stock to last me another few days and I need to find a new supplier fast. But the ones I've tried so far want to charge me so much for transportation of the stuff to here that it bites almost entirely into the margins of what I make on the sales. I don't want there to be any interruption to the offer of kosher food on our menu but it's getting close'.

'Remind me again what the deal is with kosher food?'

'Well, it's cooked in a kosher kitchen and blessed by a Rabbi. Strictly orthodox Jews try to eat only kosher food. Secular Jews are less concerned. And I play the game by keeping it in a separate freezer from all the other stuff and I heat it up in a separate oven so that it's not contaminated by non-kosher stuff'.

'You go to a lot of trouble, baby'.

'I just want to show that I care about people's particular needs being met'.

'And some little fuck out there is labelling you a terrorist just because you're a Palestinian'.

'I think that's about it, yes. I mean, I don't shout about it but it's not a secret either'.

'And that shouldn't make any difference to anything'.

'But we both know that it can do'.

'Oh yes. Being an indigenous Australian, a proud Aborigine, makes me a target for all those with sad excuses for a mind. And that's even before I open my mouth and say anything at all'.

Sadiq kissed her. 'I know'.

'But If only they knew how much you went out of your way to make sure everyone was happy' said Dawkins who was getting so frustrated at how someone out there was completely ignoring the truth of how Sadiq goes about his business. She knew that Senior Sergeant Joel Stringer and his team were looking at CCTV footage from two cameras positioned on the street where Sadiq's 'Oasis' café is situated, and that they were also canvassing the other shopkeepers in the vicinity. There were several of them on both sides of the street. There may even be witnesses, although it was a long shot, but they've appealed for them anyway. 'It really pisses me off. But Joel Stringer is one of the best. He'll be doing everything he can to find the gutless wonder who's doing this. And you're taking all the right precautions? Keeping the back door closed and locked at all times? Making sure you write down details of any customer who even looks the least bit suspicious?'

'Yea, I'm doing all that. I'm worried though about the staff. Including Sapphire, the daughter of your boss'.

'Well, Farrell hasn't said anything to me, so I guess Sapphire hasn't said anything to him' said Dawkins who knew she had to tread a fine line between saying things to support the man she loved in the situation he was in, and not getting into specific details of an actual police case. 'But your staff are loyal, Sadiq. I'm sure they'll have got your back'.

'But I hate the very idea of putting them in that position, Zoe. Sapphire and the others are all young people earning cash for whatever reason to do with their future. They plan to go to university or to go travelling or whatever. I'd be mortified if they got caught up in something just because me, their boss, is a Palestinian who some coward is labelling a terrorist. And anonymous notes I can handle, Zoe. It's what else they might be planning that worries me'.

That's what Dawkins was afraid of too.

12.

'The thing is, Zoe' Senior Sergeant Joel Stringer began after Dawkins had taken him to one side when she arrived at work that morning. She wanted to know how the investigation was going into the potentially threatening notes that were being pushed under the door of her boyfriend Sadiq's café. 'We've now got the CCTV footage and we're going to start going through it this morning. I'm also going out to speak to the postie who covers that area today'.

'So why are you sounding like it's all a waste of time?'

'No, Zoe, I don't mean to sound like that' Stringer assured in the best voice he could muster for a colleague who was also a friend and going through strife. 'What I was going to say is that the response to the canvassing of the other business owners along that street has been, shall we say, a little less than positive'.

'How do you mean?'

'They see it as something political and they don't want to get involved' Stringer explained. 'And they especially don't want to be seen as standing up for a Muslim'.

Dawkins was seething. 'Bloody bigots'

'It's not that they don't like him, Zoe'.

'But just because of his ethnicity they won't have his back'.

'I'm sorry, mate'.

'What do they even think will happen if they do?'

'They think it might look like they're standing up for a terrorist'.

Dawkins threw her head back and was open mouthed at what she was hearing. 'I've met most of those people. They all want his help when they're fighting increases in business rates, or when they want support for their mate who's the Liberal party candidate in either the state or federal elections. Even though no Australian government has ever done anything constructive to help the Palestinian people on the ground. Yes, they've given sanctuary to Palestinian refugees, including Sadiq and his family. I give them full credit for that. But they wouldn't have needed to do it if Sadiq's family and all the other Palestinians who now call Australia home, hadn't been made homeless by an illegal occupation of their land'.

'There's another way of looking at that though, Zoe' said Stringer, smiling. 'If the Turnbull government hadn't given Sadiq's family and all the others sanctuary, then he might not have ended up in Kingsbrook and the two of you might not have met'.

Dawkins gave out a quiet sort of laugh. 'God moves in mysterious ways, right?'

'He does but sometimes I wish he'd come clean with us mere humans about what his intentions for us all are'.

'Amen to that. You're sounding philosophical all of a sudden? Have you been watching stuff on SBS?'

'Please, I'd rather get addicted to sleeping pills'

'Seriously though, Joel, he's supported all of them at some time or another with something or another, and I don't mean political shit. He feels he's part of the business community. He thinks they're all genuine people with good intentions towards him. He thinks they see him as an equal, and that really does mean everything to him. He never felt an equal in his own land. He does in this one. Or at least he did'.

Dawkins tried not to carry her bad mood into the team

meeting with Farrell and Markovic. It wouldn't be fair to make them suffer it especially as she knew that neither of them would support Sadiq's detractors.

'Something she said makes a lot more sense now' said Markovic.

'With regard to what, Ryan?' asked Farrell.

'Well, she said that her family wasn't the kind that you read about who hold disgusting secrets that only come out when something devastating happens' Markovic explained as he recalled the details of his interview with Lena and her husband Gareth. 'Now, it may not be that disgusting secrets are behind the Hathaway family masquerade, but I think we can say that the happy smiley face of the family was dependent on sharing the views of and obeying the instructions of Glen and Rosemary Hathaway'.

'And we've only scratched the surface so far,' said Dawkins. 'Really. If we dug deeper, I feel we could end up finding motives for both Scott and Lena to have murdered their mum and dad'.

'I don't think we'd get that far, Zoe,' said Farrell, shaking his head. He'd already placed a picture of Ethan Morgan on the squad room white board. 'I agree that we should remain suspicious of Scott Hathaway in particular although even if it turns out that he's somehow implicated in the murder of his parents in some remote way, I still don't think he was directly involved. I also think that his wife Joanna Hathaway's affair with Ethan Morgan has no connection with whoever murdered Morgan and whoever murdered Glen and Rosemary Hathaway'.

'But you do think it was the same killers in both cases, boss?'

'Yes, Zoe' Farrell answered. 'I think it's reasonable to assume that based on what we know'.

'We need to get to what it was that Ethan Morgan had found out about Barnett Holdings, boss' said Markovic. 'It's what's going to unwrap everything'.

'Agreed, Ryan'.

'So, it has to be something pretty significant,' said Dawkins.

'Well, there's never been any police investigations into the activities of Barnett Holdings, boss' Markovic went on. 'Nothing about any area of their activity has been reported or questioned'.

'Well then, it's time we investigated a company that seems to think it's been untouchable since it set up shop here in Australia. Somewhere in the depths of that enterprise are the answers we're looking for. Now, Ryan, Dean Robson has sent us the autopsy report on Ethan Morgan. What does it tell us?'

'That he was literally beaten to death, boss' said Markovic. 'Almost every rib had been broken, his spleen was ruptured, his arms had both been broken, ankles. The list is pretty extensive. It also confirms that he was already dead when he was thrown into the water because there was no water on his lungs which means he didn't drown. Now I've managed to get hold of Martha Stone, Morgan's ex-girlfriend, and she's agreed to a video call'.

'Good' said Farrell. 'So, if you can deal with that Ryan, DS Dawkins and I will be going to offices of Barnett Holdings and see if we can get to what the Hell is going on there'.

Martha Stone had been doing her best to get back to something like a normal life. It hadn't been easy. When she'd first got together with Ethan Morgan, she'd fallen madly in love with the charismatic man who'd made her feel like the rest of her life had been settled. She'd thought she'd found 'the one'. He was a spunk. Great in bed. And he could cook. He could cook a lot better than she ever could. He was kind. He was generous. He seemed to want nothing more than to make her happy. She couldn't have wished for better.

But then it had all gone wrong.

'And when did you first realise that it had all gone wrong,

Martha?' asked Markovic as he interviewed Martha Stone on a video call from her office as the New South Wales account manager for the insurance company she now worked at in the city. She'd already said how she was building a new life for herself. She'd moved into a flat in the Parramatta district of Sydney. The rest of her family lived nearby, and she'd wanted to be around them again after her 'experience' with Ethan Morgan and Barnett Holdings. 'What made you realise it had all gone wrong, Martha?'

'It began with his affair with Joanna Hathaway'.

'And how did you find out about that?' asked Markovic who thought that Martha Stone was an attractive looking woman. Her thin lapelled green and white patterned jacket over the white shirt with the large open collar she was wearing all looked expensive. Her dark hair was wavy, parted at the side and shoulder length. She wasn't wearing much make-up which led Markovic to believe that she was the sort of intelligent, professional woman who didn't need a lot of make-up to enhance her self-esteem. She'd probably never watched Love Island and wouldn't do even if someone paid her. Her fingernails were clean and not painted in every imaginable colour with stars and different designs on each of them. Markovic hated that. A friend of him and his husband Max did that, and she was very nice and everything, but you wouldn't exactly put her up for Mastermind.

'The signs were all there and like most people in that kind of situation I ignored them' Martha admitted. 'The pauses before he told me where he'd been, the smell of another woman on him, the text messages that he was suddenly all secretive about in a way he hadn't been before, that sort of thing. I didn't believe the obvious because I didn't want to'.

'So, what happened?'

'I ended up confronting him. Ethan was good at lots of things but lying wasn't one of them'. She started to cry. 'I'm sorry' she said.

'That's all right'.

She reached for a paper tissue and dabbed at her eyes. 'I just can't believe he's dead, you know. And yet at the same time I can. I was scared because of what he was getting himself into'.

'And what can you tell me about that, Martha?' he pursued. He hadn't expected her to lose her composure so early on. She'd looked so poised when the video link had first been established. Perhaps she was more fragile than she looked. He'd have to bear that in mind. 'Just take your time. There's no rush'.

'I don't really know what to say or rather I don't really know how to say'.

'Why don't you go back to when you confronted him about the affair with Joanna Hathaway?' he suggested as he watched her take a glance out of the window which was to her right and showed nothing but another office block across the road. Markovic wouldn't want to only have that to look at every day although there might be more if he could see the full view. 'Take it from there'.

'He didn't even try to deny it' she recalled with a mixture of sorrow and fury in her eyes. 'I told him that Scott Hathaway had taken great delight in telling me about his wife Joanna's affair with him, but it didn't seem to touch Ethan's conscience. Not one little bit. Not really. He said that he was sorry that it had upset me, but he also said that he'd be lying if he said he was sorry that the affair had happened ...'

Charming, thought Markovic.

'... he said that Joanna wasn't unhappily married as such, but that there were problems between her and her husband Scott, which Ethan chose to exploit because he was into her. And like all cowards, Joanna thought the answer to her marriage problems was to take another man into her bed. My man. The rotten bitch. Don't talk to me about the bloody sisterhood.

And Ethan saw it as an opportunity to add another one to his scorecard. It really was the selfish side of him coming out and biting me in my absolute foolishness. God I was stupid. Stupid and pathetic'.

'Tell me who hasn't been, Martha' said Markovic. 'And anyone who claims that they haven't has never been in love'.

Martha managed a half smile. 'You're very kind, detective'.

'Realistic, Martha. My job tends to make you that way'.

'I'm sure it does,' said Martha. 'Anyway, Ethan and I had a furious argument and I told him to get out. You see, although we virtually did live together, I mean, we didn't really spend any nights apart, we kept our own places, and he went back to his. All kinds of things went through my mind that night. I saw Scott Hathaway at work most days. There are only about thirty people who actually work at the head office as opposed to being out on site somewhere or other, so it's hard to avoid someone even if you really tried hard to'.

'Yes, I can see that'.

'Then there was actually a scene one morning in one of the corridors between Scott and Ethan. I thought they were going to come to blows and it was getting rather tense but then someone came between them and got them both to calm down and go their separate ways'.

'So, it would be right to say that Scott Hathaway held a pretty bitter grudge against Ethan?'.

Martha paused whilst she went through the implications of what Markovic had said. 'Well, yes and understandably so. Ethan had been sleeping with his wife. But Scott Hathaway is no killer. I'm certain of that'.

'I hadn't made that leap of thought, Martha' Markovic lied. 'I'm just trying to get a picture of everything, that's all. Did you speak to Ethan after that?'

'Oh yes. A week after I ended our relationship I decided to move back to the city because most of my social life in Kingsbrook was tied up with Ethan and I felt humiliated amongst everyone. I just wanted to get away. I was going to ring Ethan and tell him what my plans were and that I needed him to come and collect the things he'd left at my place because I'd given notice that I was leaving my flat. But that was the morning he was fired from his job at Barnett's. And Scott Hathaway was the one who fired him'.

How interesting, thought Markovic. And Scott Hathaway still denies ever having known Ethan Morgan. As if he could keep that one going.

'Ethan came round to my place, but I've never seen him in such a state'.

'How do you mean?'

'He was very agitated' she began to explain. 'It was like he was looking over his shoulder the whole time and frightened of his own shadow. I asked him what the Hell was the matter. He said he couldn't tell me because if he did then that would make me a target for them. I asked him what the fuck he was talking about, but he just said that he'd found something out that had led to him being fired and that the knowledge was getting him into deep trouble. I asked him to at least tell me who or what it was all about, and he said he was all about the history of Barnett's. But he wouldn't elaborate further. He said that as soon as he'd issued instructions to his lawyer to take Barnett's to court for unfair dismissal, he'd started getting calls from someone who just hung up and he'd started hearing noises after dark as if someone was right outside his house. Then he thought he was being followed. Now as it turned out the insurance company that I'm now working for here called me and asked if I could start earlier than I agreed. I told Ethan this and he told me to say yes and get the Hell out of Kingsbrook. But I still cared for him. I still loved him. I was terrified over what might happen to him. I told him to come with me to the city and get right away from anything to do with Barnett's. He said he couldn't but wouldn't tell me why. He said he had to see it through, whatever it was. I left the next day and went to stay with my parents, but I managed to find a flat fairly quickly and I moved in at the end of last week. I lost the deposit on the one I'd rented at Kingsbrook because I hadn't stayed for the notice period, but I couldn't give a damn about that. I was just glad to be away'.

'But I take it you were still worried about Ethan?'

'I was desperately worried about him' she revealed, tearfully. 'But what could I do? He almost compelled me to leave Kingsbrook. And now when I think about what happened to him. It just beats me up inside, you know'.

'And Ethan never gave you any indication of what it was he'd found out about Barnett's?'

'No, absolutely not. He just said that he wouldn't in order to protect me. But from what, I have no idea at all'.

'Martha, you've told me a lot already, I know, and I appreciate your time' said Markovic. 'But can you tell me what kind of company Barnett Holdings is to work for?'.

Martha ran her hand through her hair. 'They don't like you talking about them to anybody outside the company. Everyone has to sign a confidentiality agreement not to talk to any third parties about the business. That's what they got Ethan on. He'd talked to someone who didn't work for the company and that was against the rules'

'But you don't know who he'd talked to?'

'No, I'm afraid not'.

'It all sounds very shadowy'.

'It is very shadowy' Martha agreed. 'It's not an open and transparent company at all. It's very secretive and, as you say, shadowy. But I've no idea why they're like that when all they do is buy and manage existing properties and construct new ones that they either sell or manage. I don't know why they feel like they have to construct a Berlin wall around that'.

13.

'You know, it's almost as if they did it on purpose,' said Farrell. Dawkins was driving them back after their decidedly unsuccessful mission to the offices of Barnett Holdings. All of the managers, except Scott Hathaway who was still on time off following the death of his parents, had gone on a team building exercise at some remote outback lodge interstate in South Australia. Even the current owners of Barnett Holdings, Raymond and Cecilia Barnett, who apparently were brother and sister as opposed to husband and wife, had gone with them. They wouldn't be back for another twenty-four hours. 'I mean, even if I'd insisted on them all coming back, especially the owners, they wouldn't have made it until late tomorrow anyway which is why I got the receptionist to tell them to call me immediately after they do get back on their agreed schedule'.

'I must admit it does sound that way, boss' Dawkins agreed. 'We couldn't have picked a worst time. Even just talking to the staff who were there was like trying to pull teeth'.

'It was bloody excruciating' said Farrell who recalled all the false smiles on false faces that covered up the fact that the good people of Barnett Holdings really didn't want to talk to them. 'They were so robotic. Like they'd all come off some obedient employee production line or something. Like one of those really bad movies that they show on arvo TV where everybody has been brainwashed and are being controlled by some sinister power. And the acting is always diabolically bad'.

Dawkins laughed. 'I know exactly what you mean, boss. I don't think any of them would be in line for a Logie'.

Farrell laughed too. 'Certainly not, Zo'.

Dawkins paused and then said 'You sound frustrated, boss'.

'Well, we're going round in bloody circles, Zo' Farrell groaned. 'We're dancing to somebody else's tune here and I don't like it. Three people have been murdered on our patch and the fog is nowhere near clearing over any of it.

'It does seem like Ryan has had more luck with Martha Stone though, boss?'

'Yea' Farrell agreed, albeit a little reluctantly. The investigation was really starting to get to him. 'And from what Martha Stone says we're going to have to bring Scott Hathaway in for more questioning. I didn't buy this insistence of his that he knew nothing of Ethan Morgan before and now we know that he was lying through his teeth. Martha Stone and his wife Joanna have both told us things that prove he's a liar'.

'His assertions were too ridiculous to start with, boss'.

'They so were. I'm still not of the opinion he's a killer though. He's just a jealous husband who didn't take too kindly to his wife putting it about with another man'.

'Another man who we now know she was contemplating leaving Scott for and taking their son with him' Dawkins added. 'Which we also now know is why he was hanging around. But the big picture answers must be somewhere within the whole Barnett Holdings organisation, boss'.

'I don't know where else they could be, Zoe. We'll get hold of the owners, Cecilia and Raymond Barnett when they get back from their little outback walkabout and in the meantime, maybe we'll get something from that notice you pinned up'.

A number for people to call if you had any information on the investigation, which went straight to the Kingsbrook cop shop, but callers could leave information anonymously, had already been made public. Dawkins pinned a notice about it on the staff information board in the hope it might spur people into phoning through with what they knew.

'I thought it might be worth a try, boss' said Dawkins. 'And you never know but maybe one or more of their managers might be itching to talk to us once they know we may be on to them. Getting in touch with nature out there under the stars might make them want to unburden themselves'

Farrell laughed. 'Well, wherever it comes from, I think we are due a break on this case, Zo. But whilst we're waiting, when we get back to the office, we'll see if Ryan has been able to check the number that those anonymous calls that Martha Stone says Ethan Morgan received came from. And like I said, we'll get Scott Hathaway back in and try and get some kind of truth out of him. But I wonder what it was that Morgan found out about the Barnett's history'.

'I know the Barnett family were able to take a lot of Aboriginal land when they first came here back in the nineteen forties' said Dawkins. 'And right the way up to the nineteen seventies. But that won't be the big secret because everybody was complicit in ripping my community off. The feelings of my community were completely ignored. And then so many in the settler community wonder why we get so bloody resentful'.

Dawkins was thinking of talking to the boss about her boyfriend Sadiq and the campaign of intimidation that seemed to be being levelled against him at his café. There'd been no more notes shoved under the door with the word 'TERRORIST' written on them in the last day or so but both he and Dawkins were nervous. A red light at a pedestrian crossing made her stop and she was about to bring up the subject with Farrell when he seemed to have been struck by the sight of the woman crossing in front of them.

'I don't believe it' he breathed in shocked tones. 'It can't be'.

'Do you know that woman, boss?'

Farrell didn't answer. Instead, he got out of the car and called after the smartly dressed woman with a figure that Dawkins would die for. And she was one of those women who was really suited to wearing high heels and a short skirt without looking like she was available for the business of pleasure. Dawkins laughed at herself for her mild duplicity. She'd never have let a man get away with saying something like that. But what was the boss up to?

'Becky!' Farrell called out. He couldn't believe he'd clapped eyes on her. What the Hell was she doing in bloody Kingsbrook? 'Becky!' He watched her stop, pause, and then turn round and look anxiously at him.

'I'm Nicole'.

'Course you are' said Farrell who couldn't believe he'd been that stupid. 'I'm sorry'.

'Boss!' Dawkins called after opening her car and leaning out. 'The light is about to change'.

'I'll see you back at the station, Zoe'.

'Boss?'

'I'll see you back there later, Zoe' he said, insistently.

Dawkins smiled resignedly before closing her door and driving off. She couldn't wait to hear what that was all about but wondered if the boss would be forthcoming. She couldn't wait to tell Markovic about it too. She wondered if he knew who the mystery woman was.

Senior Sergeant Joel Stringer scratched his head.

'So, you've got no ID for him at all?' he asked the duty nurse to confirm. The station had received a call from Kingsbrook General saying that a Caucasian man, probably in his mid to late thirties, had been literally dumped at the main entrance doors to the hospital. He was so deep into a state of unconsciousness that he was lucky there was any actual life left in him at all. But he was still in this world. Just. His right elbow had been bent the wrong way which meant it had been broken in what nurse Bao Nguyen said would've been an unbelievably excruciating experience for him. He and Nguyen were standing by his bed in the emergency room. Nguyen and the rest of the medical team looking after him weren't even thinking of transferring him to a ward yet. The priority was to make sure he was stable, despite his unconsciousness. Both he and Stringer were standing by his bed and looking down into his face. Nguyen had his arms folded across his chest and Stringer had his notebook and pen in hand. They looked up at each other fleetingly whilst they talked.

'That's no doubt why he passed out' Nguyen added. 'He must've been like this for a couple of days'

'Has he never heard of painkillers?'

'Believe me, they wouldn't have touched the sides with something like what he must've gone through,' said Nguyen.

'And he was dumped here early this morning?'

'It was just after eight' Nguyen confirmed. 'And I guess the way it was done means that somebody doesn't want you knowing who they were who did the dumping. It looks like he was involved in something he shouldn't, and his accomplices must've had an attack of some kind of conscience which is why they brought him here'.

'Injured in the field but not dead. The worst possible scenario for your average crim. Death means they don't have to be bothered about anymore. But injured leaves them all vulnerable to being found out. They must've liked him or perhaps they weren't your average crims'.

'There are no signs of any other injuries, so he probably was part of the gang rather than their victim' said Nguyen who loved to watch all the crime stuff on TV. Dramas, true life docos. It all fascinated him, and he sometimes wondered if he should've chosen a career in the police. But those moments didn't last long.

He did love being a nurse. And he prided himself on being quite a good one even if he would say so himself. 'And there was nothing in his pockets with which we could identify him'

'You've got CCTV on the outside though, yea?'

'Oh sure,' said Nguyen.

'I'll need that. They must've come pretty close so there might just be something on there that's useful to us'

'There were two eyewitnesses, both of them said that the car sped up to the doors where he was literally thrown out and the car sped off again. Neither of them got any chance to get a reggo number'.

'We'll need to talk to both of the eyewitnesses' said Stringer.

'I've got their names and addresses'.

'Thank you,' said an impressed Stringer. This Nguyen bloke was well switched on all right. He wished they had someone like him as part of every incident. 'Is the security room still on ground level behind the main reception desk?'

'Yes' Nguyen confirmed. 'And that's where you'll get the CCTV footage'.

'Thought so'.

'But look, I need to get on now so if there's nothing else?'

'No, you've been great mate, thanks'

'No worries. Anytime'

Stringer's attention was drawn when his mobile bleeped. He took it out of his pocket and saw that there was another message from his lover Tracey. The girl he was shagging outside of his marriage. The girl who'd started off being all the fun he'd needed and who'd accepted that he was never going to leave his wife. But there'd been a couple of times recently when he'd got the impression that Tracey wasn't as happy as she had been about their 'friends with benefits' situation. She'd grown a little clingy.

This was the third text message she'd sent him that morning. He'd responded to the first one but hadn't yet responded to the second one which is what this third one was about. She knew that he couldn't always respond to her messages straight away. So what the Hell was she playing at? Because if this kind of behaviour developed further, she'd be sure to lose him. He'd just walk away. He'd been absolutely honest about his intentions right from the start. She could never say that she'd gone into their affair with her eyes closed. He was going to make her wait. She had to learn that the clicking of her fingers would never control him.

He focused back to the man lying there holding on to life with the aid of all different kinds of wires and tubes going in and out of various parts of him and connected at the other end to various life supporting machines. The sight of him inspired a few more thoughts to go through his head. The team already knew that DNA had been found at the house of Ethan Morgan that wasn't found at the home of the Hathaway's. They also knew that Morgan broke into the Barnett family mansion after he'd received a payoff from the company for dropping his lawsuit against them for unfair dismissal. Then there was the question of who he was running from when he made his escape from his house. The gun he was carrying wasn't registered to him. No gun was registered to him, and he really didn't fit the picture of someone who would carry a gun or have one in his house. So, had he picked up the gun from whoever had got into his house? And what had happened to whoever had got into his house? When they'd checked the house, there'd been no sign of anybody else in there.

He took out his phone and called the forensics officer, Dean Robson. The two of them had known each other for years and didn't need to go through any long introductions. They could get straight to it and that suited them both nicely.

'Yea, Dean, you know the DNA you found in Ethan Morgan's house for which you had no match on the system and which you didn't find in the Hathaway house? ... well, can you get down to me here at Kingsbrook General with your kit, please? I've a feeling I might be looking at a vital missing link'.

They were sitting in a small coffee shop and Farrell was glad that they were on the other side of town from where the Oasis café was located. He certainly didn't want his daughter Sapphire, who worked at the Oasis, to see him with the woman who was now known as Nicole. Sapphire knew that her parents existed within a less than perfect marriage that they'd never acknowledged but he didn't want to flaunt evidence of it right in front of her. He felt guilty enough about the effect his estranged marriage was having on their daughter. If he was truly honest with himself, he'd say he needed to grow a pair and sort it one way or another.

'When it's just you and me, please call me Becky. It'll take me back to a time when I was happy. With you'.

'If that's what you want' said Farrell, looking round. 'It looks like we'll be safe enough to do that in here'.

'I never thought it would be like this' said Becky as she smiled across the table at Farrell. With Farrell in his suit and Nicole in her black leather skirt with white linen shirt that she was wearing pretty low cut and outside the waist of her skirt, they did look a little out of place amongst a clientele that was made up mainly of tradies. Not that either of them could care less about that.

'I'm sure you've been in much more salubrious places'

'I wasn't always rich, Jason'.

'I know'.

'And I was only rich then because my husband was'.

'Some would say you'd married well'.

'And they'd be so very wrong,' said Becky. 'As you well know'.

Farrell smiled. Her eyes were as bright and as sad as they ever were. But when they were on him, they made him feel so bloody wonderful. And that's what made it all so dangerous.

'So, what did you mean by what you said before?' he asked.

'That I didn't think we'd meet again over a flat black and a cappuccino'.

'I didn't think we'd ever meet again at all'.

Becky licked her spoon clean. She'd just stirred two packets of brown sugar into her cappuccino. It was good to see Jason again. Oh God it was good to see him again. They'd met when Farrell had been a detective in the city and assigned to an operation to bring down the activities of one of Australia's most notorious drug barons. His name was George Rothwell. And he was Becky's husband. But she'd decided to help the police with everything they'd need to put her husband George away for a very long time because he'd diversified from dealing drugs to being involved in what is described as 'modern slavery'. Desperately poor people across Asia were loaned money by Rothwell's associates and he then organised the trafficking of one of their children into Australia to be used as 'debt bondage'. They were then hired out by illegal networks to who Becky had described as 'evil, sick bastards' to be used as slave labour in households where nobody had ever heard of a conscience. Some of them were as young as ten. That's when Becky had decided that she couldn't turn a blind eye to her husband's activities any longer and besides, there were only so many Gucci bags a girl could have without her conscience stabbing away at her about how the money had been earned to buy it for her. Farrell had been given the job of handling Becky after she'd approached the police and the attraction between them had been instant. Farrell knew it had been completely the wrong thing to do on every level and he should've resisted. Course he should've. But he couldn't. Neither of them could. Then just when there was enough information for the net to close in around Rothwell, a police officer who'd been involved in the surveillance of George Rothwell was shot dead outside his home after he got out of his car. A team of officers raided Rothwell's house, but he was nowhere to be found. Becky was placed under suspicion of having tipped him off at the last minute and facilitating his escape, but she was adamant that she hadn't. She didn't convince some of Farrell's superiors and when they found out about Farrell's affair with her it almost cost him his job. Not surprisingly they'd been absolutely furious with him but in the end no action was taken against him. His previous record as an officer had saved him. It was then accepted that Rothwell had absconded and escaped justice without his wife's help and that's when it had been decided that she would be given a new identity of Nicole Wilson and moved to start a new life in Adelaide under the rules of witness protection because if she hadn't helped him then it probably wouldn't take Rothwell much to work out that she'd been helping the police. That's when she and Farrell had been forced to bring an end to their involvement with each other and it had torn them both apart.

And despite what they'd done to get her out of harm's way, Farrell knew that she remained under suspicion by some in the Sydney high command who simply refused to accept that Rothwell could've made his escape without his wife's help.

And they still had no idea of his whereabouts.

'I didn't think I'd see you again either,' said Becky.

'So, what are you doing here? I mean, it's not like I'm not pleased to see you. I'm more than pleased to see you'.

'You're just worried about the possible implications'

'Yes'.

'Sounds like they've kept you in the dark about everything,' said Becky.

'And that scares me,' said Farrell. Why hadn't the high command in the city told him that they were moving Nicole into the very town where he was? What the Hell was it all about?

'And me,' said Becky. She looked into Farrell's eyes and just wanted to cry. Since she'd been placed under witness protection it had felt like her life hadn't been her own anymore. It had felt like she was being treated as some kind of criminal without ever having done anything. And she'd had no choice in being moved to Kingsbrook. 'But they only gave me twenty-four hours to get ready to leave Adelaide. I didn't know where I was going until I was on the way here'.

'And they didn't tell you that I live and work her now?'

'No' she said. 'No, they didn't. But look, before I say anything else, I want you to tell me something'.

Farrell breathed in deep. 'I will if I can'.

'I want you to tell me that your life has meant absolutely nothing since you and I were forced apart'. She could feel the tears begin to fill her eyes. 'Or failing that, just tell me that you missed me, Jason'.

Farrell took hold of her hand and linked his fingers with hers. She'd been moved here for some reason, and he was going to find out what that reason was. But for now, he was just happy in the moment of breathing the same air as her.

'Even if I never saw you again,' he said. 'I'd never forget you'.

Becky bit her lip. 'The same'.

14.

Oliver Townsend was having an absolute disaster of a day. He'd come all the way from the other side of the world and Kingsbrook hadn't been difficult to find but trying to see Cecilia Barnett was like trying to get an appointment to see the bloody Queen. In fact, it was probably easier to get to see the Queen. He'd given the Barnett's 'staff' his full name which he thought would cover the cost of his admission to the apparent fortress that masqueraded as a mansion, but it hadn't proved to be the case. At least so far. And it's not as if he didn't have a reason to be there. And they knew full well what that reason was.

He wondered what kind of emotion Raymond and Cecilia Barnett would show when he did finally get to see them. Especially Cecilia. How they would react to him. Once they knew why he might have to end up demanding to see them. After all, they were descendants of British aristocratic stock. They'd been constructed from the same gene pool as the Royals, but would they show that they have emotional intelligence when the Royals never have? He was frustrated to Hell. His father had told him during one of their video calls that he had to remain patient because it would all come good in the end. Oliver knew his dad was right. His dad was always right. He was so lucky to be his son.

That night for dinner he decided to try the Korean restaurant in Kingsbrook that had been recommended to him by the Olympic champion of a flirt that was Katrina who worked behind the reception desk at the hotel. Well, she did the morning shift and she appeared to have a rather active social life. She'd clearly not heard of the concept of getting enough rest before going to work. When her face wasn't ignited by her flirting with a male guest who'd taken her fancy, she looked like she could fall asleep at any moment and sipped constantly from a can of high energy fizzy drink that she quite brazenly kept on the desk in front of her. Back home doctor Oliver had been strongly advising his patients lately not to consume those energy drinks. They were full of the most insane amounts of sugar and only provided a temporary fix from a very avoidable problem. Not even when he'd been going through his final exams at medical school in the British city of Liverpool had Oliver ever succumbed to them even when he'd been exhausted with studying. They were lethal.

Before he'd gone for dinner the owner of the hotel, Polly Henshaw, had been making great play of letting everyone know that she was taking it easy by staying on the diet cokes tonight. This was whether they wanted to know or not but since most of the guests had already been treated to her drunken behaviour, she probably thought she'd shout about her laudable new- found self-control. Like most alcoholics she wanted to turn her own environment into the Globe theatre stage and put on a Shakespearean play out of trying to convince everyone, but mostly herself, that she was in control of the drink when everybody could see that the drink was in control of her. Sad bitch. She needed help. But with his doctor's hat on once more Oliver knew that she had to make that decision for herself. There was no way she'd let herself be forced into it. It was the same with all addicts. They had to make the decision to get off whatever was bringing them down.

He had thought about going for a drink at a bar in town, but in the end, he didn't think he was in the mood and couldn't be bothered. He got back to the hotel and wasn't surprised to see that Polly Henshaw had got rather bored with diet coke and was back on the chardonnay. She was well on the way to putting sobriety behind her, until the next time she wanted to put on the Shakespearean play, and poor old Nathan who was doubling up as usual on the late shift as both reception desk agent and barman, really had his work cut out. Polly was acting as if Nathan had multiple pairs of hands and shouting out orders for drinks for everyone who was in the bar. She really did take liberties with Nathan. But tonight, the cavalry had arrived in the shape of Polly's husband Andrew who was helping Nathan with some of the bar orders. Andrew the truckie.

He caught Oliver's eye alright.

Oliver had always known he was gay from a very early age. He'd confided in his parents, and they'd encouraged him to come out and be himself. They couldn't have been more supportive. He'd been so lucky. He'd had a couple of fairly serious boyfriends in his life, plus several 'liaisons', but he was currently single and would like to settle down with someone. He wanted to share his life. And Andrew was hot. Oliver would certainly have a lot of difficulty saying no if Andrew knocked on his door.

But he was married.

So why was he shaking his hand and fixing a smile on Oliver that made him feel like he'd been hit by a strike of lightening? He almost had to catch his breath. This man was naughty.

During an unexpected lull in the evening festivities, Andrew came round from helping Nathan behind the bar and over to where Oliver was sitting at it. He brought him another glass of the red wine he'd been drinking. Andrew was having a beer, holding his glass in those big hands on which the skin was a little rough as Oliver remembered from when they'd shaken hands. Oliver could imagine those hands in all kinds of places. He could also just picture him in his truck, driving up and down the highways contributing to the transport of goods around Australia. He probably thought nothing of driving for eight hours or more. He might indeed think that was a pretty short run. He liked looking at Andrew. He was tall with big, wide shoulders, a dimple in his chin, square jaw, face covered in stubble, short jet- black hair with amazing blue eyes. Oliver had always loved that combination. He had a very engaging smile which turned into short bursts of laughter, and he looked good in his light blue denim shirt with press stud fastenings for buttons and which he wore outside his darker blue jeans. The sleeves of his shirt were rolled up to his elbows, exposing his fury arms.

And a thick gold wedding ring was shining brightly on his finger.

Oliver was enjoying being in his company, and he couldn't help but entertain the idea that Andrew was the sort of man who was gay on the inside but straight on the outside. Oliver had been there, done that a couple of times back home in the UK and got his fingers burned both times. It had made him wary of getting involved with anyone who brought third party complications with them. And with Andrew an alcoholic wife was a rather big complication. He told himself to shut the fuck up and stop letting his libido put two and two together and make what his libido wanted the numbers to add up to. Then he told himself to let his libido add up the numbers to any fucking number it wanted to. He didn't care. He fancied the pants off him.

But he was married to a woman who was sitting just a few metres away.

'So' said Andrew, leaning against the bar counter and with his usual light-hearted grin across his open face. 'What's our mysterious pom been doing today?'

'There's nothing mysterious about me, Andrew' said Oliver, innocently.

'Tell me why you're here then?'

'Do you put all the guests through the third degree?'

'No'.

'Because I thought Australia was a free country where no explanations were needed'.

'It is' said Andrew. 'All of that. I'm just curious as I get to know you'.

'And do you get to know all the guests?'

'No. If they're only here for one night then there isn't much chance. Especially if I'm away on an interstate run. But if they're here for a few days and I'm on some time off from the day job then it's sometimes good to get to know people. And we don't get that many foreign guests here. We're not really on the tourist trail. We're just a small country town not far out of the city. So, people tend to either stay in the city or go further out than where we are here. And as you can see most of our guests are either people doing business in the area or they're visiting family but don't want to actually stay with them. Or they're Aussies who are touring round and like the look of the place so decide to stay. All of which makes me even more curious to know why you're here. Because you're not any of those I've just described'.

Oliver laughed. 'Nice try, Andrew'.

'Damn!' exclaimed Andrew, playfully. 'I must be losing my touch'.

'I doubt that' said Oliver, unable to stop himself from a minor flirt. It was hard not to be captivated by those incredible blue eyes. 'So have you always been a truckie?'

'Since I was nineteen years old, yes, so for seventeen years now'.

'You obviously enjoy it'.

'I love being out on the open road and being my own boss' said Andrew who was very taken with this gentle voiced Brit. His dark green eyes and brown hair, his wide very smiley mouth. Very taken indeed. He wondered if he'd be up for play. It's often said that nobody else knows what goes on behind the closed doors of someone else's marriage. And in the case of Andrew and Polly that was all very true. Nobody else in Kingsbrook knew the truth of how their marriage worked. Or didn't work. But Andrew sometimes thought that some of them had worked it out. People aren't stupid. They see signs and read into them. There was a growing part of him that hoped Oliver would read the signs.

'Yea, I get that'.

'It must be different for you though being a doctor?'

'How do you mean? I work collaboratively. I don't always have all the answers'

'I thought you doctors all believed that you always did have all the answers' Andrew teased.

Oliver smirked. 'We haven't all got a God complex, Andrew'.

'And there was me thinking that you did'.

They both laughed and Oliver ordered more drinks for them from Nathan who was looking more relaxed now. Less stressed. But there were a lot of dirty glasses and various other debris across all the tables in the bar so Andrew did a quick circuit and picked up as much as he could.

'Nathan is lucky you're here' said Oliver when Andrew came back. He'd taken all the glasses and placed them in the dishwasher behind the bar.

'He's a good kid,' said Andrew.

'He sure is' Oliver agreed.

Andrew took a first gulp of the beer Oliver had ordered for him. 'And he has to work bloody hard here. Cheers for this by the way'.

'Cheers' said Oliver as he raised his glass of red and clinked it with Andrew's glass of VB. He wanted to turn the table and ask Andrew what the story was behind his marriage to Polly. He could well understand what Polly saw in Andrew physically. But what had she meant when she'd drunkenly said that there were 'issues' between her and her husband? He'd love to know the answer to that one.

'And tell me, what kind of doctor are you?' Andrew asked. He wouldn't mind an examination. A very thorough one.

'I'm a GP at a practice in Windsor which is west of London. It suits me well. I like the whole community medicine thing, you know. Have you ever been to the UK?'

'No' said Andrew. 'I'd like to have done but I never have. Like most Aussies I've been to Bali. And I've been to New Zealand. But I've never been any further. When I was younger, I couldn't really afford it and then since Polly and I bought this place we've never really had the chance to take a proper break. It's been hard work making a success of this hotel'.

'But it's doing okay now?'

'It's doing all right, yea. It could be doing better but then all business owners say that. But it has been a long journey. It was pretty run down when we got it. But we decorated throughout and got some good staff in like Nathan behind the bar here. And we started advertising in all the right places that made people think of us when they're planning their trips for business or whatever. Believe it or not, my wife is a pretty astute businesswoman by day. It's just at night when she loses it to alcohol'.

'And is it every night, Andrew?' Oliver asked as he followed Andrew's eyes to where Polly was sitting with two male guests at a table over in the far corner of the bar and looking like she was already way past the point of no return. What goes on inside that head of hers that leads to her getting into this state every night? She was an addict. But she was an addict for a reason. He'd learned that very simple truth as a doctor. An addictive personality doesn't help but there was always a reason why someone is an addict. There's always something that's provoked someone's consciousness into being that way.

'Yes. She's dependent. She can't go one evening without alcohol'.

'What's she dealing with, Andrew?'

'Having a husband like me is what she's dealing with, Oliver'.

Before Oliver had the chance to think of a response to what Andrew had just said, Andrew excused himself saying he'd better go and rescue his wife. 'Or rather, I'd better go and rescue the guests from my wife' is what he went on to say. Oliver's glass was empty, but he didn't want to remain in the bar. He had some wine in his room anyway so he could have himself a little nightcap whilst reading another couple of chapters of the Finnish crime novel that he currently had on the go or watching some late- night telly. He wasn't quite ready to go to sleep yet.

He slipped out of the bar quietly without looking over at Andrew and Polly Henshaw playing out their marriage with issues.

Oliver didn't know how long he'd been asleep when he was woken by the sound of a knock at the door. He lifted himself up and switched on the bedside lamp. He turned his head to the door and swung himself out of bed to go and answer it. He only had his underpants on but didn't think that would matter because he kind of knew who it would be. He opened the door and sure enough, there was Andrew standing there with a bottle of scotch and two glasses, looking him up and down as Oliver put a hand on the side of the door. Andrew was in just a t-shirt and shorts. Nothing on his feet. But there was a look in his eyes that made Oliver think of the Stevie Nicks song when she talks about something inevitable happening between two people that could nevertheless lead to a whole lot of trouble.

'I hope you don't mind' said Andrew, holding up the bottle and the two glasses. 'I thought we could share a nightcap'.

Oliver stood back to let Andrew through and then closed the door. 'I'm not entirely surprised that you're here' he said. He was indeed very pleased to see Andrew. 'But what about Polly?'

'Polly has passed out like she always does' said Andrew who stepped forward and placed the scotch and the two glasses on the desk type table in the corner of the room. He poured them both a measure and handed one to Oliver. 'Cheers'.

Oliver clicked glasses with his gentleman caller. 'Cheers'.

'She's in our little flat which is above reception. I put her to bed. She won't be back in this world before the morning. I need you tonight, Oliver and I don't think I'm alone in feeling that there's something between us'

Oliver placed his glass on the table and Andrew did the same. Oliver caressed the side of Andrew's face with his hand and then they went for it. Kissing, hands everywhere. Oliver frantically pulled Andrew's t-shirt off. He had a thick chest rug that extended over his stomach. Oliver loved that and ran his hands through it all. Then he slid one hand into the back of Andrew's shorts. 'Right, get these off and get in bed'.

They were wrapped in each other's arms when they woke up at the same time in the early hours. The rising sun was seeping through the cracks in the curtains, bathing the room in shadow light. They smiled at each other and then kissed. Then they each said, 'Good Morning'.

'Well, this is the kind of room service that isn't offered in every hotel,' said Oliver.

'And on a scale of one to ten, Sir, where would you rate the room service you've received?'

'Oh, it would definitely be an eleven'.

'Nothing we could improve on?'

'Absolutely nothing at all'.

'Well how about I run down to the kitchen and grab us some brekky that we could have here in bed?'

'The only thing I want in bed for breakfast is you'.

They started kissing and even though they'd been at it well into the night, it wasn't long before they were making love once more. When they were done, Andrew held Oliver in his arms. He'd never felt like this before. He'd felt it from the moment he'd set eyes on Oliver. It was wonderful. But it scared the living Hell out of him.

'Haven't you got a run in the truck today?' asked Oliver as he ran his fingers up and down Andrew's fury arm.

'Yea, to a town called Mudgee. It's only a couple of hours each way plus time to load and unload the truck. I haven't got another overnight run until next week'.

'I've caught you at the right time then'.

'I reckon you have, yea'. And in more ways than one he thought.

Oliver turned himself round to face Andrew. 'Andrew, are you going to explain about you and Polly?'

'It's complicated, Oliver'.

'Well, I'd worked that much out for myself,' said Oliver.

'Course you had' said Andrew as he gently stroked the side of Oliver's face. This man had the face of an angel with no doubt a heart to match.

'The last thing I want is to cause any trouble, Andrew'.

'I know and trust me, you won't be. I will make my life as uncomplicated as it can be so that we can enjoy what we've found with each other whilst you're here in Australia'.

15.

After Andrew had left to go to work, Oliver took a shower and got dressed before making himself a coffee using the kettle in his room. He'd decided not to go to the hotel restaurant for breakfast. He really didn't want to bump into Polly and so he intended to go and find a café downtown. He knew there were several of them so it wouldn't be a problem. He'd also decided not to head to the Barnett family mansion today. Instead, he was going to go to the offices of Barnett Holdings to see if he could organise a meeting with Raymond and Cecilia Barnett through someone there. It may be something of a long shot, but he was going to see the Barnett supremos one way or another whether they liked it or not. He was going to get his answers and only they could provide them.

He couldn't help but smile as he went about things. He'd been knocked sideways by Andrew. He'd never had any intention to get romantically involved during this trip to Australia. Indeed, it was the last thing he would've wanted. But these things come along at the behest of the universe and when you're least expecting them. And he liked Andrew. He really liked Andrew and the connection they'd made had come out of nowhere which made him believe even more than it was meant to be. He had no choice but to accept that it was happening. He wasn't going to be stupid enough to deny it. He couldn't ignore it. This kind of feeling doesn't come along often in life and when it did you just had to grab it despite whatever difficulties it might present.

And besides, some intentions were meant to be broken.

He collected his things together. His mobile, his laptop, his notebook, and put them in his bag which he then, as usual, threw over his shoulder. He headed out of his room and down the corridor with rooms on either side. The housekeepers were starting to replenish the newly vacated rooms that would now be waiting for new guests along with sprucing up those rooms, like Oliver's, that belonged to guests who were in the middle of their stay. He knew they would probably re-make the bed and that made him feel embarrassed. There were damp patch stains all over his sheets after his night with Andrew. But it couldn't be helped. And he was sure the housekeepers would've seen it all before. And worse.

He walked through reception where Katrina the flirt was busy checking people out. There were five people in the line waiting for her attention, a couple of whom looked like they were growing a little impatient at having to wait. The main glass doors were fixed open, and he was about to go through when the voice he didn't want to hear called out to him.

'Oliver!'

He stopped and thought for a moment. Could he act as if he hadn't heard her and just keep walking? No. Ridiculous idea. The reception area wasn't exactly cavernous and of course he'd be able to hear her. He chastised himself. He was a doctor for fuck's sake. He was used to all kinds of situations being thrown at him and having to take responsible decisions accordingly. He hadn't had any doubts about shagging this woman's husband all night and this morning so to ignore her now would be pretty cowardly of him. He turned round.

'Polly?'

'Could we have a talk, please?'.

She led him out into the garden area in front of the hotel. There were a few benches and she gestured for him to take a seat at one of them. She sat down beside him but with a little distance between them. She was dressed in a smart light blue business suit, her skirt just above her knee. The jacket was buttoned and the top one was reasonably high. She wasn't wearing anything underneath. She took a packet of cigarettes out of her pocket and offered him one. He declined.

'I suppose as a doctor you disapprove of smoking' she said in measured tones whilst lighting up. 'But you clearly do approve of sleeping with a woman's husband'.

'I'm not having a slanging match with you, Polly'.

'I'm not after a bloody slanging match' she retorted. She'd taken a drag of her cigarette and closed her eyes whilst holding her hand to her forehead. 'I just thought you might be wondering why I married a man who'd rather stick it up your shitter instead of my jut'.

There was a part of Oliver that wanted to laugh at that, but he didn't think he'd better. She looked tense. She looked really tense. She was an attractive woman with her shoulder length auburn wavy hair. But her eyes looked troubled. And she was thin. She was so thin. He wondered if she ate anything at all.

'Only if you want to talk to me about it,' said Oliver. 'And it looks like you clearly do'.

'Sorry about that' said Polly who was looking everywhere except at him. She'd liked him before he'd slept with her husband. That little detail shouldn't really change anything between them considering the state of her marriage. But it did. A little. But enough.

'Don't be' said Oliver who noted the sarcasm of her voice with a mixture of amusement and irritation. If she thought that she could bully him with words into some kind of admission of guilt, then he was afraid she'd picked on the wrong one.

'I don't want to take the shine off your night'

'You won't'.

'It was a good night then?'

'I'm not going to lie to you, Polly'.

'I thought so. Andrew had a look on his face this morning

that made him look like the cat who'd got the bloody cream. I take it you had no conscience about taking my husband to bed?'

'No'.

'I suppose I should thank you for your honesty'.

'That's not to say I didn't think twice'.

'Well, that's something I suppose. Throughout my life people don't seem to have given a second thought about hurting me. You're probably the first if my memory serves me correctly'.

'I don't know what else to say, Polly' said Oliver who could see that she was growing more tense. She'd already lit a second cigarette and he could see the characteristic shakes in her hands that most alcoholics have when they're desperate for their dependency drug of choice. He couldn't help but feel sorry for her. She looked like the bottom had fallen out of her world a long time ago.

'There's nothing else to say. You'll just be joining a very long list of people who think I'm this pathetic clown who can somehow run a successful business'

'I'm sure they don't look at you like that'.

'How would you know? You don't know me. Or what a sad bloody case I am'.

'Then why don't you tell me?'

She crossed her legs and lit her third cigarette. 'I was born and brought up in Gosford which is north of Sydney on the New South Wales coast. Remember I told you I was just a little kid when my parents died?'

'Yea, I remember'.

'Well, they were both killed in a car accident. I was four years old. I didn't have any brothers or sisters. I remember wondering at the funeral why nobody was holding my hand. Because nobody was. I went to live with my aunt who was my mum's sister. I was nine when her husband started coming to my room at night. I had to wank him off at first. Then after he got bored with that, he got me to suck him off. He said if I told anybody, especially my aunt, then everyone would accuse me of lying and they'd send me to a children's home and forget about me. I was twelve when he started fucking me'.

'Oh Jesus, Polly, I'm so sorry'.

'Why? You weren't the one doing it to me. Anyway, when I got to about fourteen, I became too old for him, and he stopped. But the damage had been well and truly done. I don't know if he did it to any other girls after that'.

'I take it your aunt and uncle didn't have any children of their own?'

'No. They didn't. My aunt called it nature's curse. I never knew if she knew what her husband had been doing to me for all those years'.

'So, what did you do?'

'I was nineteen. I'd finished school and by some miracle had done pretty well. But I couldn't stand playing happy families with them anymore. Every time I looked at my uncle, I wanted to grab a knife and stab him in the heart and twist it round and round whilst watching the look of horror on his face. Whilst watching him die and knowing that I'd done it'.

'I don't think anybody would blame you for feeling like that'.

'Yea, well, there's still a thing called law that stops everybody's fun'.

'So, what did you do instead of stabbing him?'

'I ran off to Sydney. My aunt and uncle were out shopping one day, and I packed a bag. I'd had a job in the admin office of a local engineering company, so I had some money put by. I went to the bank, withdrew the lot, then I jumped on the bus. I stayed in this little hotel for a couple of nights then I found a house share up at the cross. That's the King's Cross area of Sydney'.

'I know it well. This is not my first trip to Australia'.

'And what was the reason for this trip?'

'I don't think you've finished your story yet'.

'Okay. Well Andrew was one of the other house mates. I fell for him straight away. Oh God I was nuts for him'.

'But you knew he was gay?'

'Oh yea. I mean, it's not obvious with Andrew and a lot of people are surprised when they find out. But neither does he try and hide it once you get to know him. Anyway, we were all really drunk one night. And I mean we were totally wasted and out there. He was lying on the couch, and I jumped on him. I suppose you could say I raped him really. He was too gone to do anything about it but not gone enough not to do anything about it if you see what I mean'.

'I think I get it, yea'.

'It only happened that once, but it was enough to make me pregnant. And those were the happiest nine months of my life. Andrew said he'd do the right thing and I took him up on it. We got married. I'd already contacted my aunt and uncle. I wanted to let especially my uncle know that I was happy. That somebody had made me happy after all the shit he'd put me through and even though it wasn't exactly a fairy tale romance, Andrew was and still is my best friend. My aunt and uncle paid for a very nice little wedding with a reception at a local hotel up in Gosford. But it was all a masquerade because my husband and I don't share the same sexuality'.

'So why did you go through with it?'

'Because I wanted a family of my own to make up for all that I'd missed'. Tears started to fall down her cheeks as she continued to recall. 'It's a stupid fucking cliché of modern times but it was how I felt. Anyway, I was very close to full-term when all of a sudden, I stopped feeling my baby kick or move at all. They gave me a scan at the maternity clinic. The doctor said he was sorry to have to tell me that my baby was dead. I gave birth to a still born. He was a little boy and we'd been planning to call the baby Ivan if it had been a boy. My beautiful boy had been taken from me. I ended up having a breakdown and I didn't know if I'd ever be able to put myself back together again. I felt like I'd lost so much. My parents, my innocence to my evil uncle, and now my son. There was no guardian angel looking after me. But it was Andrew who put me back together. He really was a tower of strength. And I made him promise that we'd stay married even though we weren't together as such. I couldn't lose anybody else'.

'My God Polly you've been through such a lot of Hell,' said Oliver. Polly's story was so unbelievably sad, and his heart really did go out to her. He was though trying to work out where it left him and Andrew. He knew that he couldn't wait to see Andrew later on as they'd planned. He also knew that Andrew felt the same.

'Oh, I've pointed my finger up at the heavens in absolute frustration more times than the politicians in Canberra have lied, believe me' said Polly. She wiped her face with her fingers. The tears were still flowing but not as much as before. 'But then I did have a stroke of good luck. My aunt and uncle died with months of each other. And I copped for the lot. Their entire estate. It was enough to buy this place. It wouldn't have been enough to buy anywhere in the city which is why we cast our net a little further and found this place. And I'm pretty good at running it, you know …

Oliver wondered about that. He thought about Nathan and all the extra 'duties' he had to undertake to save Polly's skin.

… and I like watching all the happy couples come and go. Trying to beat Andrew to all the good- looking men who are travelling on their own'.

Oliver smiled. He fitted into that category himself. 'I see'.

'And look Oliver, me and Andrew are done. You know. We're

done. I've made him put up with me for too long and he deserves to be happy with someone who can love him in the way that he needs. And that's not me. Or any woman for that matter'.

'I think we're getting a bit ahead of ourselves here'.

'I'm going on the way he was this morning. And the look that comes into your eyes when you talk about him. It's obvious. And sometimes it doesn't take weeks and months of seeing somebody to realise that. It can happen in an instant. And like I say, Andrew deserves to be happy'.

'And so do you' Oliver emphasised. 'Especially after everything you've been through'.

Polly dragged on her cigarette. 'Yea well, happy endings are a bit thin on the ground in my life'.

'Polly, when you had your breakdown did you have any therapy or psychiatric help of any kind?'

'I refused it. I told you. Andrew got me through'.

'Well, I'm not a psychiatrist but I think you need professional help to deal with the loss of your parents, what happened with your uncle, and then what happened with your baby'.

'All of that is what chardonnay is for'.

'No, Polly, that's not the answer'.

'You've put your doctor's hat back on then'.

'Guilty as charged, your Honour. We medics can't help ourselves. But I'm also saying it as a human being who wants to see you move on from all the pain that you've never dealt with'.

'You're right. I know that'.

'Polly, I want to help you. I feel honoured that you've shared your story with me, and we can't just leave it like that'.

'I'm one of life's tragedies, Oliver. I just have to suck it up'.

'No, you don't. You can get help'.

'I felt like I wanted to tell you and that doesn't happen very often, believe me, so there must be something special about you. I don't disclose my inner most secrets to everybody'.

'Neither do I' said Oliver with no hint of irony. He was glad she didn't pick up on it. He didn't want to have to start sharing his secrets. 'And like I said, you deserve to be happy too, Polly. You're still a young woman and you've got years of life ahead of you'.

'Yea, well sometimes I really wish I hadn't'.

Andrew joined Oliver for dinner that evening, and they went back to the Malaysian restaurant that Oliver had gone to on his first night. In between mouthfuls they talked non-stop. No awkward silences. No silences at all. It was almost as if they'd always been together. When they got back to the hotel, Polly greeted them both with a kiss and insisted the three of them had a drink together. Andrew did his usual thing of helping Nathan the receptionist and barman for a while and that left Oliver and Polly with time to talk some more.

'What you said earlier?' Oliver began, 'About wishing you didn't have years of life ahead of you? Did you mean it?'

'Yes' Polly answered after taking another slurp of her chardonnay. 'Why do you ask?'

'But you can't be happy with that?'

'I am if it means feeling like I do every day'.

'Then get the help that I know must be out there for you'.

'Oliver, darling, I promise I will think about it. I promise you'.

Andrew then came back to them and sat down with his glass of VB. 'Have I missed anything?'

'No' said Polly. 'Now will you two piss off and spend the night together like two people who will be falling for each other pretty soon even if they haven't already'.

Andrew and Oliver looked at each other and neither of them knew quite what to say to that.

'But it's still early,' said Oliver, a little lamely. 'Don't you want some company?'

'I've got my eye on Mr glassware salesman from Melbourne who's sitting on his own over there pretending to miss his darling wife whilst secretly wanting to get lucky because he's far away from home and up for it. And he's not bad in that middle aged married man whose wife probably buys all his clothes for him type of way. So, stop cramping my style and get the Hell out of here'.

When they got back to Oliver's room, he and Andrew were quick to undress each other and get down to business. Afterwards, Andrew turned onto his back whilst Oliver snuggled up on his side and propped his head up with his arm bent at the elbow. He ran his hand through Andrew's black chest rug whilst they talked.

'Well, that was a first,' said Oliver. 'Getting the green light from the wife of a man to have my wicked way with him'.

'And you sure made the most of it' said Andrew, sighing contentedly. He stretched out his body. 'The good doctor certainly gives his patients a very thorough examination'.

Oliver leaned forward and kissed Andrew tenderly.

'God, you taste good,' said Andrew who then opened up his arms. 'Come here Mr Godsend'.

Oliver gladly slipped into Andrew's embrace 'I wonder how Polly got on with the glass salesman from Melbourne'.

'She can be pretty determined when she really wants her man,' said Andrew. 'She's had more men than me'.

'Seriously?'

'Oh yea. And we're both as bad as each other. Most of my fun has come from casual hook-ups too. Hitchhikers, men I've met when I've been staying over somewhere, men who are like me in that they're married to a woman but secretly of the other persuasion. And Polly has been pretty good at targeting men who want nothing more than she does which is to fuck all night'.

'Doesn't it all get a bit, for want of a better word, empty?'

'Yea, that's a pretty accurate word for the kind of open marriage we have'.

'Don't you ever think about the future?'

'I've thought about little else since you arrived on the scene to be honest'.

Oliver lifted up his head and rested his chin on Andrew's chest. 'Andrew, Polly told me her life story today. All of it. I'm so sorry for your loss of Ivan'.

'Thanks, mate' said Andrew, softly and staring out into the space in front of him. 'I think about him every day. He'd be six years old now'.

'Have you been to any kind of grief counselling?'

'Naw. It helped me to help Polly if you see what I mean. And I haven't got all the emotional scars that she has. I grew up in a stable family background. My mum and dad and both my sister and brother are all in the city and I'm close to them. I had a happy childhood and that's what gives me the strength to deal with Polly and all that she carries deep down inside of her. You know?'

'Well, yes, I do. I can't believe the amount of pain that the universe has thrown at her. An unbelievable amount of loss. It really isn't fair'.

'It certainly isn't. She's been through it alright'.

'She's clearly a mess, Andrew and I can well understand why.

But you've committed yourself to living a lie'.

'I know'.

'Polly needs help, Andrew. There's so much she hasn't dealt with'.

'You don't need to tell me' Andrew said. He then began to gently stroke the side of Oliver's face with his fingers. 'And what I need to deal with is the feeling I get when I look at you. For the first time you've made me think how I'm wasting my life. How I'm not helping Polly by keeping up with our arrangement'.

'You're not helping yourself either'.

'No, you're right, I'm not. And though we've barely known other five minutes I feel like I've known you all my life, Oliver. And I don't want to ignore that. I can't ignore it. You do feel the same?'

'Yes, I do but we haven't been dealt with a particularly easy set of circumstances'

'No, we haven't, but I'm sure we can find a way through especially as Polly seems to think that she and I have reached a turning point now that she's admitted that we can't make each other happy with the arrangement we've got, and it isn't fair to impose each other on each other like we've been doing'.

'And I get all of that'.

'But look, there's something I need to know from you. I mean, I'm bloody glad you're here but why are you here? Why have you come to a place like Kingsbrook? I've opened up my heart to you, mate. You need to get fair dinkum with me now. Where do you go each day? Is there somebody you're looking for or something?'.

Oliver thought for a moment. Andrew was right. He did need to come clean and tell him why he was here.

'I came here to try and meet with Cecilia Barnett. Of Barnett Holdings?'

'Well yea, I know who she is, and I know the reputation that she and her brother Raymond have got round here. There's always been talk about them that hasn't exactly been favourable but lately it's grown way more sinister'.

'How so?'

'One of their employees, Ethan Morgan, was dismissed from the company and threatened to take them to court. Then he suddenly dropped the case and then he was found murdered'.

'Murdered? I read about him when I was in Sydney. All about how he was wanted in connection with the murder of a couple. Wasn't their name Hathaway?'

'Absolutely and then Morgan also turns up dead and they're now looking for two other people who, according to our local paper, they think are responsible for all three murders. Oliver, it also said in the paper that Morgan had found something out about the Barnett family that they didn't want to get out and it hinted that because of that they may have silenced him'.

'And they think that whoever murdered the Hathaway couple also murdered Morgan?'

'Correct' said Andrew. They both sat up and Andrew placed his hands on Oliver's shoulders. 'You wanting to see Cecilia whilst whatever the fuck is going on is going on is making me very nervous. Very nervous indeed. Oliver, why do you need to see Cecilia Barnett?'

'I was adopted, Andrew. And I recently discovered that Cecilia Barnett is my birth mother'.

16.

Farrell put in another call to his area commander, Tara O'Brien, who was based at NSW state police headquarters in the city. This was more than a little complicated. Tara O'Brien was his ex. But so was the woman he was calling her about, Becky Rothwell. She was the wife of notorious Sydney drug baron, George Rothwell, and she'd turned up in Kingsbrook. A couple of years ago she'd turned informer on her husband and Farrell had been assigned to handle her. And that had ended up with them having an affair and just when they were ready to go after George Rothwell, he'd shot through, and nobody now knows where he is, or even if he's still in Australia. For her protection, not only from her husband but also from his associates, Becky had been given a new identity of Nicole Wilson and moved to Adelaide. Now she'd been moved to Kingsbrook. Nobody had told Farrell and he should've been told given that since he is the commander of the Kingsbrook police. But he knew that Tara O'Brien would be behind it, and he knew that she had her own particular axe to grind with him. After his affair with Becky Rothwell had been abruptly curtailed, a few months later he'd started an affair with Tara O'Brien who, like him, was also married. It had gone on for several months until Farrell had ended the affair saying that he wanted to try again with his wife to try and make their marriage work. That had been true. But it hadn't worked, and he was also, though he never admitted it at the time, still in love with Becky Rothwell. When Tara had been promoted above him, she made sure he was moved to Kingsbrook where she knew the local officers had been involved in the sexual abuse of children for years and she knew that Farrell would expose them once he found evidence. Which he did. She also believed that it would make him a pariah amongst his colleagues for grassing on his own and it was all about getting back at him for finishing with her. But it didn't make him a pariah. Some went against him, but others considered him a hero. And he knew that it frustrated the Hell out of her.

'Detective Inspector Farrell, good morning to you' she greeted in a wholesome and familiar way after she'd picked up. 'Just to say that I'm talking to a group of new recruits at police college and you're on loudspeaker. So, what can I do for you?'

The bitch. He'd tried twice to call her, and it had gone to voicemail both times. And now on the third attempt she'd put him in a situation where she knew he couldn't talk about what she knew he was calling about.

'I'm calling about a highly sensitive operational matter so I'd appreciate it if you would call me when we can speak confidentially. I have left you two messages already. Thank you and good luck to all the new recruits there'.

He hung up. He was seething. Tara was such a fucking twisted bitch. He wished to God he'd never got intimately involved with her. But he had. He'd let his prick do the reasoning. And now this business with Becky Rothwell was a consequence of it. Trouble was written all over it and it was the very last thing he needed right now. Three still unsolved murders. Glen and Rosemary Hathaway. Ethan Morgan. The ever- increasing shadow of Barnett Holdings hanging over all of it. But now it looked like they might be on to something of a breakthrough thanks to something that had come courtesy of the diligent work of senior sergeant Joel Stringer.

'His name is Adam Petrie' declared Stringer, referring to the man who'd been dumped outside Kingsbrook General Hospital with the broken arm. Stringer had been asked to join the latest detectives briefing. 'Dean Robson, our forensics supremo, took the necessaries from our friend here although he hasn't regained consciousness and that's still the case'. He added the quip 'And

I'm referring to Adam Petrie and not Robson'. He cleared his throat before carrying on. Only Markovic had appreciated the joke he'd made with a light laugh. Farrell and Dawkins both seemed to be a little bit pre-occupied this morning. 'Now Petrie's DNA is on the system because of his previous conviction for assault'.

'And when and where did that happen?' Farrell wanted to know.

Good, thought Stringer. The boss is paying attention after all. Just not to Stringer's jokes. 'This was from an incident in a pub in the city when a fight broke out between Petrie and another bloke who Petrie thought was looking a little too closely at Petrie's then girlfriend. And what stirs the pot even further here, boss, is that Adam Petrie, just like Ethan Morgan was, is an employee of Barnett Holdings. Believe it or not he's employed as a security consultant and his boss is the operations director, Russell Wallace'.

'Is that right?' said Farrell, his mind now working overtime.

'And his DNA has been matched with what was found in Ethan Morgan's house, boss' said Dawkins.

'So, what do we know about him?' Farrell asked.

'He lives up on the Chase Creek Road with his wife Marie-Ann and their four- year-old son Arthur' Dawkins added.

'And I take it his wife hasn't reported him missing?'

'No, boss' Dawkins answered. 'She hasn't. Since he was admitted to hospital, his parents have been there almost constantly, and his sister has visited several times too. But strangely his wife hasn't been anywhere near according to the hospital staff'.

'And that tells us a lot,' said Farrell. 'I want her brought in. I'm sick of playing nice with these people. There's got to be a reason why she hasn't visited her husband in hospital. I also want the house searched and I want all computers confiscated and brought here for analysis'

'I'll get that organised, boss' said Markovic.

'Thanks, Ryan. And I think that what we're looking at here is that an armed Petrie let himself into Ethan Morgan's house and was challenged by Morgan who managed to get the gun off him and in the process, broke his arm in the way that he did. Morgan then ran from the house and the other two mystery suspects we're looking for, went in pursuit'.

'It seems that way, boss' said Stringer.

'Which means that Adam Petrie and the other two suspects must've been working together,' Dawkins asserted.

'They just couldn't not have been, Zo' Farrell concurred.

'And Morgan did not have a firearm license, boss' Markovic added. 'As far as anybody knows he didn't own a gun and certainly didn't have one in his house. Neither his lover Joanna Hathaway nor his ex- girlfriend Martha Stone had ever seen a gun anywhere in the property'.

'Morgan knew they were after him,' said Dawkins.

'I agree, he must've done,' said Farrell. 'But look, it could be argued that it's circumstantial at best but I'm more than ever sure that Barnett Holdings are involved in some way in the murders we're investigating. Now Joel, whilst we're questioning Adam Petrie's wife, I want you to get a team of uniformed officers together. I'm going to get a search warrant and we are going to descend on the head office of Barnett Holdings without warning. We'll gather all the staff in one place, and we'll bring the operations director of Barnett Holdings, this Russell Wallace character, back here for questioning. But we're going to make him wait'.

'Wait for what, boss?'

'Wait whilst we go back to the Barnett Holdings offices where you and the rest of the uniformed team give the place a thorough going over. Whilst that's taking place. Me and detectives Dawkins and Markovic will split the staff into three groups. We'll take one group each and question them individually. And Joel, I want the building turned upside down. I mean really upside down. Leave absolutely nowhere out of your detailed scrutiny. Go through files, confiscate the computers that hold all the staff personnel records, plus Russell Wallace's laptop. It'll all be covered by the warrant. By the time all of that is done, Mr Wallace will have worked himself right up and we'll come back here and start getting him talking'.

'What if he refuses to co-operate, boss?' asked Markovic.

'Then we'll arrest him on suspicion of conspiracy to murder the Hathaway's and Ethan Morgan'.

Stella Rosenberg was proudly walking down the main street of Kingsbrook on the arm of her husband of forty-five years, Lionel Rosenberg. She considered them to be a sprightly old pair of ducks. She caught their reflection in shop windows. And they looked sprightly too. Lionel still had a full head of hair, cut short at the sides and back and still with some black in the growing change to white, and Stella went to the hair salon every Thursday morning, unless she and Lionel were out of the country. They dressed good too. They could afford it. Lionel had run his business highly successfully for decades. He'd made heaps of money running a chain of second- hand car shops which was now being run by their eldest son, Binyamin. Their second son, Isaac, was a dentist with his own practice in the Double Bay area of Sydney. And their youngest, their baby, Eva, had married one of the top criminal defence lawyers down in Melbourne and they'd just moved into a rather lovely house in the Toorak area of the city. Eva was way too busy styling the house to go out to work. Besides, she and her husband were busy trying to make their first baby and she didn't want any distractions. Stella and Lionel couldn't wait to become grandparents. Neither of the boys seemed keen to bless the family with children yet so Stella prayed to God every month that Eva would've conceived. It hadn't worked yet. But it would. They'd led solid lives according to their Jewish faith and deserved the reward.

They were staying with their friends David and Anna Brownstein. They had a lot in common. They were more or less the same age and Anna had been a stay- at- home Mum whilst her husband David had run the family business importing furniture from specialist factories in Thailand and China and then selling it in their own stores across NSW and Victoria. They were both from Kingsbrook and had always lived there. David was also now retired and had handed over the business to their eldest son. This morning they were at the hospital where David was having his usual regular check-up after having had a benign tumour removed from his stomach a couple of years ago. So, Stella and Lionel were taking the opportunity for some time to themselves and a wander round town.

'This place looks alright, Lionel' said Stella after they stopped outside the Oasis café. She saw the menu that was fixed to the wall by the entrance door and stepped forward to take a look. 'And look, they've got a kosher menu. It was meant to be. Come on'.

They took a table one row back from the window. The three next to the window were all taken and that was the first thing that bothered Stella. She liked to sit in the window of places. She liked to be seen. But it was all smiles when Sapphire came up and greeted them before giving each of them a menu.

'Welcome to the Oasis' said Sapphire, cheerfully. Her notepad and pen were at the ready to write down the customers' order. 'Will you be having lunch with us today?'

'Yes, please, dear' Stella replied. 'And we're going to take something from the kosher selection on the menu'.

'Oh, I'm really sorry,' said Sapphire. 'But the thing is, I'm afraid the kosher items on the menu are not available today and for the next few days'

Stella's face straightened. 'And why is that?'

'It's because our supplier of kosher food has gone out of business, and we haven't been able to find a replacement yet' Sapphire explained in her best apologetic voice. She was genuinely sorry. She knew that Sadiq the owner was too, but she got the feeling that with these two it wouldn't be the end of it. 'I really am sorry'.

'No, you're not'.

'Excuse me?'

'You're just being anti- semitic like everybody else' Stella sneered.

'I can assure you we are not being anti- semitic'.

'Don't argue with me, you're only a slip of a girl'.

'I beg your pardon?'

'Don't speak to my wife like that' Lionel spat.

'Look, she started on me and am I supposed to not stand up for myself?'

'Show some respect, girl!' Lionel ordered in a slightly raised voice that caught the attention of the other customers.

'That has to go both ways' Sapphire retorted. Her anger was growing. This couple were so bloody rude.

'Is there a problem with the rest of the items on the menu?' Stella wanted to know.

'No, there isn't'.

'Which proves my point that you're being blatantly anti-semitic!'

'Did you not hear what I said to you? The suppliers of the kosher food we normally offer have gone out of business'

'Liar'.

'It's not a lie' Sapphire insisted. She wasn't going to let this awful couple get the better of her. She wasn't going to lose it with them because that's probably exactly what they wanted.

'Yes, it is a lie' Lionel shot at her. 'People have been using bare faced lies to hide their bigotry against us Jews for centuries'.

Sapphire had never been religious and called herself an agnostic. But she could see that some of the other customers were getting uncomfortable. A lot of hushed voices were circling round the room. She was starting to feel rather uncomfortable herself. It was all making her think of the notes Sadiq had been receiving with the word 'TERRORIST' written on them and she wondered if this couple had anything to do with them. The encounter was starting to unnerve her. Then Sadiq came over.

'Are you okay, Sapphire?' Sadiq asked.

'And who are you?' Lionel demanded.

'My name is Sadiq and I own and manage this place'

'Sadiq?' Stella questioned, her eyes narrowing as she regarded him. 'Are you an Arab?'

'I'm an Australian now' Sadiq replied, his suspicions rising from the tone in her voice. As if being an Arab was some kind of criminal offence. This was going to be trouble. 'I've been here ten years. By birth I'm a Palestinian'.

Stella and Lionel both laughed sardonically. It was as if they'd achieved some kind of victory.

'Then we're right' Stella asserted.

'In what exactly?' Sadiq wanted to know. He didn't really but he didn't think he had any choice.

'Your removal of kosher food from the menu is a deliberate act of anti- semitism because you hate us! Because you refuse to acknowledge who is the boss on the West Bank. And because you're all terrorists!'.

'Look, Sadiq goes out of his way to make sure his kosher customers are looked after and your attack on him is wholly unjustified!' Sapphire charged. 'He's trying his best to find a new supplier, but in the meantime, he won't compromise on how the kosher food is kept and prepared. That's how far he's prepared to go to make sure those who order kosher food get it just how it's meant to be'.

Stella and Lionel smirked as if there was a bad smell right under their noses as they slowly hand clapped.

'And how long did it take you to rehearse that pack of absolute lies?' Stella charged.

'It is not a lie' Sadiq asserted.

'It is a lie because you're a terrorist and you all lie!'

'I'm a victim of terrorism not a perpetrator of it' Sadiq threw back at them, trying to keep his fury under control. 'My father, my unarmed father, was shot dead by Israeli soldiers whilst protesting against the Israeli occupiers forcing Palestinian children through a checkpoint on the way to and from school adding over an hour a day to their journey'.

'You're a terrorist liar and I don't believe you,' Stella barked. 'I don't believe that your father was unarmed because he was a terrorist … '

'… he was not a terrorist!'

'You're all terrorists! And do you know what? I'm glad your father was shot dead. It's called defending Israel's interests because your father was a terrorist because you all are! And one dead Palestinian in a box in the ground is one less terrorist lining up to murder an Israeli. So, I'm glad. Very glad that he's dead. Very glad indeed'.

Sapphire was open mouthed at this woman's callousness. So were the other staff. To say that about Sadiq's father was unforgiveable. And unbelievable.

'You have no right to say that to Sadiq!' Sapphire hissed at her.

'I've got every right! We live in a free country and that gives us a right to free speech!'

Sadiq could barely believe what was happening. Or what he was hearing. He knew his father had not been armed on the day he was murdered by Israeli 'defence' forces. He'd never carried a gun or any other kind of offensive weapon. It just wasn't in him. And for this woman to dishonour his memory in the way that she had was beyond all reason. And all because he'd had to take the kosher selection off the menu. And that wasn't even his fault! The supplier had gone bankrupt for fuck's sake! It just wasn't fair. It wasn't fair at all. But then he noticed that the other three members of his staff had gathered by his side and some of his customers, some of whom he knew as regulars, were also standing up in support of him. He was gratified of course. How could he not be? But he wished it didn't have to happen. He wished it wasn't necessary. He wasn't in the least bit anti-semitic. He'd never allowed himself to fall into that trap. Then one of the other customers who was standing up, a local doctor called Hugh who came in most days during the week, started to speak out in support of Sadiq.

'And I'm now exercising my right to free speech by suggesting that you should leave so that the rest of us can enjoy our lunch without having to listen to you insult our friend Sadiq,' said Hugh.

'Oh, this is what Germany must've been like in the thirties!' Stella hit back. 'The fourth Reich is rising!'

Hugh looked at her pitifully. 'If you only knew how ridiculous you sound. I've been coming in here for two years and this is the first time that the kosher menu has not been available. You are totally out of order to accuse Sadiq of anti-semitism. Totally out of order'.

Lionel and Stella stood up and Stella looked Sadiq up

and down contemptuously. 'We should put a stop to all immigration'.

'And can I ask how you and your family came to be Australians?' asked Hugh. 'I suspect it might've been because your family migrated here?'.

'Our grandparents on both my husband's side and mine, were welcomed here after the second world war because of something called the Holocaust and the taking over of Eastern Europe by the Soviet Union. Do you know about the Holocaust? Six million of our people were murdered by the Nazis. Does that matter to you at all?'

'So, Australia rightfully gave your family sanctuary back in the forties' said Sapphire. 'Because they'd been through one of the most evil periods of history and they'd survived. Yes, I do know all about the Holocaust, and we should never forget that it happened, but it's no justification for you throwing out your nasty accusations to Sadiq, especially when it was your people who stole his homeland and made refuges of his family. And now you want to deny to others the sanctuary that your family were given by Australia? How utterly selfish are you'.

Stella ignored Sapphire and on her way to the door, flanked by her husband Lionel, she stopped in front of Sadiq and shouted into his face. 'Terrorist!'

After they'd gone, Sapphire and the other members of staff wrapped their arms around Sadiq in a group hug, whilst the customers all stood up and applauded. Sadiq was so touched by the response that it was bringing him close to tears. But the woman had more or less spat on his father's grave with what she'd said. It had broken his heart.

He'd come to Australia for a peaceful life and to contribute to the country that had given his family what he thought was a safe home where they wouldn't be victims anymore.

But it seems like thousands of miles mean nothing when

people have got hatred in their hearts.

Markovic took two uniformed officers with him to the home of Adam Petrie who was still lying unconscious in his hospital bed. But it was his wife Marie-Ann Petrie who he needed to speak to and when she opened the door, she had a suitcase in her hand. She looked a little confused when she looked at him. He held up his ID card in front of her.

'Mrs Petrie? I'm detective constable Ryan Markovic. Are you going somewhere?'

'Why do you need to know that?'

'Mrs Petrie, I need you to come with me to the police station'.

'Why?'

'We need to ask you a few questions' Markovic went on. 'It won't take long if you co-operate'.

'But what about my son? Who's going to take care of him?'

'If there isn't a relative who can take care of him then you can bring him with you. He'll be looked after whilst you're answering our questions'.

'But I don't know what I can tell you'.

'Well, you can start by telling us why you haven't been to see your husband since he was admitted to hospital, why you haven't even called the hospital for a progress report, and why, on the basis of what I can see right now, why you're clearly planning a trip out of town when your husband still hasn't regained consciousness. Don't you care about what happens to him?'

17.

Marie-Ann Petrie looked like the sort of girl who thought that her sense of entitlement in a first world country like Australia was way more important than anything as boring as world hunger or millions of people in a faraway country being displaced by war. Markovic had been through the usual shit for the benefit of the tape about her having turned down her right to have a lawyer present and Farrell, who was sitting beside Markovic on the opposite side of the table from Marie-Ann Petrie in the interview room, had been watching her throughout. Her shiny black hair was straight and went halfway down her back. There were probably extensions in it, Farrell thought. She was wearing a fair amount of make-up from the looks of it. The eyelashes were clearly false. She'd had botox injections on her top lip. Her fingernails looked like they'd been 'done' by a professional and were painted alternatively in orange and blue which to Farrell looked hideous. She was wearing tight black leggings that looked like she'd been poured into, and a red vest like top with no bra underneath. He knew that would have absolutely no effect on Markovic, but Farrell had clocked it for one singularly alpha male moment. He couldn't be blamed for noticing. But there was nothing real about her appearance. Nothing at all.

But it was her manner that was intriguing him most. She was acting like this was just a chore she had to get through before she could fly up to the Gold Coast or wherever the fuck she was planning to go. It was written all over her royally enhanced face. This was all proving to be an irritation. A minor obstacle on the way to her having some fun. But where did that indifference come from. And where did it leave her relationship with her husband who was effectively lying on a thin line between normal life and something else.

'I don't intend being here for long' she said as if she'd love to just dismiss them completely. She was running her fingers through the bottom half of her hair, like a recalcitrant teenager who couldn't give a damn about what some teacher dork was trying to teach her. She was totally bored stiff with it all.

'That's for us to decide, Mrs Petrie' Markovic reminded her.

'But you can't keep me here. I can't just leave my son with my mum for however long you decide'.

'I'm afraid you're going to have to, Mrs Petrie'.

'But what is it you want from me?'

'We need you to answer a few questions and if you give us satisfactory answers, in other words, the truth, then you'll be back with your son before he's even noticed that Grandma cooked his dinner tonight and not you. Except you weren't going to be cooking his dinner tonight were you. You were going away somewhere. You'd packed your suitcase and you were planning to go away. I presume, you were taking your son with you?'

'What do you think?' she questioned sarcastically.

'I don't know. Why don't you tell me?'

'Course I was. Do you think I'd leave my four- year-old son to his own devices? What kind of mother would that make me?'

'Well what kind of wife does it make you to leave her unconscious husband lying there in hospital without calling the hospital to check on him let alone actually going to be there at his bedside. And neither did you report him missing for the last three days. Care to shine a light on all that for us, Mrs Petrie?'

Marie-Ann lowered her head. 'It's none of your business'.

'Speak up, Mrs Petrie or else the machine won't hear you'.

Marie-Ann sighed and then raised her voice. 'I said it's none of your business'.

Markovic put on an equally stern voice back. 'Well, it is our business when it becomes clear that your husband may be connected, indirectly or directly, with the murder of three people that we're investigating. So, forgive me for not being sorry for probing into the reasons for your little trip'.

Farrell smiled inwardly. Markovic's skill in interviewing had grown considerably over the past months. When he'd first met him, Farrell had found Markovic somewhat tentative at times and better suited to a softer interview style necessary if you were in someone's home. But those days were long gone. Markovic was a much more accomplished interviewer overall now, whether it be in someone's home or the police officer's home turf of a cop shop interview room. It all contributed to Farrell's satisfaction with the team altogether. He, Dawkins, and Markovic were tight. Really tight. There were no tensions. Any serious disagreements on cases they were investigating, or anything else for that matter, were sorted out over a drink or two in Ned's Place after work. They were mature in their approach. They respected each other's professionalism as police officers. And better still, they liked each other.

Marie-Ann was almost laughing. 'This is crazy. I really shouldn't be here'.

'Yes, we get that you feel that Mrs Petrie, but you haven't come anywhere near to telling us why'.

'I don't need to tell you why'.

'You do need to tell us why, Mrs Petrie' Markovic insisted. 'At the risk of repeating myself, this is a murder investigation, and you need to answer our questions so that we can use your answers to assess whether or not your husband was involved in any of them. Now I ask again, why have you seemingly ignored the fact that your husband is in hospital? And why didn't you report his disappearance?'

'Because it's not the first time it's happened, and on those other times he always came back safe and bloody sound. I'd no reason to believe it wouldn't be like that again this time. As for him being unconscious, again, he's been in hospital before, and I was assured that I'd be kept informed but that his condition wasn't life threatening. And that's all I needed to know because they've never let me down before'.

'Who told you, Mrs Petrie?'

'Look, don't you blokes talk to each other?'

'What do you mean?'

Marie-Ann sucked in air through her clenched teeth. 'I was told to pack some things together for me and my son and we would be taken to an address in the city. As soon as Adam was well enough, he will be joining us there. They wouldn't say if we would end up coming back to Kingsbrook. They said it depended. But on what I really don't know'.

Markovic and Farrell looked at each other as it suddenly hit them what Marie-Ann Petrie was talking about. They just needed her to confirm it.

Markovic leaned forward. 'But who told you this, Mrs Petrie?'

'Your colleagues in the city police force' she blurted out with exasperation. 'That special unit. You don't ever see them wearing uniforms. They turn up on the doorstep and Adam has to do what they say. I shouldn't need to tell you that he's a former dealer. Low level drugs, nothing big like heroin. But enough to bring him to the attention of that unit a few years back. He did a deal with them to avoid being prosecuted and I live with the fear of him turning up on the doorstep with a bullet through his head. He'll be known as a grass. Now I've lived with their control of Adam since I met him and whatever you think you might have on him means nothing. I shouldn't have to tell you any of this, but you'll never be able to charge him with anything. Your colleagues in that special unit won't let you. He's untouchable.

He's a police informer'.

When detective Dawkins got down to the Oasis café that was owned by her partner Sadiq her heart sank at what she saw. The glass in the windows of the café which took up two-thirds of the frontage starting from the top on either side of the glass panelled front door had been shattered by bricks having been thrown through them. The same with the glass in the front door itself. All the shards of broken glass had been swept up into three separate piles across the floor of the café. Senior sergeant Joel Stringer was there with two uniformed officers. He was talking to the boss's daughter Sapphire who'd just arrived for work when the 'incident' had taken place. She'd been joined by the other two full-time staff members. Pieces of paper had been attached by rubber bands to some of the bricks on which had been written various messages. 'THIS CAFÉ IS OWNED BY A TERRORIST', and 'MONEY FROM THIS CAFÉ FUNDS THE MURDER OF ISRAELI CHILDREN' and 'WE MUST FIGHT ANTI-SEMITISM'.

'Oh baby!' cried Dawkins. She rushed over to where Sadiq was sitting on the floor with his back against the counter where cakes and pastries were displayed, and the till was next to them. She knelt down and threw her arms around him. She hugged him to her. 'I got your call and came straight down here. What happened?'

'Everybody was here, and we were preparing to open' Sadiq answered in a low voice. He'd been pretty spooked by the whole thing but thanked God for the fact that nobody had been hurt. This kind of violence was commonplace and everyday back on the West Bank. The enemy had been visible then. In full colour all around them the Israeli Defence force had provoked the Palestinian population into reacting. But the enemy here was invisible. And that made it a whole lot worse. 'Then all of a sudden, these bricks came flying through. It was lucky nobody was hit by one of them'.

'You must all have been terrified'.

'I didn't really have time to think until we heard what sounded like people running' Sadiq explained. 'That's when we thought it must be over and I called the police. And you. If you see what I mean'.

They both allowed each other to smile a little.

'Do you think it was the same people who've been leaving all those notes under the door?' Dawkins asked.

'I don't know, Zoe. We had a couple in here yesterday who caused a scene because I couldn't provide the items on the kosher menu. It could've been them I suppose. Or people who they know'.

Dawkins stroked the side of her lover's face. She felt incredibly guilty. She knew that the resources of the Kingsbrook cop shop had virtually all been taken by the current murder investigation and that everything pertaining to the notes being pushed under the door of the Oasis with 'TERRORIST' written on them had been placed on the back burner. Eyes had been taken off the ball. That meant that whoever was behind it had been able to escalate their campaign.

'We will get to the bottom of this, baby' she said, determined and yet unsure of whether or not she could deliver on what she was promising. 'We will get justice for you'.

'Justice and Palestinian never go in the same sentence,' said Sadiq in a surprisingly composed and calm sounding voice. 'And you know, what makes all of this even worse is that my family moved to the other side of the world to escape the constant tensions in our homeland and lead a normal, peaceful life. But it's just followed us here. Will they ever leave us alone, Zoe? Will they ever leave us alone? Will they ever let us live like normal people?'

Dawkins could see just how much Sadiq's heart was breaking. It was right there in his eyes. Her own heart was breaking for him. But where was all this shit coming from? He'd had the café for three years and he hadn't known any trouble before. So why now? What's triggered it? She'd like to be able to take the day off and help clear the place up and be there for Sadiq, but she knew she wouldn't be able to. The current murder investigation was at a critical point, and she just wouldn't feel right about asking the boss for time off anyway. He'd probably okay it, but he'd do it reluctantly. Even the good guys of this world have their limits. She could say that about Sadiq too and it was concerning her a little that he hadn't chucked a mental over what was happening. He seemed to be internalising his feelings and only expressed them when she went looking for them. She knew that. And it did bother her. He was bottling it all up too much.

They both turned their heads when they heard raised voices at the front of the café where one of the windows used to be. Dawkins saw that Sapphire, who worked for Sadiq and was the daughter of her boss Farrell, was confronting a couple who must be in their sixties and who were dressed in casual but rather expensive looking clothes.

'How dare you show your faces here!' Sapphire raged at Stella and Lionel Rosenberg with whom she'd locked swords the day before when they'd accused Sadiq of anti-Semitism. 'Look at what you've done!' She waved her arm around. 'Look! Are you happy now?'

'We had nothing to do with this' Stella pleaded. 'I swear to you we didn't'.

'You're a liar! This happened only a few hours after you launched your tirade of verbal abuse against my boss which was cruel, nasty and wholly unjustified. You're responsible for this, and for the fact that it's going to take days before we can reopen, and I will not believe your denials'.

'Have you finished young lady?' Stella asked. She knew she had no right to, and that the moment clearly wasn't what could be called opportune. Although maybe it was?

Sapphire folded her arms across her chest. 'Until I have to challenge more of your lies, yes'.

'Then could we please see Sadiq?' Lionel requested. 'We do need to speak to him'.

'Okay, but I'd like you to know that my father is the most senior police officer in this town, and I will call him if you cause any more trouble'.

Sadiq stood up and whispered to Dawkins, telling her who the couple were. He then walked over to them. Dawkins followed discreetly behind him. She didn't want to undermine him. This was his stage. But she wanted to show that she was there for him. And he could count on her.

'What do you want?' asked Sadiq briskly. Sapphire and the other two members of staff were there too.

'I was hoping we could talk privately,' said Stella.

'It's either like this or not at all' Sadiq answered impassively.

'Very well' said Stella who was holding hands with her husband Lionel. 'Sadiq, I owe you a massive apology. I completely over-reacted yesterday. We're staying with our friends David and Anna Brownstein. I think you know them?'

'Yes,' said Sadiq, his heart warming as he thought of the Brownstein's. 'I know them well. They are regular customers,'

'And they told us that. They told us that they'd been coming in here since you opened, and that yesterday was the first day you'd never had the kosher menu available. They also told us about the effort you go to in order to help the local Jewish community celebrate our festival of Passover. You've got a big heart, Sadiq. I should never have laid into you like I did. I should never have accused you of anti-Semitism. Will you forgive me? Please?'

Sadiq couldn't help it. He stepped forward and hugged Stella.

Lionel then joined them and once they were done, they each stepped back.

'Course I forgive you' said Sadiq. 'What kind of man would I be if I didn't? I'd just spend my life being eaten up by bitterness and I'm not going to let anyone, or anything do that to me'. He felt Dawkins rub her hand up and down his back tenderly. He always loved it when she did that but today it felt even better than before. He had love to see him through his strife. He felt lucky. Some people have to go through all the darkness in their life without anyone to hold their hand. Or rub their back.

'Thank you,' said Stella. Lionel then also said 'thank you' and shook Sadiq's hand.

'And please believe us, Sadiq,' said Lionel. 'We had absolutely nothing to do with all this trouble you've had this morning. We'd never have been part of it'.

'I believe you'.

'You'll probably need to make a statement to my colleague Senior Sergeant Joel Stringer over there' said Dawkins who gestured over to where Stringer was discussing something with the other two uniformed cops' he'd brought with him. She then held up her ID. 'I'm a police officer too, and I'm also Sadiq's girlfriend'.

'We'll co-operate as much as we can,' said Stella. 'But we don't know anything'.

'Then just say that in your statement and give an account of the argument you had here yesterday,' said Dawkins. 'It'll be fine I'm sure'.

'It must've taken a lot for you to come here and apologise this morning,' said Sadiq.

'I agree' said Sapphire, smiling at Stella and Lionel. 'Good on you'.

'We spoke to you very badly too, young lady,' said Lionel.

'And we're sorry'.

Sapphire was still smiling. It wasn't quite a happy ending. The shop was still in a dreadful mess. But at least these two had held their hands up. 'Accepted. Thank you'.

'There is one more thing, Sadiq' Stella began. 'We want to apologise for the death of your father and for the way it happened'.

'We would never support the state of Israel gunning down unarmed civilians' Lionel added. 'We want you to understand that'.

Sadiq felt a lump come into his throat as he thought of his father. He thought of his smile. He thought of his bright eyes. Sadiq had got his big heart from his father. He'd never been a bitter man despite having been turned into a refugee. The morning he'd gone out on the demonstration he'd been happy. He'd been determined to show that peaceful non-violent means of fighting back can overcome even the mightiest of military power. And he'd paid for it with his life. Sadiq would never forget going to see him in the mortuary. Helping to carry his coffin in the funeral procession. Trying to comfort his mother and the rest of his family. It had been a period where time had appeared to stand still.

'And I do,' said Sadiq. 'I just wish my father was still alive to hear you say that'.

'Well look,' said Lionel who handed Sadiq his business card. 'If for any reason the insurers don't come good, or you end up in difficulties because of the loss of trade, or you need financial help for whatever reason with getting this place back into shape, then please call and we'll do whatever we can'.

'We so will, Sadiq,' said Stella. 'We very much want to help after what we put you through yesterday. Some of the things I said were unforgivable'.

'Thank you. It's very much appreciated'.

'That is very good of you' Dawkins agreed.

'Some of the things you said did cut pretty deep but when you grow up in what is essentially a war zone you get to be able to harden your heart when you need to'.

'You shouldn't have to'.

'No, I shouldn't. But let's not get into the whole Israel and Palestine debate now. Let's just be grateful for the fact that we're on the opposite side of the world which means that we can be friends because here we're not enemies'

'Can we help you clear up in here?' Lionel asked.

Sadiq smiled. 'No, thank you for the offer but we'll be right. We know where everything goes, and I've got to get some professional blokes in to board up the front until I can get new windows fitted'.

'Well, we'll give our statement to the police and then head back to the city,' said Stella.

'Whereabouts in the city do you live?' asked Sapphire. 'Me and my parents used to live in Manly'.

'Well, we live in Rose Bay, dear' Stella answered, a little self-consciously. Admitting to living in one of the more exclusive parts of Sydney can sometimes induce a somewhat less than balanced form of envy in people. And she didn't want to add to the possible fragility of the positive vibe that had broken out here. It was all smiles at this very moment, but they might be hiding harder feelings.

'Oh, right' said Sapphire with a knowing smile. She'd heard all about Rose Bay. 'I've never been to that part of the city, but I've heard it's a pretty nice address'.

'Well, we like it,' said Stella. 'Our two sons and their families both live in the next suburb, Double Bay, and they still come to us for Friday night dinner, but our daughter is married to one of the top lawyers down in Melbourne and lives there now'.

Dawkins wondered why she'd had to emphasise that her son-in-law was 'one of the top lawyers down in Melbourne?' Why couldn't she have just said that he was a lawyer? She hated braggers. It was so unnecessary and just got people's backs up. And she'd bet that it would be a million times harder for an Aborigine like herself to be even thought of as a top lawyer in any Australian city. And yet her tribe had been here for thousands of years compared to this Stella woman and her tribe who'd only been here for five minutes in comparison. But that's part of what it means to be human. It really does depend on where you are in the pecking order. And if you're an Aborigine, just like if you're a Palestinian, you don't come anywhere near the top of the human race pecking order. You have to fight to get wherever you want to go. Tribes that are higher up don't have to fight. She was musing on her perspectives when Senior Sergeant Joel Stringer came up to her.

'I know what you're going to say, Joel' she said.

'We haven't been able to go through any of the CCTV footage following all the notes being pushed under the door,' said Stringer. 'Zoe, I just don't know when we're going to get to a full and proper investigation into this. I'll make it the priority right behind the murder investigation. We're going to interview people in the vicinity once again and we'll flag it up to the media. I'll do my best, Zoe'.

Dawkins smiled and patted his arm. 'I know you will, mate. I'm desperately worried about Sadiq though. First, it's notes, now it's bricks through the window. Who is out there doing this? Do they know where we live? Are the staff safe on their way to and from work?'

'Including our boss's daughter'.

'Including her, yes'.

'Do you believe our friends Stella and Lionel when they say they had nothing to do with it?'

'I do,' said Dawkins as she looked round at the bomb site of a mess all around her. Sadiq and his folks would be cleaning up all day and still they'd finds bits of glass for days to come. Pieces of smashed glass got absolutely everywhere. 'My instincts tell me they're speaking the truth, given though that I've only spoken to them briefly. But the old copper's nose isn't twitching. I believe them'.

'Well, we'll take their statements and then take it from there if we need to refer back to them,' said Stringer. 'But we also both know that criminals don't often look like criminals these days. They either look like drug addicts or people like Stella and Lionel Rosenberg. People you wouldn't think twice about if you passed them in the street and that provides the best cover'.

Dawkins lifted her phone out of her jacket pocket when it started to ring. The news she received sounded promising.

'Adam Petrie has woken up in hospital' she declared. 'And apparently, he's keen to talk. So, the raid on the Barnett Holdings offices has been put on hold. I've got to go. See you back at the cop shop, Joel'.

Dawkins then went over to her boyfriend Sadiq, and they embraced one more time after she told him she had to get back to work.

'I'm sorry, babe.'

'It's okay,' said Sadiq. 'You know I understand. Now get back to work and I'll see you tonight'.

Dawkins kissed him and then said, 'See you tonight'.

18.

Oliver Townsend woke up and it took him a moment or two to remember where the Hell he was. His immediate surroundings were clear enough. He was lying on a bed, a large bed, in a bedroom that was fitted out with the usual wardrobe and set of drawers, all in a very modern style. The curtains were drawn closed, but he could see that it was daylight outside from the light that was shining its way through on either side. He tried to lift his head off the pillow and that's when the pain struck him. He pulled a face and rubbed the back of his head. Shit. It was bloody painful.

Then he remembered.

He remembered the blow he took to the back of his head whilst he'd been waiting for his 'mother' Cecilia Barnett. Her secretary, a rather severe looking woman who'd introduced herself only as Miss Barnett's 'secretary' without giving any name, had shown him through to the rather grand living room of the mansion after she'd let him in. It had struck him that he could probably have fitted three or four living rooms the size of his own back in the UK, into this one. And everything looked mightily expensive. From the four- seater couch, the two elegant high- backed armchairs, the mirror that looked like it would crack if it didn't like the look of whoever was looking into it, and all the soft furnishings of cushions and wraps. Everything looked expensive. The ill- gotten gains of those who'd traded on the wrong side of what would be acceptable to most normal people and his research into the family had shown him that the Barnett's were anything but a normal family. They'd been under police investigation on several occasions, but nothing had been able to stick. They seemed to have got through life like Teflon. Nothing had ever stuck. Oliver wondered if they'd simply paid people off. They must've done. Nobody sails as close to the wind as they have without having paid people off. It's how some people who are rich make their money. Application to the task at hand without any sign of anything resembling a conscience.

Just like handing over an unwanted child for adoption. He still didn't know the precise circumstances but from what he had gathered about his birth mother, he couldn't imagine Cecilia Barnett having had any feeling for him at all when she handed him over.

The view from the floor to ceiling windows in the living room was pretty awesome. Fields, bush, trees for as far as the eye could see. Oliver had thought it was the best thing he'd seen about the mansion so far. The view from the inside to the outside.

As he'd stood there, he suddenly started to wonder why the fuck he'd come. What was he hoping to gain from this? He certainly didn't want any of the Barnett money. He wasn't rich. He was comfortable. As a doctor he earned not a bad packet really. It meant he didn't have to worry too much about making ends meet at the end of the month when his salary went into his bank account. He'd managed to put some by since he'd qualified too. His Mum had also left him something and he'd used a portion of that to put down the deposit on the terraced two-up, two-down in Windsor that he called home. His dad had helped him with that too. He'd been lucky. He'd been adopted. And he still missed his mum. Because she'd been his real mother. She'd been the one who'd been there when he needed her. She'd been the one who'd wiped his nose and dried his tears. She'd been the one who'd looked after him when he'd been sick. She'd been the one who'd given him the love that had inspired the confidence in him to become a doctor. She'd been there with her comforting arms when his first boyfriend had broken his heart. She and his dad had both been there exactly at the precise moments when he'd needed them. So why had he flown to the other side of the stupid world on some stupid emotional quest? Because she was his birth mother. And he wanted something from her.

But what?

He'd been contemplating what he should've thought more about before he left the UK when he felt the first strike against the back of his head. It had made him see stars. It had made him unsteady on his feet. He'd started to try and turn round when the second blow struck.

And he hadn't known anything after that.

Until now.

He wondered how long he'd been out for. They must've taken his mobile phone because he didn't have it and he couldn't see it anywhere around. He thought of Andrew. The man he'd just met but was already crazy about. The man who hadn't wanted him to come out here to the mansion. The man who'd tried to warn him of the potential dangers from a family that operated outside of the normal ways of everybody else. The man whose wife was an alcoholic and an extremely troubled soul with a very sad past. He'd felt for her. He really had.

He swung his legs out and planted his feet as firmly as he could on the floor. He leaned his head back. God, it was hurting like bloody hell. Where was ibuprofen when you needed it? He clenched his fists and put them on the edge of the bed to push himself up. And it worked. He stood there for a moment. His head started to spin a little. Then it stopped. The back of his head, his neck and shoulders, were all throbbing. But he put one foot in front of the other and was able to carry himself forward. He was walking okay. He pulled back the curtains and realised that the room he was in must be directly above the living room because the view was the same as that he'd seen whilst he'd been 'waiting' for Cecilia. His birth mother. The woman whose birth canal he'd come down but who had never been a mother to him. She'd given him away instead.

And she'd probably done him a favour in that regard.

He tried the windows, but they were locked shut. He went over to the door and that was locked too. What the fuck was happening here? Who'd knocked him out earlier? Who'd locked him away up here? What were they planning to do with him?

Farrell and Dawkins stood by the bed that Adam Petrie was lying in. Senior nurse Bao Nguyen had been responsible for his nursing care throughout and made sure he was comfortable, before checking the fitting of his oxygen mask and a drip that was going into his arm, plus a couple of other monitors that were helping to manage his progress to recovery. He then turned to Farrell and Dawkins.

'I'll leave you to it,' said Nguyen.

'Thanks' said Farrell.

'He's still a little groggy so don't press him too hard on anything'.

'No worries. Thanks again, mate'

Once Nguyen had left the room, Farrell turned to Petrie. 'I must say Adam, you don't look bad considering'.

'Yea, well, the morphine helps' said Petrie. 'But it does feel like I've got my whole-bloody body weight of plaster on my arm here'.

'Yea, that doesn't look too comfortable' said Farrell as he looked at Petrie's injured arm. The plaster went from his wrist right up to his upper arm and it was thick. It didn't make Farrell feel particularly sorry for him though. Not until he'd heard what he had to say. His wife had 'outed' him as a police informer. But to which department? And about what? Once again Farrell was angry at having been kept in the dark by those higher up the chain. He'd been in contact with people in the NSW police headquarters in the city, wanting to know who was handling

Petrie, but had not received anything like a definitive answer. All he was told for certain was that it was to do with the organised crime unit. He did of course know about the organised crime unit but trying to engage with it was like trying to engage with some kind of secret society, like trying to get into the Prime Minister's office if you were from an opposing party. It made him wonder if everyone in the force was on the same bloody side. There'd always been corruption in the force. Farrell had seen a lot of it himself without letting himself get touched by it. Was this just another example of it? He hadn't even tried to contact his area commander, Tara O'Brien. Farrell's ex. And what made it ever more complicated was that he couldn't rely on her to remain professional and keep an unbiased view of things where he was concerned. He strongly suspected that she had a hand in it somewhere just like he strongly suspected that she also had a hand in bringing Farrell's former lover, a woman he really had loved, Becky Rothwell, wife of Sydney crime boss, George Rothwell, to Kingsbrook under her new identity they'd given her after she'd turned informer on her husband. Farrell wished to God he'd never got involved with Tara in the first place. She was a wonderful woman in many ways, but he had been led by what was in his pants. And he'd never felt anywhere near the same for her as he had done for Becky Rothwell.

'It isn't. Believe me'.

'So, what have you got to tell us, Adam?' asked Dawkins.

'I've never seen you two before' said Petrie as he looked them up and down, a little suspiciously. 'You're not from the organised crime unit, are you? Where's Tommo?"

Farrell introduced both himself and Dawkins and they held up their ID cards. 'We're from the local police here in Kingsbrook, Adam. Certain crimes have taken place in the town that we're investigating, and we believe that you could provide some very useful information'.

'I don't know if I'm authorised to talk to you about it'.

'Adam, I'm chief of the police in this town and I'm authorising you' said Farrell, firmly. Enough of all this bloody bullshit. 'Now we need you to tell us about what's been happening. Bearing in mind that we know that you were in Ethan Morgan's house on the afternoon he ran and was chased into finding sanctuary in the car of Glen and Rosemary Hathaway who were then brutally murdered in their own home. Then Ethan Morgan himself turns up dead two days later. What happened to you in the meantime, Adam? How did you end up being dumped here at the hospital? Who dumped you here? We need answers, Adam. We need them from you'

Petrie shifted slightly in his bed. It wasn't a comfortable position to be in, either in regard to his injury or to the pressure he was under with these two. But things had got out of hand. He was scared. Scared for himself. Scared for his wife and his kid. He had to do something.

'I was told to go into Ethan Morgan's house and bring him in'.

'Who told you to do that, Adam?' asked Dawkins. 'And bring him in to where?'

'Look, you've got to protect me and my family' Adam pleaded. 'I won't tell you anymore until you give me that assurance'.

'Who would we be protecting you and your family from, Adam?'

'From Barnett Holdings! I work for them. Russell Wallace, their head of operations, is my boss. He employed me and a couple of others to help maintain the darker side of their business. You don't know what they're capable of. You've got to protect me and my family. You've got to'.

'Adam, I get that,' said Farrell. 'Now your wife and son have been moved to an address in the city and you'll be joining them when you're done here'. He'd managed to find that much out at least from the organised crime unit in the city. They were such generous bastards with their info.

'Then you'll have to protect me whilst I'm in here' Petrie insisted.

'And I promise you that we will' said Farrell, a little exasperatedly. 'But you've got to tell us everything, Adam. You've got to help us untangle all of this mess'.

'You don't ask for much,' said Petrie. He then managed a half-smile. 'I knew the two of you weren't from the usual unit I deal with because you look too much like police officers'

'Well, we'll take that as a compliment,' said Farrell, with a glance at Dawkins. 'So, I presume this Tommo character is your usual handler?'

'Yes. Didn't you know that?'

'Look, just forget him for the moment, Adam. You'll just have to make do with us'

'And you can start by telling us why you had to bring Morgan in,' said Dawkins. 'You went to Ethan Morgan's house that day and you were armed. We want to know why, Adam. Bring him in to who and for what reason?'

'Ethan Morgan was fired from his job at Barnett Holdings because he'd found out a secret about the Barnett family that he was threatening to make public'.

'It must've been a pretty big secret,' said Farrell.

'It was something to do with how and why the Barnett family moved from the UK to Australia at the end of the second world war' Petrie went on. 'I don't know what that secret is'

'You don't?'

'I seriously don't' Petrie insisted. 'But what I do know is that they are prepared to do anything to protect it'.

'Including murder?'

'It looks that way, yes'.

'But why did they fire him which to me would increase the risk of him going public with what he'd found out?'

'That doesn't make sense to me either, but you'd have to ask the Barnett's about that. You see, they send their orders down through Russell Wallace and he has to carry them out'.

'And did you go into Ethan Morgan's house on his instructions?'

'Yes. They'd paid him off, but he hung around which made them suspicious that he'd spill the beans anyway. We knew that he was waiting to see if his lover Joanna Hathaway would come with him and make a new start with the money he'd been given. But the Barnett's grew paranoid, and they wanted him taken out. I went into the house, but he was waiting for me behind a doorway. Ethan was no fool. And he knew they might try something, but I guess that the love he felt for Joanna Hathaway made him quite reckless. He jumped me and that's when he broke my arm. I saw him pick up the gun I'd been carrying which he'd knocked out of my hand and run off with it. I didn't know much after that because I was in such fucking pain. And I must've passed out'.

'Who were the two others you were with, Adam?'

'You will protect me and my family?'

'Yes'.

'I have your word?'

'You have my absolute word. Adam'.

'Their names are Adrian Porter and Steve Bellamy. They're also on the payroll at Barnett Holdings thanks to Russell Wallace. They hoped my arm would heal. When it became clear it wasn't going to and needed medical help, it was Porter and Bellamy who dropped me, literally, at the doors of the hospital'.

'Adam, was it Adrian Porter and Steve Bellamy who murdered Glen and Rosemary Hathaway?'

'Yes. They followed Ethan Morgan after he'd been picked up by the Hathaway couple. Later they came back to pick me up and Morgan was tied up in the boot of the car. At the house of Adrian Porter, I knew they were keeping him in an upstairs room, but they always took him somewhere else to beat the living daylights out of him. Where that was, I don't know. They told me that he kept on insisting that he hadn't told anybody about the secret the Barnett family were carrying. But they kept beating him. Then they told me they'd killed him and dumped him in the river. Sometime after that they dropped me at the hospital'.

'But why did they murder Glen and Rosemary Hathaway?'

'They thought they were associates of Ethan Morgan and were willing to grass on the Barnett family. But of course, they weren't associates at all. They were innocent bystanders who got caught up in it all by sheer fluke of driving their car in that place at that time. Ethan Morgan thought he'd been able to escape. But he hadn't counted on Adrian Porter and Steve Bellamy following them'.

'So, Porter and Bellamy truly believed that the Hathaway's knew the Barnett family's big secret?' Dawkins questioned. 'Just because they'd seen them picking Morgan up and therefore assumed they were collaborators?'

'Yes' Petrie answered. 'Like I say, they followed them and used their guns to threaten them into letting them into the house. They beat Morgan up and started their fun and games with the Hathaway's. When they'd done with the Hathaway's they took Morgan away. They picked me up on the way to Porter's house. They're both very violent men. That's why Wallace hired them. But look, I got involved in the seedier side of the Barnett business because of some low- level drug dealing I got into in the city which brought me under the radar of Russell Wallace. He said he wouldn't dobb me into the cops if I came to work for him. He already knew that I had a conviction for assault because of a fight I'd had in a pub'.

'That was how we identified you, Adam'.

'Yes, I knew it would be. But those hours I was trying to recover from my broken arm that was causing me more and more pain as the hours went on, I knew they were holding Ethan Morgan in a room upstairs and were beating the living Hell out of him. I heard him screaming and calling out for them to stop. They were convinced he was talking to the media, and he kept on denying it. But they wouldn't believe him. And eventually it all went quiet. That told me that Morgan was no longer of this world'.

'Did you fear for your own safety?' Dawkins asked.

'Not really' Petrie replied. 'I was on the same side as them. But then again, that wouldn't have stopped them turning on me if they thought they had due cause. I was literally in absolute agony and went unconscious with it. That's when they must've dumped me outside the hospital here'.

'You're taking a big risk now, Adam' said Farrell who nevertheless couldn't wait to start working on the substantive information Petrie had given them. 'What's made you turn now?'

'The murder of the Hathaway's. They were a pair of old ducks who'd done nothing against the Barnett empire. And the way they were murdered was way beyond anything. Porter and Bellamy seemed to have enjoyed it, you know. I could tell when they were boasting about it. I also got to know that they were thinking of going after Joanna Hathaway because of her affair with Ethan Morgan. She's just a woman with a kid, you know, just like my wife. And yea, she had an affair with Ethan Morgan but the last time I looked adultery wasn't punishable by death in this country'.

'So they would've killed her?' Farrell asked.

'If she hadn't told them what they wanted which she wouldn't have because I'm convinced that she knew nothing,' said Petrie. 'Because there was nothing to know. Morgan had not gone to the press about the Barnett family secret. He knew it but he just wanted Joanna to run away with him'.

'Adam, how come the organised crime unit got involved with all this?' Farrell wanted to know. They hadn't been involved before when Farrell had been investigating George Rothwell in the city.

'The Barnett family have made huge amounts of money, and I mean huge amounts, from people trafficking into Australia. Their associates loan money to really poor people in Asian countries and those families have to hand over one of their teenage daughters as part payment for the loan. These girls are then trafficked into Australia to be used as debt bondage or to put it another way, slaves. Usually in the underage sex market. That's why the organised crime unit got involved. But what's complicated it all recently is that their business partner, if you can call him that, in this whole people trafficking enterprise, is a Sydney crime boss called George Rothwell. The city police were about to swoop on him last year, but he conveniently disappeared when they went to pick him up. But I know for a fact that the Barnett's are hiding him somewhere, maybe even somewhere here in Kingsbrook. What I also know is that he's still working with them. They're still trafficking these young and very vulnerable girls. They take their passports off them and tell them they'll be killed if they say anything to anyone about their situation'.

The mentioning of the name George Rothwell was like a light going on inside Farrell. So much was now making perfect sense. The organised crime unit must've known that George Rothwell had been working with the Barnett's in their odious people trafficking enterprises and that's why they moved Becky Rothwell here. They wanted to draw him out. They must've known that the Barnett's were hiding him out somewhere. And yet he'd heard nothing from them. He knew that Markovic would've been right on top of entering every new development into the system. After this little bit of a yarn with Petrie he'd have a lot more to enter. Farrell hadn't been a member of the organised crime unit when he'd been involved in investigating George Rothwell back in the city. The organised crime unit hadn't been investigating Rothwell then. It had been the serious crimes team within the existing CID. What the fuck were they playing at now? Why were they seemingly leaving everything to Farrell?

'Adam, is there anything else you want to tell us about? Anything else you think we need to know about?'

'Jeez, haven't I spilt enough?'

'Well, we can leave it there. For now. But we may not have finished with you. That will be a judgment that we'll make. You see, whilst you're busy breaking the law, we're busy upholding it. Whilst you're busy playing your little game of double agent, we're busy on the right side of the law at all times'.

'Entertaining though that little speech was, detective, I have given you almost everything you wanted on a plate'.

'Yes, and the crucial word there is almost. You haven't divulged the big Barnett secret'.

'Because I don't bloody know it! I told you that. Now I need you to protect me in here'.

'And we will. There'll be a guard on your door at all times and regular patrols will be made of the entrance to the building. Now just one more thing, Adam. I assume you're going to be willing to put everything you've told us today in a statement which we can use in court?'

Petrie took a deep breath. 'It wouldn't have been worth telling you otherwise'.

'Good. Hope the rest of your recovery goes well. We'll be in touch'.

The expression on the face of Russell Wallace, operations director of Barnett Holdings, was grave as Farrell and Markovic, with a team of uniformed colleagues, arrested him in his office. And it didn't change as he was led away in handcuffs after being charged with conspiracy to murder.

'And we're just getting started' said Markovic as he held Wallace's arm as they walked through the building where they were being watched by all the staff.

When they got back to the cop shop, Farrell and Markovic left Wallace to stew a little in the interview room whilst Farrell held a press briefing. All of the national TV news channels were there, along with representatives of the local and national print and internet media organisations. Warrants had been issued for the arrests of Adrian Porter and Steve Bellamy. Raids had been made on their homes in the town and certain personal belongings had been confiscated, like laptops. Dawkins and Senior Sergeant Joel Stringer would be going to the Barnett mansion to arrest Cecilia and Raymond Barnett on charges in connection with people trafficking. That had received the loudest audible response. The Barnett's were powerful to say the least and it seemed like nobody had ever questioned their activities before. That became everything the journos wanted to know about, but Farrell only answered half a dozen questions before saying he had to move on.

Farrell and Markovic then went into the interview room where Wallace was sitting alongside his lawyer, Louise Bateman, who'd come down from the city and looked the epitome of a tiger roaring defence counsel. Farrell had heard the name of Louise Bateman many times before. She'd represented several high- profile cases involving Sydney's underworld over the years, managing to secure the freedom of some of the most evil- minded low life in the contemporary criminal history of not only Sydney, but also the rest of Australia too. Her clothes, her make-up, her hair, the bag she'd brought her laptop and paperwork in. It all shouted loudly the huge amount of dollars she must be able to spend on her appearance. Farrell wondered how she could sleep at night knowing that she worked to secure the freedom of individuals who make a business out of killing. It was their money that went to make her look so cheap.

Farrell went through the usual preliminaries but before he was able to hand things over to Markovic who was going to lead the interview, Bateman answered a call on her mobile. Whoever had called her obviously wasn't a great talker because for the few seconds she was on the phone, Bateman remained composed and didn't give anything away on her face. She then ended the call and asked if she and her client could have some time alone with her client. Farrell said she could have five minutes and no longer. He and Markovic then left the room and desk Sergeant Mary Chung came up to them.

'Boss, we've had a call from the owner of the Clarendon hotel, just on the edge of the centre of town,' said Chung. 'Her name is Polly Henshaw and she and her husband Andrew say that they've had a guest staying at the hotel, a UK national by the name of Oliver Townsend, who yesterday had a meeting with Cecilia Barnett out at the Barnett mansion. He left for that meeting over twenty-four hours ago, boss and he hasn't been seen or heard of since. They've been ringing his phone, but it keeps going to voicemail. Now, Andrew Henshaw was already concerned about their guest's intended visit because of the reputation of the Barnett's and because of the reason why Oliver Townsend was going to see them. So, he had a tracker placed on Oliver Townsend's phone. It's been at the Barnett mansion since half an hour after he left the hotel yesterday morning'.

'But he's not been answering it?'

'No, boss. Not even late into yesterday evening and early on this morning'.

'And why did this Townsend character want to see the

Barnett's?' Farrell asked.

'Boss, he apparently told Andrew Henshaw that he'd been adopted as a small baby back in the UK in 1992. His adopted mother died of cancer a couple of years ago and, like a lot of people in that position, he decided to trace his birth mother'.

'And she turned out to be Cecilia Barnett?'

'Bull's eye, boss. He's been trying to contact her for months from the UK and received no response at all. Phone calls, letters, emails. All of them had been ignored which is why he took the plunge and flew out here to try and make contact with her. Henshaw drove out to the mansion yesterday evening, but they wouldn't let him past the electronic security gates at the entrance to the driveway leading up to the front door, and they told him that they'd never heard of an Oliver Townsend. Because it's been more than twenty-four hours, the Henshaw's have now officially reported him as a missing person. They're concerned about what's happened to him and it sounds like we should be too'.

19.

Farrell shared the concern for the safety of Oliver Townsend. It didn't seem like the Barnett family would do emotional reunions with children they'd once given up for adoption and he was nervous about what might have happened to Townsend. He'd called Dawkins who was on her way to the mansion with Senior Sergeant Joel Stringer and a team of uniformed officers and brought her up to speed. Townsend must be somewhere on the property. He'd certainly been there for his mobile phone to have seemingly been abandoned there. Farrell told Dawkins that he wanted Townsend found as a matter of urgency. His description had been given to them by Andrew Henshaw, husband of the owner of the Clarendon Hotel, and it had been circulated to every officer on patrol and to neighbouring cop shops too.

'Well, well, well' said Farrell after he and Markovic had gone back into the interview room where Russell Wallace was still sitting there, still looking like he had the weight of the world on his shoulders. Which he probably did have. But then again those who live by the sword die by the sword, and Wallace had been involved with the Barnett's long enough to understand that if the walls came tumbling down, he'd be buried in the rubble.

'Where's Mrs Bateman?' Wallace wanted to know.

'On her way back to the city' Farrell told him. He looked at his watch. 'She'll have got through town and be on the freeway by now. I'm sure she'll soon be sipping cocktails in her swanky apartment. Because I'm sure it is pretty swanky. Lawyers like her who make their money from saving evil bastards from answering for their crimes always do have pretty swanky addresses'.

'Where is she?' Wallace repeated testily.

'Don't you think you can trust the word of a police officer? Or are you getting a little short of patience, Russell? Or do you prefer being called Russ? Is that what your friends call you? Russ? I'll bet your mother doesn't call you that. I'll bet she calls you Russell. I'll bet your wife insists on calling you Russell too. Doesn't she? Does she know what you really get up to when you tell her you're at work? Does she know that you hire people to do the Barnett's dirty work for them?'.

'Where is Louise Bateman?' Wallace roared.

'She's left you high and dry!' Farrell shot back. 'Hadn't you worked that out for yourself? Or did I underestimate just how stupid you are?'

Farrell watched as Wallace sat back before leaning forward and burying his face in his hands. He looked absolutely conflicted. Like he really didn't know which way to go. The Barnett's must have quite a hold over him. Or had quite a hold on him. They've thrown him away now.

'Let me spell it out to you in words you might be able to understand, Russ' Markovic began with a note of sarcasm. 'Louise Bateman will no longer be representing you. She's been instructed by her bosses, Cecilia and Raymond Barnett, to drop you. To leave you to your own devices. People like the Barnett's see people like you coming, Russ. They chew you up and make you think that you're mixing with the high life and that you're right up there with them. The fact that their activities are largely criminal is just a detail once you've been drawn in. You're high on the excitement of it all by then though. High on that over-rated sense of your own importance that they've given you. And you were too stupid to see through it all. Or they were too clever. You can look at it either way. The conclusion is the same. Once things go wrong, you're on your own. And that's where you are now. On your own. The ones who made you what you are wouldn't spit on you now if you were on fire'.

'Alright, alright, enough!' Wallace pleaded. He lifted his face back up and looked anxiously at Markovic. 'What do you want from me?'

'What do we want from you?' Markovic repeated in an exasperated tone. 'Russ, we've already got enough on you to charge you with conspiracy to murder. You'll be going down. But you can help yourself and us. You can help us conclude this investigation and get justice for all those who need it. Like Glen and Rosemary Hathaway. Like Ethan Morgan. And you can tell us what's happened to a British citizen called Oliver Townsend who went for an arranged meeting with Cecilia Barnett yesterday and, according to the people who run the hotel he was staying at, never returned. Where does he fit into it all? Just start wherever you like, Russ. But give us the truth. Otherwise, your co-operation will mean nothing in terms of your defence. Zilch. Zero. Complete fuck all'.

'You really think it's that easy for me?'

'Well, you tell us why it isn't?'

'You don't know the kind of people you're dealing with here'.

'Well then you need to enlighten us' said Markovic. 'I mean, did you know that Adam Petrie had been informing on your activities, Russ?'

'I had suspected' Wallace replied. The police were right. He had been stabbed in the back. The Barnett's would deny everything. And they'd probably find some way of getting away with it. That's what was sticking in his throat more than anything. He'd controlled everything at Barnett's. Now everything was going to control him. The man who'd thought he was mighty for all these years had fallen in a matter of seconds. 'It was just an instinct. Nothing more. And I never challenged him about it'.

'Did you inform the Barnett's of your suspicions?'

'He wouldn't still be alive if I had'.

'And what about Adrian Porter and Steve Bellamy? They killed for you'.

'For the Barnett's'.

'Aw don't embarrass yourself by trying to be bloody clever, Russ. It makes you sound pathetic. You ordered the murder of Glen and Rosemary Hathaway because you were acting on instructions from the Barnett's. You ordered the murder of Ethan Morgan even after you'd authorised the transfer of his hush money from the offshore account in Vanuatu. We know that because we managed to trace the transaction order back to your laptop. You ordered those murders and the boys you'd employed, namely Porter and Bellamy, carried them out for you'.

'They thought that the Hathaway's were working for Ethan Morgan in some way' Wallace tried to reason.

'Yea, funnily enough, Russ, we had worked that out for ourselves' Markovic scoffed. He had nothing but contempt for this Wallace idiot. He added 'And of course, Ethan Morgan was such a Mr Big kind of character, wasn't he? Such a rival for the Barnett's and for their mate, George Rothwell'.

'Alright, alright, he got caught up in it all. In them all. I've told you already that he wasn't guilty of any crime'.

'Easy to say now that he's dead' Markovic hit back. 'All he was doing was waiting for his married girlfriend to agree to run away with him. But you. You, Russ. You thought he was up to much more than that and it was enough to get him killed. By your instructions. You really need to watch that paranoia of yours because it leads to innocent people getting killed. Glen and Rosemary Hathaway. Just started the continuation of life's journey with their superannuation. And they met their end with torture and a bullet through their heads. So where are your two little torturers, Russ? Adrian Porter and Steve Bellamy'.

'I don't have any idea'.

'You're lying'.

'I'm not'.

'You're lying!' Markovic charged. 'You knew that we were getting close, and you made it possible for them to think that they could escape justice'.

Wallace shot Markovic a warning look. 'Don't you dare. Don't you dare talk to me about escaping justice. I served in the Australian army. I was in Afghanistan protecting the western world. I saw daily examples of people escaping justice'.

'I'm sure that is the case' said Markovic. 'What you did for the country is what brings many of us out on ANZAC day. But let's be realistic here, Russ. Let's get real. You sacrificed the good work that you did in Afghanistan, on behalf of all Australians and the wider world, on a line of coke. And that's where I pull my sympathy back from you. Because many members of the Australian armed forces went through horrors that the rest of us just cannot even begin to imagine. But they didn't all come back and become so addicted to coke or other drugs that they fell under the radar of criminal gang lords like George Rothwell. He was the one who got you the job with the Barnett's, wasn't he?'

'Why ask me the question when you think you already know the answer'.

'Oh, so I've got it all wrong, have I?'

'I didn't say that'.

'So, what do you say, Russ? What do you say?'

'That you don't know what the fuck you're talking about when it comes to serving in Afghanistan'

'That's true, I don't' said Markovic in a voice that was as calm as that of Wallace had been agitated. 'But I do know that you threw away the memory of the service you gave to your country protecting us from terrorist attacks by becoming involved in organised crime. You threw it all away, Russ. All of it. After being so heroic you now couldn't get any lower than where you are right now'. Markovic linked his fingers together and placed his hands on the table. He leaned forward. 'Who delivered the fatal blow to Ethan Morgan, Russ?'

'I wasn't involved directly in beating him up'.

'But your torturers were. So, I ask again, where are Porter and Bellamy?'

'I don't know where they are now'.

'You expect me to believe that?'

'You can please yourself. It's the truth'.

'Where is George Rothwell?' Markovic demanded. 'Is he being kept at the mansion? My colleagues are on the way there right now so you may as well tell us'.

'Look, the Barnett's think nothing of having someone killed if they cross them' Wallace pleaded. 'No matter who they are and what you've done for them in the past. If they take against you for whatever reason, then you're dead. I'm divorced but I still have to protect my ex-wife and my kids'.

'You should've thought about that before' said Markovic, wearily. 'I want answers, Russ. I want to know where Adrian Porter and Steve Bellamy are. I want to know where George Rothwell is. I want to know what's happened to a British citizen called Oliver Townsend who hasn't been heard of since he went to the mansion yesterday. I want you to make a statement giving answers to those questions as well as a detailed account of all your activities whilst working for the Barnett's'.

'I'm not saying anything without there being a deal in place'.

'You're in no position to force us into a deal, Russ'.

'You're not getting anything out of me without one'.

'We'll find out what we need to know with or without your help, Russ. But if you volunteer the information to us now then it could make life easier for you on the other side of what you're going to be charged with. Your co-operation could be used to help you. But I want that statement first, Russ. Otherwise, you're on your own'.

Oliver didn't know what the Hell to do. He couldn't contact anyone because they'd taken his phone. He'd tried forcing the door open but even though he'd put his whole strength into it, the blessed thing had barely budged. He'd thought about trying to get out through the window, but not only would that draw attention with the smashing of the glass, but what would he do then? It was a fair way down to the ground. He really wished he hadn't tried getting to his birth mother. What was his dad going to do if something happened to him? His dad had already lost his wife, Oliver's mum. This had been an act of pure bloody self-indulgence.

Then the sound came of a key being placed into the lock of the door. He heard the key turn. His mouth went dry. Suddenly he was extremely apprehensive. He couldn't move. He'd frozen. What if someone was coming in with a gun and these were his last seconds on this earth?

Then she stepped into the room. She didn't look at all bad for someone in her early fifties. But then again that wasn't old, and she'd had the financial means all her life to make sure that everyone knew she considered herself to be 'worth it'. She was wearing make-up, but it had been applied with subtlety rather than in a Joan Collins all you can eat buffet type of way, and her long- sleeved knee-length dress covered in a blue flowery print, with a high round neck and a smart looking thick black belt all looked, like everything in the house, expensive. Her hair was brushed back and shoulder length.

'Hello?' she opened, softly. 'I'm Cecilia and I can see without any shadow of a doubt that I'm looking at my son. The same colour hair, the same bone structure. It's like I'm seeing my baby all over again. Which of course, I am'.

Something in her eyes made the anger he felt subside. He'd

always been a bit of a soft touch. And what's a bit of forced confinement between mother and son?

'What happened earlier?'

'My security guard saw you snooping about and thought you were an intruder' she explained. 'I hadn't explained anything to him about your visit'.

'Clearly you were ashamed'.

'Clearly, I was too embarrassed to explain who you were. I mean, look at you. Anybody who knows me would know that you're my son'.

'So why the locked door?'

'I didn't want you to leave before I'd had the chance to explain myself,' said Cecilia. This was a first for her. She didn't feel in control. 'You've got to believe me when I say that I never meant you any harm. How could I? Look, it was a crass thing to do but I'm far from being a perfect individual and I'm sorry'.

'I expect we can put it behind us' said Oliver with a half-smile.

'So, will you come downstairs with me now and we can talk? I'll get us some coffee or tea or something stronger?'

'Tea would be good, thanks' said Oliver. He rubbed the back of his head which was still aching like nobody's business. 'And can you throw in a couple of ibuprofen tablets too?'

Cecilia smiled. 'I think we can manage that, yes'.

'Okay, but I need my phone back'.

The two of them walked down the stairs and some man who she introduced as her security guard gave Oliver back his phone. He looked and there were 12 missed calls from Andrew Henshaw, plus numerous text messages. He gave Andrew a quick call and assured him he was okay. He said that he'd be back at the hotel later and would explain everything then. There were also two text messages from his dad. They'd been due to zoom call and he wanted to know where he was. He texted him back to apologise and to say that he'd contact him later that day UK time. He looked at Cecilia and wondered. He wondered how this was going to play out although he felt better now about having crossed the world to meet her.

Cecilia led Oliver into the living room he'd been shown into when he'd first arrived at the mansion and the tea arrived swiftly along with the ibuprofen tablets. They were sitting in two high backed red armchairs that were positioned close together and slightly inclined to each other. Oliver looked at Cecilia. He really wanted to like this woman. He really wanted to like her.

'I'm so sorry, Oliver' said Cecilia as she watched him down the two ibuprofens, followed by a large gulp of his tea.

'Well like I say, let's put it behind us. These will probably kick in fairly soon'.

'Well, you would know being a doctor,' said Cecilia. 'And that must be in the genes. Your father was a doctor'.

Oliver was astonished. 'He was?'

Cecilia didn't have to search through the recesses of her memory. She'd been thinking a lot about Oliver's father in recent weeks since Oliver had first tried to contact her.

'His name was Marcus. Marcus Littlewood. Dr Marcus Littlewood. He was the only man I've ever really loved in my life. Nobody since has ever come remotely close to replacing him in my heart'.

'So why couldn't you be together?' asked Oliver who was glad they were getting straight down to business and cutting out all the usual shit about whether or not you had a good journey or how good a summer everyone was having. He really wouldn't have wanted any of that.

'Because he was married to someone else' Cecilia explained with a heart that was suddenly heavy. 'I went to the UK to meet with my relatives. As you probably know, my grandparents were British. I got on well with them all and I decided to stay in London for a while. Now even though I was of independent financial means I decided to get a job so I could meet different people. I got one in the admin department of Guy's hospital in London and that's where I met your father. He was an ophthalmic surgeon there. I fell madly for him even though I knew he was married with two children. We had an affair for a year and then I found I was pregnant with you. So, you see it wasn't just a brief, casual fling. We loved each other and when I told him I was pregnant he was delighted. Then the next day he turned up on my doorstep, I'd rented a flat in Chelsea, and he moved in with me'

'So, he left his wife?'

'Oh yes. And we talked about the future. I was going to stay with him in the UK because he didn't want to be on the other side of the world from the two children he already had. I thought that was fair enough and I emotionally settled on spending the rest of my life in the UK with the love of my life and our child'.

'And what got in the way of this apparent bliss?'

'His wife' Cecilia stated, bluntly. The hatred she felt for the woman was still palpable. 'She threatened that if he didn't go back to her then she'd make it impossible for him to see the children. Even if a court confirmed his access rights, she'd make it as awkward as hell. To cut a long story short he decided to go back to her. I was heartbroken. I thought I'd never recover. My mother flew over from Australia and stopped me from having an abortion'.

'You wanted to get rid of me?'

'Can you blame me? Considering the position that I was in?'

'No, and I've always supported a woman's right to choose' Oliver replied. 'It just seems strange to take in that it was because of a grandmother I never met that I actually exist'.

'Well, that's a way of putting it, yes' Cecilia agreed. She

glanced out of the window for a moment then turned her eyes back on him. 'But I gave you up for adoption because I didn't love you, Oliver. You came out of me and because I'd lost your father, I hated you and could never have gone forward as a single mother'.

Oliver swallowed hard. 'Well, I certainly respect your honesty and I can appreciate why you felt the way you did'.

'That's very ... generous of you'.

'I'm a doctor, Cecilia. It's my job to show empathy even when it cuts as close as it gets to home'.

'My family paid a part in it too' she went on. 'If I'd taken a baby home as an unmarried mother, I'd have brought disgrace on the family. My brother Raymond has fathered at least three or four kids dotted around Australia but that's alright because he's a boy. My mother completely supported my decision to have you adopted and would've forced me into doing that even if I hadn't decided on doing that myself'.

'Did you ever have contact with my father again?'

'This is the bit that you might have more trouble understanding than any of the rest' Cecilia began. 'After I gave you up, I went into a very deep depression and one day I saw your father and his wife walking along the street, hand in hand, laughing, enjoying being together. It looked like it hadn't taken him long to get over me. And he'd never contacted me to see what I'd done with you. He'd cut me off completely as if he'd never loved me in the first place. And looking at them that day I wanted to kill them. I wanted to kill them both. I'd become a very bitter and twisted woman, Oliver. And in many ways, it's stayed with me. But going back to then. I decided to exact my revenge'.

'What the Hell did you do?'

'I could've had them killed' said Cecilia as casually as if she was explaining that she wanted to stay up but she was too tired. 'My family had the right contacts. But that would've been too easy and too quick. I wanted them to suffer like I was doing. So, I used our contacts to destroy your father's career. It sent him on a downward spiral. He ended up having the family home taken back into the possession of the bank who'd given him the mortgage. He ended up taking his own life. And on the day that I found out, I broke out the champagne'.

Oliver sat back slightly in his chair. She meant what she'd just said. She really meant it. He could see it in her eyes. She'd celebrated his father's suicide with champagne, and she didn't regret it one little bit. If he was being wholly rational, he'd say that he understood. He'd say that he got it. His father had broken her heart. She'd been shattered by his duplicity. But this was his father. He'd been an absolute bastard, but did she have to set the wheels in motion that led to him doing what he did? He now knew that he had two half-siblings and they'd lost their father when they can't have been more than children.

'I'll need some time to process all of that,' said Oliver. He was exhausted with all her revelations concerning his father. 'I presume there's a graveside I could go to?'

'Yes. It's in south London. I'll give you the address'.

'You go there?'

'Whenever I go to London, yes'.

Christ, thought Oliver. She's got more bloody front than Brighton.

'You probably think that's … inappropriate' she went on.

'Just a little'.

'My family have never been what you'd call … conventional'.

'Sounds to me like that's putting it mildly'.

Cecilia stood up. She looked as if she'd suddenly remembered she had to do something. She went over and opened two of the full- length windows out onto the grounds at the back of the house. Oliver noticed that she peered out. What was she looking for? Who was she looking for? The part of the room they were sitting in looked like it had been an extension to the rest of the long back wall of the mansion. It stuck out like a shag on a rock. Though not unattractively. Like everything in this mansion. It wouldn't be to Oliver's own taste. It was just too big for a start. His own two-up, two down terraced cottage back in Windsor was more than big enough for him to manage. He hated housework. God, he hated it. He'd much rather be reading a good book or catching a good drama on TV. No, this place wouldn't suit him at all. He'd feel exposed.

After a moment Cecilia turned and came back and sat down again. 'It was just after I came back from London. My brother Raymond had always had associates in the criminal world. I'd refused my permission for us to get involved with them. We both had to agree, you see. But after everything that had happened, I changed my mind. I agreed with my brother Raymond that we go into business with George Rothwell'.

'He's the Sydney crime boss, right?'

'If that's what you want to call him'.

'Well, you don't strike me as someone who would dress anything up'.

Cecilia allowed herself a short laugh. 'You read me well'.

'Didn't George Rothwell go missing last year?'

'You really have done your research, haven't you?'

'I was always first in my group to hand in my assignments at med school' Oliver revealed. He couldn't shake the suspicious feeling that had come over him though. That feeling of foreboding. He just couldn't shake it. But maybe it was what she had to tell him that was giving him that feeling. 'I read all about George Rothwell in the papers after I arrived in Australia. It was all over the TV news too. News was breaking about the murder of a middle-aged couple here in Kingsbrook. And then of one of your former employees. Someone called Ethan Morgan. So, are you saying what I think you're saying?'

'Which is what exactly?'

'That your company, Barnett Holdings, is a front for other activities'.

Cecilia rubbed the palms of her hands together and looked down. 'With George Rothwell, we run protection rackets, people trafficking, drug dealing. We've got it all detailed in files in the office upstairs. The whole shooting match'.

'You sound almost proud of it all'.

'It's given me something to do'.

'But a lot of people must've got hurt in the process. Don't you give a damn?'

'Your father destroyed all of my feelings'.

'How convenient for you that you had him to blame for the despicable way you must've destroyed thousands of lives over the years,'

For what felt like the first time in her life, Cecilia looked at her son and knew that if he couldn't forgive her, it would break her heart all over again. Just like his father had done.

'Could you ever try to understand, Oliver?'

'I can't save you from what you've done'.

'I'll take that as a no then'.

'You had a property business that made the family heaps of cash. That should've been enough. But you …you then went and started this whole other income stream out of trading on the absolute misery and desperation of others. How many souls did it take to be dragged to this country to work as slaves just because you were bitter?'

'It was only after you contacted me that I started to feel any conscience about it at all'.

'And that's why you resisted my reaching out to you. Because it made you take a long, hard look at yourself'.

'I'm sorry, Oliver'.

'It's too late for that now,' said Oliver. 'And I want nothing more than for us to get to know each other properly. But I can only be part of your life if you make certain very big changes to it and that means dropping everything to do with this George Rothwell character'.

Cecilia was almost tearful as she said, 'I think I owe your parents an awful lot'.

'I had a fantastic childhood with fantastic parents' said Oliver, although he didn't want to rub it in. 'They brought me up well'.

'I can see that'.

'They taught me to have respect for other people and not to be a user'.

'It sounds like giving you up for adoption was the best thing that I as your mother could've done for you'.

The shot went straight into the back of Cecilia's head. Suddenly there was blood spurting out everywhere. Oliver was shocked beyond belief and could feel himself shaking as he leapt up and took her in his arms. He wanted to do something. He was a doctor for god's sake. But she was already dead. Her head had been almost blown off. His mouth was wide open. He was gasping.

'No, no, no!' he roared.

'Don't shed any tears over her, mate'.

Oliver twisted his head round and saw a man standing just inside the house holding up a gun that he was pointing at him.

'I'm George Rothwell. You and I need to have a bit of a yarn'.

20.

Oliver couldn't believe what had just happened. When he'd first started to plan to come out to Australia to meet his birth mother, he had all kinds of questions for her with regard to how she came to giving him up and who his father had been. The more he'd researched her and her family though the more it had started to feel like it would be a confrontation. His values and hers were light years apart. He couldn't describe their brief exchange as either a disclosure talk, or a confrontation but as he squatted there with his arms round her dead body, he couldn't help but feel absolutely wretched. His breathing was rapid. He used his thumbs to close the lids over her eyes. It was the least he could do to restore a little dignity to her. And now he had a notorious Sydney gangster pointing his gun at him. This wasn't exactly how he imagined things would work out. It's not exactly what he'd like to detail on the back of a postcard home.

'I've got nothing to say to you' Oliver spat. 'You have just murdered my mother in front of me. I'd known her for the briefest of moments and now you've taken her away. You're scum! You're evil scum! I have nothing but contempt for you'.

'That's all very brave talk for someone in your position'.

'My feelings about you go way beyond mere hatred right now'.

'You really didn't know your mummy, did you?'

'You fucking know I didn't' Oliver shot back. He was surprising himself by how close he was getting to losing it emotionally. This woman he was holding in his arms had been his mother. A very flawed individual, but she'd been his mother, nevertheless. She'd confessed to having been instrumental in driving his father to suicide. But she was still his mother. And she'd been murdered in front of him. Then he heard the police sirens.

The next thing he knew there were flashing lights all around the property and two police cars screeched to a halt outside the back of the house. A number of uniformed officers leapt out and took up their positions with their own firearms. Then a woman who looked like she was a detective because she was in plain clothes, stepped forward and pointed her gun at George Rothwell's back.

'Put the gun down, George' she commanded in albeit a calm voice. She started to step further towards him.

'Stop right there or he loses it!' Rothwell commanded.

'George, I'm detective Zoe Dawkins of Kingsbrook police. You're surrounded. You have no way of escaping. You need to drop your weapon and turn to us with your hands up'.

Dawkins could see through to where the man she took to be the British guy Oliver Townsend was holding the dead body of Cecilia Barnett in his arms. Her blood was all over him too. The scene was macabre in one sense and bizarre in another. Probably one of the most expensively furnished rooms in Kingsbrook was covered in the blood of a woman who'd taken a bullet straight through the head.

'It's over, George,' said Dawkins. 'You've got nowhere to go'.

'I'm starting to really get sick of the sound of your voice' Rothwell hissed.

'Well, that's too bad, George, because the only way to shut me up is to do as I've already told you'.

At that moment, Rothwell lunged forward to grab Oliver, but Dawkins reacted and shot him in the leg. She did that because she didn't want him dead. She wanted him to be stopped in his tracks now but able to pay for his crimes later on. He collapsed onto the floor in agony, dropping his gun which she then rushed to pick up. She couldn't resist charging him there and then with the murder of Cecilia Barnett even though he was crying out in pain.

'And we're just getting started, Georgie' Dawkins added.

Farrell, Dawkins, and Markovic, were sitting in the team room reviewing an investigation that had now almost come to a conclusion. There were still a few loose ends to tie together and successfully unite with the rest of the bundle, like the fact that Adam Petrie was still in hospital, but the back had been broken on the investigation and the main perpetrators were now behind bars.

At least, the ones who were still alive.

George Rothwell had now been charged with multiple counts of murder, extortion, racketeering, people trafficking and, the ubiquitous trade of modern criminals, drug dealing. It all added up to the certainty that Rothwell would never see the light of day again. He was being held in a maximum security facility on the edge of the city and the court had agreed with Farrell's fervently argued plea that the court reject the application by Rothwell's lawyer, Louise Bateman, that he be granted bail whilst awaiting trial. Farrell had argued that he would simply disappear just like he'd done before, and that the kidney disease he'd been diagnosed with could be as easily treated whilst he was incarcerated.

'I don't know which is worse,' said Dawkins. 'A criminal who brings Hell to people on earth like Rothwell or a lawyer like Louise Bateman who stands there and defends him'. She shook her head. 'I don't know how either of them can sleep at night. And if what Rothwell had done already wasn't enough, he then goes and murders his two associates of the last thirty years'.

One of the murders George Rothwell had been charged with

was that of Cecilia Barnett but he also confessed to the murder of her brother Raymond too. He told Farrell and Dawkins where the body could be found on a disused farm thirty k's outside of the city. And true enough, the body had been found exactly where he said it would be.

'The lives of other people meant nothing to Rothwell' said Markovic. 'That's how he could do what he did for all his adult life. He was a psychopath who used the protected status of the Barnett's to hide his and their crimes behind. But then he turned on them once they all knew that they weren't being protected any longer because that made him vulnerable'.

Rothwell had told Farrell and Dawkins during their lengthy interviews of him that the Barnett family were protected by the national government in Canberra because of a long- standing agreement with the British government. It was how the family had come to be in Australia after the second world war but even he didn't know what the big secret was that led to them being protected. So, Farrell had contacted the Department of Home Affairs in Canberra and they'd been surprising willing to talk to him. It transpired that the grandparents of Cecilia and Raymond Barnett, Lord and Lady Hamilton, had been close friends and associates of King Edward who'd abdicated the throne to marry Wallis Simpson in 1936. And that closeness had included a shared support for Hitler and the Nazi regime in Germany. It's known that Edward, who is now known as the traitor King, helped to facilitate the Nazi invasion of France when he and Wallis were living in Paris by sending the Nazis military secrets that Edward was privy to. At the same time, and indeed throughout the war and the Nazi occupation of France, the Hamilton family informed on people in Paris who were hiding Jewish families to avoid them being deported to the death camps. Those people who'd been hiding the Jewish families were executed by the Nazi occupiers, and the Jewish families were first placed in a detention camp in the Paris suburb of Drancy before being put on trains there and deported to the death camps in other parts of Nazi occupied Europe. They'd been destined for murder. Literally hundreds of local families in Paris and the Jewish families they were hiding, were sent to their deaths because of the treachery of the Hamilton family. But when all of this was found out at the end of the war after France was liberated by the allies, British Prime Minister Winston Churchill thought that the scandal would be too much at a time when the country needed to pull together after six years of war. He also thought it would reflect badly on the monarchy and their associates in the titled classes, many of whom had been suspected, like the Hamilton's, of supporting the Nazi cause. So, he arranged to have the Hamilton family shipped out to Australia where they were given the new identity of Barnett but were able to keep their enormous wealth. That's how they got Barnett Holdings started with their acquisitions of property across the country. They stopped any form of criminal activity and neither did Cecilia and Raymond's parents get involved in anything untoward either. It was only when Raymond Barnett met George Rothwell that the criminal tendency in their genes came out once more. Had Cecilia and Raymond Barnett lived they'd have been facing the same charges as Rothwell. And they'd been informed that the new Australian government were not going to continue the protection of the true identity of the Barnett's that successive Australians governments had done in agreement with successive British governments since 1945. The new Australian government felt like justice for the families of those that the Barnett's ancestors had sent to their deaths must finally be done. Indeed, the department were contributing to a documentary being made about the whole business by channel 9's 'A Current Affair' which would be broadcast in a few weeks, perhaps to coincide with Rothwell's trial. Rothwell had not wanted to get caught up in their mess and that's another reason why he got rid of them.

'The protection of those bastards should never have been there in the first place' opined Markovic. 'I don't agree with the death penalty in this day and age but back then, just at the end of a war that had slaughtered millions, they should've been hanged for sending all those people needlessly to their deaths'.

'I couldn't agree more, Ryan,' said Farrell.

'That makes three of us' Dawkins concurred.

'But the protection wasn't taken away before Ethan Morgan found out the big secret,' said Farrell. 'And that's what cost him his life. And the Hathaway's too. Adrian Porter and Steve Bellamy thought that the Hathaway's were involved when really, they were just in the wrong place at the wrong time. And now we've got Porter and Bellamy's confession to all three murders'

'And we've got the down and out Terry Patterson to thank for that, boss' Dawkins reminded them.

Terry Patterson really had played fair dinkum with them even though it had not been made easy for him by desk sergeant Mary Chung.

Patterson had witnessed the murder of Ethan Morgan by Adrian Porter and Steve Bellamy. It had been carried out in the back of a disused shop unit on Avalon Street where Patterson had been sleeping rough. They hadn't seen him because he'd been using a small stockroom just inside the front door. They'd used the upstairs for their 'interrogation' of Morgan who they brought from and took back to some other place. They entered and exited the building through the back door. Patterson had been too scared to do anything directly about what he could hear was happening to the poor bugger, but he'd gone straight down to the cop shop, only to be confronted by desk Sergeant Chung who had dismissed his plea to speak to a detective because he stank, and she assumed he was drunk and was just going to waste their time. She'd done it not once, not twice, but three times to him. Then when he saw them take Morgan's dead body out of the unit, presumably on the way to where the two kids had found him floating in the river, he went again to the cop shop where Mary Chung again dismissed him and told him to go away.

He'd wanted to tell her that the two mongrels who'd done away with the 'poor bugger' were also the ones he'd seen pushing offensive notes under the door of the Oasis café and then threw bricks at the place, smashing all the front windows. It was only when Sadiq, boyfriend of Detective Zoe Dawkins and owner of the Oasis café called her to tell her what Patterson had told him, that she went and interviewed Patterson to confirm it all. She and Senior Sergeant Joel Stringer led a team to the disused shop where Patterson told them the 'two mongrels' were now hiding out and were able to arrest them. Farrell had been absolutely furious with Mary Chung. If she'd stopped looking down her nose at Patterson just because he slept rough and listened to what he had to say, then the life of Ethan Morgan might've been saved, and Sadiq may not have had his windows smashed. She didn't try and defend herself or show any remorse for the failings she'd shown. She'd listened when he told her that the police listen to all members of the public if they say they've got information for them, no matter what kind of state their life may be in. He said that he shouldn't have needed to have told her that. It was basic stuff. Her only excuse was that she'd assumed that Patterson had been after the food her husband had cooked and which she brought in for all of them in the cop shop every day. She thought he'd just been after a free feed. He said he'd have to record what had happened. Mary had then applied to take some extended leave and it had approved. She said that she'd be back, but Farrell wasn't sure if she would be. He wouldn't be surprised if he received her resignation.

'I thought it might be too good to be true,' said Dawkins. 'Mary has been showing signs of her heart melting recently, but it only goes to show that you can't run away from your true self'.

'Well enough said about that,' said Farrell. 'And speaking of a person's true self, Zoe, how long has your Sadiq been feeding Kingsbrook's down and outs with leftover food at the end of each day that he'd otherwise have to throw away because it would go past it's sell-by date? He really is a man amongst men that one'

Dawkins pulled herself close and smiled tenderly. 'I know'. She'd looked at Sadiq the night before and realised that men like him only come along once in a thousand years and she couldn't believe how the universe had seen fit to send him to her. She wasn't going to think about it any longer. She'd agreed to marry him, and this was the first time she'd told Farrell and Markovic. They both leapt up excitedly and hugged her, wishing her congratulations. They were over the moon for her.

'And now we also know that Porter and Bellamy were hiding in the disused shop after they knew that we were on to them, and that they'd been working for a Jewish terrorist group that has become active in Australia in recent years' said Markovic. 'They target anyone they see as an enemy of Israel, including any Palestinians who've now settled here. All the information that Porter and Bellamy gave us about them has now been passed on to the anti-terrorist unit at HQ in the city. They hope to be making some arrests from it which is a good thing. And the really sickening thing about it is that neither Porter nor Bellamy are even Jewish. They just did it for money. The greedy bastards pushed hatred in the community just for money. Hired intimidators. Unbelievable'.

'It certainly is, Ryan' Farrell agreed.

'The one I feel really sorry for in all of this is the British guy Oliver Townsend,' said Dawkins. 'I mean, he flies to the other side of the world to meet his birth mother and he gets a lot more besides. Including having to watch her being shot dead in front of him and then being held at gunpoint himself. And all of that was on top of what he found out about Cecilia Barnett. The poor bloke. Devastated probably doesn't even cover it'.

Oliver Townsend and Andrew Henshaw were lying in bed together in Oliver's room at the Clarendon Hotel. They'd spent the night together but hadn't had sex. After the events of the last twenty-four hours all they'd wanted to do was to hold onto each other. And Oliver lay there in Andrew's tender, loving arms with his face against Andrew's beautiful chest rug.

'I love to listen to your heart beating,' said Oliver.

'I think it stopped yesterday when I heard about all the shooting that had taken place up at the Barnett mansion' Andrew admitted. 'I've never been more relieved than when you rang me, and I heard your voice' He kissed the top of Oliver's head. 'Never been more relieved'.

Oliver still shivered when he thought about what had happened the previous day. He'll never be able to lose from his memory the picture of Cecilia's head being blown off in front of him. All the blood. Christ, all the blood. Her eyes that had been like beacons as she passed from this world and into the next. Had it all been his fault? He knew that it hadn't been, but he couldn't help questioning himself. But it had been her own decision to get herself involved in criminal activity although she had argued that his father's duplicity and betrayal had been a major contributor. He wasn't sure about that. But he hadn't wished her dead. He'd wanted to establish a relationship with her that they could've built on as the years passed. But it just hadn't turned out that way. And he didn't think he'd ever get over it.

'I can't help thinking that she knew what was going to happen and she needed me there as a witness'.

'What makes you say that?'

'I could just see something in her eyes during those last few moments. It was like she was expecting something. It was as if she had to unburden herself to me before the end came'.

'That would make sense considering what had happened to her brother,' said Andrew. 'And she must've known that George Rothwell had been responsible. But would she really have wanted to put you through that? I mean, to put you in that kind of danger and to actually witness what happened?'

'She confessed to having brought about the circumstances that drove my father to suicide, Andrew. She'd held on to her bitterness for all those years since my father left her to go back to his wife. Who knows what she could justify to herself in that state of mind'?

Oliver knew that the events of the last few hours wouldn't let him go for a long time, maybe even never. But he already had an idea of how mad it was all going to be. He'd already had the newspaper and TV media onto him and some of them were camped outside the mansion. With a little help from the Kingsbrook police who were investigating the whole nightmare, they'd managed to give them all the slip and get back to the hotel.

'I've got to get out and about, Andrew,' said Oliver. 'Much as I'd like to stay here with you like this forever, reality checks keep going off inside my head'.

'Are you hungry?'

'Hungry? I'm absolutely famished'.

'Me too, so that's the first thing we'll do. I'll ring young Nathan on the desk and get him to bring us some brekky. By the way, he told me yesterday that he's been accepted by the police'.

'Good for him,' said Oliver. 'Did you know he'd applied to join the police force?'

'No, but then I guess he wouldn't feel it was appropriate until he knew whether or not he'd got it. And now he has'.

'Well looking after this situation will be good practice for him' said Oliver who then thought of all the things Cecilia had told him and he couldn't help it. He started to cry.

'Hey, baby' said Andrew who squeezed him tight.

'My family, Andrew' Oliver blubbered. 'They did such evil

things'

'And none of it was your fault, Oliver. You've got to remember that my love'.

Andrew's soothing words stopped Oliver's tears, but he was an emotional wreck. He tried concentrating on the things he had to do. It was a long list. He had to zoom call his dad back in the UK. And his sister. Those calls were an absolute priority. He also had to zoom call the manager of the medical centre in Windsor where he was a G.P and tell him what had happened. Apart from anything else, he needed to know in case the media contacted him. He'd do the same with the other three G. Ps at the practice who were all friends of his anyway. Then he had to return the call of a lawyer in Sydney who said he needed to speak to him urgently with regard to Cecilia Barnett's estate which was valued at several hundred million dollars. It was all her family fortune gained from the business of Barnett Holdings. All her 'other' money was in offshore accounts that was now being chased by federal authorities as part of the ongoing investigation into the organised crime activities of Cecilia and her brother Raymond, in association with George Rothwell. But Oliver was her sole heir and she'd recently had that written into her Will. He was now a very rich man. But he wouldn't be for long. He planned to give it all away, mostly to Jewish charitable organisations. He just couldn't have anything to do with it. It was covered in the blood of Jewish men, women and children who'd been sent to their deaths in Nazi concentration camps by Oliver's ancestors. His great-grandparents had turned people into victims of Nazi gas chambers. The only crime of those people had been that they were Jewish. It had been an act of pure evil. And the world should never forget.

But he'd also be giving some money to the Palestinians who Oliver felt strongly deserved justice of their own kind in today's world. They were also the victims now.

'I'm taking you away,' said Andrew.

'Where to?'

'We're going on a road trip. We'll pack a few things and then jump in the car. We'll head out to the outback, and it'll just be you, me and the open road. Just for a few days. I need to put you back together and I'm not going to be able to do that if we stay around here. So, we'll get away, let the dust settle, and then come back and deal with everything'.

'Sounds like Heaven,' said Oliver. 'And then when we get back, we've got a big decision to make'.

'About what?'

'Which one of us is going to move to the other side of the world so we can be together'.

'Is that what you really want? For us to be together?'

'More than anything'.

'So do I' said Andrew who thought he was going to start crying himself any second. 'Oh my God, so do I. The first time I looked at you, life suddenly started to make sense for the first time in years. And now that Polly has come to believe that we are wasting each other's lives it means I can be free to live my own life again and I can be with you'.

'She's going to need a lot of help though, Andrew' Oliver cautioned.

'And I'll make sure she gets it because we'll always be good friends'

'And I'll be with you on that,' said Oliver. He gently stroked the side of Andrew's face. 'I'm crazy about you, Andrew'.

'I'm crazy about you too' said Andrew who gently took Oliver's hand and kissed the palm of it.

'The universe brought me out to Australia to put right a massive wrong done by my ancestors' said Oliver. 'But looking at you I know it brought me out here for another reason too'.

'To save me'.

'And you've saved me too, big boy. And now that you have, I'm never going to let you go'.

Farrell had gone outside the back of the cop shop just to catch some fresh air. He'd taken his coffee with him and was happily drinking away whilst thinking about life, love and the pursuit of happiness, when a call came through from regional commander Tara O'Brien. He wasn't feeling especially well disposed towards his boss and former lover.

'Tara? I thought you'd lost my number'.

'Jason' answered Tara flatly. She didn't want to rise to it. If she could help it. 'I've been flat out recently'.

'Too busy to return one of the four calls made to you by one of your station commanders?'

'I knew you'd be handling things in your usual professional way'.

'Bullshit'.

'I beg your pardon?'

'Tara, you should've told me about Adam Petrie being a police informant, you should've told me about George Rothwell being associated with Cecilia and Raymond Barnett and what that meant in terms of criminal activity, and you certainly should've told me about moving Becky Rothwell into Kingsbrook under her new identity'.

'You don't get to tell me what I should do, Farrell'.

'Oh, so when you know I'm right it goes back to Farrell, does it? You set me up to fail, Tara. You set me up to make a complete mess of everything and put the life of a British citizen in danger to do it. But instead, and disappointingly for you, me and my team have done the job of the organised crime unit for them and brought down one of the most dangerous gangsters in the country. All in a day's work, Tara. All in a day's work'.

'Do you want a bloody medal or something?' Tara demanded angrily.

'I want you to start treating me like all your other regional commanders instead of singling me out because of our previous personal relationship!'

'Just remember who you're talking to!'

'Oh, I remember. I'm talking to the woman I rejected and who just won't get over it'.

That night all the team got together at Ned's Place for an impromptu party to celebrate the engagement of Zoe Dawkins and her Sadiq. Markovic's husband Max also joined them along with Farrell's daughter Sapphire and her boyfriend Dylan. They were looking increasingly tight together and Farrell was becoming increasingly concerned that Sapphire wouldn't be taking up her place at Sydney university when the next term year started. But he'd have to wait and see. He also apologised to Markovic's husband Max because of Markovic having to postpose the leave he'd booked to take Max away for his birthday. But Max assured him it was no drama. He'd married a copper and sometimes these things happen. It's the nature of the job and he knew that when he married him. Markovic's leave had been confirmed and they were heading off to Palm Beach, north of Sydney tomorrow afternoon for a belated birthday celebration. Farrell really liked Max. He thought he was a top bloke and the perfect partner for Markovic who Farrell knew had a good career ahead of him in the force.

They all stayed and had dinner at Ned's Place before having more drinks and Zoe and Sadiq led the dancing with the first song selected on the jukebox which was INXS's 'Never Tear Us Apart'.

Zoe and Sadiq looked into each other's eyes and knew that nobody ever would.

The next morning, they were all feeling somewhat the worse for wear when they attended the re-opening of Sadiq's café 'Oasis'. It was attended by the Rabbi of the local synagogue who'd brought half a dozen of his congregation with him, all of whom were known customers of Sadiq's. The mayor of the town presented Sadiq with a good citizen award for his work in embracing all communities and for bothering to reach out and feed the town's down and outs. Applauding the loudest to this was Terry Patterson for whom Sadiq had converted a stock room upstairs that he no longer used, into a small bedsit for Terry. It had a bed, a table with a chair, an armchair, a TV, a small kitchen area and a separate toilet and shower. All the items of furniture had been donated by various officers at the cop shop, including Farrell and Markovic. Sadiq had built an outside staircase so that Terry could have his own front door and it would be a place where he could be off the streets, safe, look after himself, and think about starting life again. Dawkins had put a large bouquet of flowers in a vase on the table and hung a painting of the centre of the town just to break up the plain walls. Terry had agreed with Sadiq to take a job in the café kitchen washing up which would mean he'd be paid something and that would help to restore his dignity. Terry had cried when Sadiq and Dawkins had taken him in there for the first time. And since then, he'd never stopped smiling. Farrell had already apologised to Terry for Mary Chung not having taken any notice of him trying to report his observations and suspicions. Terry had told him it didn't matter. He had somewhere to live now. And that's all that mattered.

That afternoon, Farrell took some time out and went to see Becky Rothwell in the house they'd put her up in. She was still under witness protection but was being moved back to the city. Now that her husband George was in custody, she was considered as being at less of a risk.

'I'm glad I caught you' he said after she opened the door and led him through. He could see that she was in the middle of packing a suitcase. The door to the bedroom was open and it was lying on her bed.

'They're picking me up tomorrow'.

'I see' he said, standing there. Everyone seemed to be moving. Scott Hathaway and his wife Joanna with their son were moving to the city. So was Scott's sister and her husband. They all wanted to get right away from where their parents had been murdered.

'So, are you just going to stand there or are you going to make a move on me?'

The sex they shared was awesome just like it always had been between them. They fucked twice and the second time it had been with Farrell on his back and Becky riding him up and down after she'd straddled him. Their connection was frenzied and had knocked them both into another world for a while. They were both panting with delirium when Farrell's phone started ringing.

'Ignore it' urged Becky as she ran her hand across his stomach.

'I'd better not,' said Farrell. He reluctantly lifted himself up and picked up his phone that had been sitting on the small table beside the bed. He looked at the screen. 'It's my daughter'. He pressed the green tab to answer. 'Hi sweetheart. What's up?'

'Nothing's up, dad' Sapphire answered. 'Well, not really. Mum's here. She didn't tell us she was coming home because she wanted it to be a surprise'.

THE END

But Detective Inspector Jason Farrell will be back.

Some of the locations used in the telling of 'DESTINED FOR MURDER' are real places that I would highly recommend. Here are some details.

PALM BEACH, NSW.

PALM BEACH B AND B. 122 Pacific Road, Palm Beach. NSW 2108. Tel- 61 409 000 013

www.palmbeachbandb.com.au

The real Rudi and Avalon will warmly welcome you to their b and b just up from where the outside filming for the TV drama 'Home and Away' is done.

BARRENJOEY HOUSE PALM BEACH. 1108 Barrenjoey Road, Palm Beach, NSW 2108. Tel – 61 2 9974 4001

www.barrenjoeyhouse.com.au

A great restaurant with excellent service. Rooms are available too.

THE ROCKS, SYDNEY

ZIA PINA. 93 George Street, The Rocks. NSW 2000 Tel – 61 2 9247 2255

www.ziapinatherocks.com.au

Superb Italian food and an absolute 'must' for me when I'm in Sydney. Comfortable and unpretentious – great service too.

MERCANTILE. 25 George Street, The Rocks. NSW 2000 Tel – 61 2

9247 3570

www.themercantilehotel.com.au

Even if you're not staying here, it's great for a fun night out, especially when they have musicians playing. Great food too.

My best to all – David, June 2022.

And why not try one of David Menon's other Australian crime fiction books? Like 'WHAT HAPPENED TO LIAM?' which is available worldwide on Amazon. Here's the first chapter to arouse your interest.

ONE

Stephanie Marshall was a Sydneysider who'd run her own business as a private investigator for the last ten years. Her office was in Beaconsfield on the way into the city from the airport and was on the top floor of a grey three-storey office block that was sandwiched between a Vietnamese restaurant and a bottle shop. If word of mouth was anything to go by, she'd be as rich as bloody shit. She was good at her job. She did what she said she would do, and she was reliable enough to have gained an enviable reputation in the trade. She just wished her clients could be as reliable when it came to paying her fee after she'd got them their desired result. But too many of them seemed to run short of funds when it came time to pay up and that made her cash flow situation an absolute nightmare at times. But it went with the territory. She couldn't take the full fee in advance because the nature of the work meant that it was so unpredictable, and she couldn't accurately forecast her costs. So, it was a case of sucking it all up and hoping that at least some clients would come through the door who could pay their invoice in one go instead of dribs and drabs.

She grabbed herself a coffee from the café on the corner where Ricardo the Italian owner flirted madly with her whilst his wife who also worked there stood by and laughed. Louisa was well used to her husband taking the traditional Italian male view of the female species. Stephanie sometimes used it to her advantage though. Ricardo knew a lot of people who would talk to him and not the police and that made him a mine of useful information for her on some cases. She was still smiling at his rueful wickedness when she reached the building she'd grown to know so well and pressed the number of the security code on the panel to open the door. There were four businesses who had their offices in there and none of them wanted uncontrolled access to visitors. She knew that some very modern and strident women would savage the likes of Ricardo for the way he acted around women. Calling him sexist would be one of the least punishing words they'd use. But whilst Stephanie wasn't in the least bit old fashioned and wouldn't take any shit from anyone that was aimed at her gender, she didn't want to lose her sense of humour entirely when it came to relationships between men and women. And in any case, she could flirt with the best of them. She enjoyed it.

On the landing outside her office, she caught herself in the long wall mirror. She should do something with her hair. It was the most boring shade of brown and just sat there, parted in the middle and the length catching her shoulders. She thought about maybe putting a colour on it, but she had no idea what. Then there was the question of her hips. They were starting to be the first thing she saw when she looked at her body. Too many takeaway sandwiches eaten whilst conducting surveillance work were to blame for that. Too many curries, fish and chips, microwave meals, late night liquid suppers involving a bottle of Shiraz because she couldn't be bothered to do anything with food. The skirt she was wearing had room to spare six months ago. Now she could barely get her hand down the front. She was going to have to do something to arrest this particular development. Her white shirt looked alright, and her black jacket was okay if she left it undone. She laughed at how ridiculously deceiving human beings can be with themselves. She wasn't fat and she hadn't lost it. She just needed to lose a bit to help her get some of it back. That's all.

It was almost ten and the early morning clouds had yet to liberate the morning sky. Stephanie looked out of the window. There were definite signs of the sun trying its best to get through. She had someone coming to see her on the hour and when the security buzzer downstairs was activated, she looked briefly at the video shot and let her visitor in, telling her over the intercom to take the lift to the third floor.

The woman who Stephanie greeted warmly at the door with a handshake had clearly been a particularly alluring beauty in her youth. She was still a very attractive woman now with her short white hair and large bewitching eyes. Stephanie would put her in her early sixties, but she was preserving well and her light brown suede jacket and skirt also helped to take the years off her. She'd also taken care that her jewellery and make-up were subtle additions to her appearance and didn't overwhelm her look. She had a poise about her that told Stephanie that she could be the best friend you'd ever had but also warned you not to cross her or you'd regret it. Vulnerable, insecure and yet with a barely hidden ferociousness that wouldn't take much to be provoked into showing itself.

'I'm Valerie Gardner,' said her visitor. 'Mrs. Valerie Gardner'. Her voice was deep and throaty. She must be a pretty heavy smoker, thought Stephanie.

'Yes, please come in, Mrs. Gardner and sit down'.

'Oh, please call me Valerie'.

'And I'm Stephanie. Would you like a cup of tea or coffee?'

'No, thanks' said Valerie, smiling as she sat down in the chair in front of Stephanie's desk. 'I'm fine. It's not been long since breakfast'.

Stephanie sat down at her desk and folded her hands before resting them in front of her. 'So, Valerie, how did you find me?'

'You have a particular reputation for finding people,' said Valerie. 'We saw the feature about you recently in one of the Sunday papers. That's when I decided to get in touch'.

'We?'

'Me and my husband Ed' Valerie explained. 'He's waiting outside in the car'.

'He's not coming in?'

'No, he prefers to let me handle this kind of thing. We have a farm in the country and that's his domain as it were'

'I see,' said Stephanie. 'So do I take it there's someone you want me to try and find?'

'Yes,' said Valerie. She took a paper tissue out of her handbag and dabbed at her eyes. 'I want you to try and find a friend of mine who went missing a year ago. He was my best friend actually and I miss him terribly'.

'Okay' said Stephanie. 'What was his name?'

'Liam Jenkins'.

'And when you say he went missing, how do you mean exactly?'

'His car was found abandoned on a quiet road near to some cliffs up at Palm Beach. The door to the drivers' side was open and the keys were still in the ignition'.

'Very mysterious' said Stephanie. 'And there was no sign of him I take it?'

'No' said Valerie. She stole herself for a moment and then carried on. 'Sorry. It's just that ... well he was almost like a son to us'.

'So how did you get to know him?'

'He was one of the tenants at a block of apartments we own over at Manly. When he moved in, we just hit it off. He'd been estranged from his mother since he was little, and he'd never met his father. I think perhaps that my husband Ed and I kind of filled those roles for him in a way, you know?'

'I do. Did he have a job?'

'Yes. At the Southern Cross bank downtown. He looked after the business accounts including ours'.

'Girlfriend or boyfriend?'

'Neither' said Valerie. 'When it came to personal relationships, he was rather confused about himself. He wanted to have relationships with women but it didn't feel right and yet he insisted he didn't feel gay either'.

'Do you have a photograph of him?'

'Yes, of course' said Valerie. She took the photo of Liam out of her handbag and gave it to Stephanie. Liam was sitting on a chair in the back garden of her house dressed in a vest like top and shorts. He had a can of VB in his hand and he looked very relaxed.

'He's certainly handsome' said Stephanie. 'Where does he get his dark looks from?'

'His mother was a white Australian but his father was Syrian'.

'Hence the dark eyes and black hair?'

'That's right'.

'Could he have just taken off and tried to start again somewhere else?'

'No' said Valerie, firmly. She leaned forward to make her point. 'I've gone through that over and over in my head and I really don't think that was the case. I knew Liam. I was probably closer to him than anybody. He wouldn't do that to his friends and all the people who cared about him. He'd been given the cold shoulder by all of his family but he'd built his own family with his circle of friends and he wouldn't have done that to us. If he'd wanted to do that he'd have told us and planned it. He wouldn't have just taken off and abandoned his car like that. Something happened to make him act in that way. He wouldn't have done it off his own back'.

'When did you last see him?'

'The night before he disappeared he came over to our place. He had dinner with Ed and I, we talked, we watched telly for a while and then he went home. I rang him the next day, like I rang him most days, and left him a message which I often did because he was at work. But when he didn't return it I rang him again because he always returned my calls. Then I rang him again and then again and then I saw the item on the local evening news which showed his car'.

'And that's when you knew?'

'Yes. It was a terrible shock as you can imagine. I've never heard anything from him since then. Nobody has'.

'What do the police say about it?'

'They've concluded that it was suicide and closed the case' said Valerie, her voice full of exasperation. 'Traces of his DNA were found in the space between his car and the cliff top. They think it all got too much for him and in a moment of despair he threw himself off. But they've never found a body'.

'That's not unusual in the cases of people throwing themselves into the Tasman' Stephanie pointed out.

'I know and if he didn't throw himself off that cliff then it looks like he simply vanished into thin air which of course is ridiculous' Valerie went on. 'But I've come to you, Stephanie, because I'm convinced that Liam didn't commit suicide. As mixed up as he was Liam wouldn't have done that. He had an inner strength that got him through all the adversities he'd faced in life'.

'You seem pretty certain of what he wouldn't have done, Valerie'.

'Because I knew him, Stephanie' said Valerie, intensely. 'Suicide may have crossed his mind, but he'd never have gone through with it. He wanted to be happy. He wanted to lay his demons to rest, and he would've done sooner or later'.

'Not everybody finds happiness in life, Valerie'.

'No but they don't all commit suicide either,' said Valerie. 'And Liam wouldn't have done. He just wouldn't'.

'Okay, well tell me more about yourself, Valerie'
 'Why?'
 'To help me gain an understanding of those close to him'
 'Why don't you tell me about yourself first?' Valerie asked. She preferred to gain the upper hand on someone before they gained it on her. 'Your accent is native but there's somewhere else in there?'

    Stephanie smiled. This lady was good. She'd successfully turned the focus away from herself. She was manipulative and there was far more to her than you'd get from any first impression. 'Well, you're right my accent isn't native although I've lived here for over fifteen years. I'm originally from the UK'.

'Do you go back very often?'

'I haven't been back since my father's funeral almost a couple of years ago'.

'I'm sorry,' said Valerie.

'He'd been ill for some time' Stephanie explained. 'It was a relief to be honest'.

'I understand,' said Valerie. 'So how come you were living here in the first place?'

'I moved out here from Nottingham in the East Midlands region of England with my husband and our two children for a better life like so many Brits do' Stephanie remembered. 'Two years later he moved back, and I stayed here'.

'And your children?'

'They went back with their father'.

'Ouch. And it still hurts?'

'Only every day' Stephanie admitted. 'I've missed out on so much to do with them. I used to go back every year to see them but then that had to stop'.

'Why?' asked Valerie. She liked Stephanie. Beneath the veneer she thought she might be detecting the same fragility that Valerie would acknowledge about herself.

'My ex-husband remarried, and his new wife thought it was unsettling to have me turn up every year' Stephanie explained. 'You know what it's like with some second wives. They have to make their mark and damn the consequences for everybody else. I wanted to fight it, but I didn't have the money and my ex-husband had legal custody. Besides, my kids didn't want to come back to Australia'.

'Why did your husband go back without you?'

'Because I was having an affair'.

'Ah. So that's why you stayed?'

'Yes,' said Stephanie. 'And God I've paid a high price for that decision'.

'Everybody judged you as a bad mother, right?'

'Oh, I was the wicked witch from Hell even as far as my own parents were concerned. I was hoping though that my children would grow up to hate their stepmother more for refusing to let me see them than they hated me for staying out here. But they've shown no signs of it yet. I have two boys, James and Matthew. James is taking a gap year soon before going to university and I'm hoping he'll come down here to see his old Mum. I'd be so happy if he did. Anyway, it sounds like you know a thing or two about this sort of thing?'

'Oh, believe me I wrote the book on screwed up relationships between mothers and children,' said Valerie. 'And I do know what it's like when it feels like the whole world is judging you for it. I have a daughter. Her name is Alison. She lives up in Queensland and runs a hotel in Port Douglas with her husband Rory. They've got three children who we see from time to time and one of my grandsons is at university here in Sydney, so we see him a fair amount which is lovely. He seems to like his grandma and granddad and we've become good mates'.

'How long have you been married to Ed?'

'Getting on for thirty years. I wasn't always sure that Ed and I would end up together. We went through a hell of a lot in the early days and we both wasted far too many years married to other people. But you can't fight your destiny'.

'True love?'

'Well, yes, I think it is true love' said Valerie, smiling broadly. She worshipped the ground Ed walked on. She always had done. 'But what about you? Are you with anyone now?'

'No' said Stephanie who quite envied Valerie's position in her personal life. She'd love to have some family around her, and it had been a while since she'd even been out with anyone. She didn't like being on her own. She didn't suit it. 'I'm between men as they say'.

'It didn't work out with the man you stayed here for?'

'We were happy for a few years, but I'd had a difficult time with Matthew's delivery and couldn't have any more children. He said it didn't matter to him and he was happy just with me. Then he had an affair with a girl he worked with, and she subsequently became pregnant. All of a sudden being a father meant everything to him. So, he left me for her'.

'That must've hurt?'

'Oh, it did at the time, yes' Stephanie agreed. 'I thought it was judgement on me for having done the dirty on my ex-husband, but I got over that and started to move on. Now tell me, did Liam get on as well with Ed as he did with you?'

'Oh yes' said Valerie. 'He was close to us both'.

'And do all of his friends believe as you do that he didn't take off for somewhere else or commit suicide?'

'Yes, they all absolutely do agree with me,' said Valerie.

'Stephanie, something happened to Liam that night. I want to know what that was. I miss him. I miss his laughter and I want him back in our lives'.

'I'll do my best, Valerie. It isn't encouraging that the police put it down to suicide but I'll do some preliminary research and then I'll be back to you for some more details'.

Stephanie went through her fees and Valerie paid the deposit with her bank card.

Would you say that Liam was happy when he disappeared?' Stephanie asked.

'No, but deep down he was never happy. He was a tortured soul. But he was desperate to belong, and he did belong with us and the rest of his friends'.

'And he gave no indication that anything like this would happen?'

'No' said Valerie. 'None of it makes any sense at all, Stephanie, absolutely none of it'.

Valerie walked briskly over to where Ed's car was parked a little way down the street. He looked up from doing the crossword in the morning paper when Valerie got in.

'How did that go?' he asked.

'Pretty well, I think,' said Valerie. 'She seems very capable and quite understanding. I really quite liked her'.

'Did you tell her the real reason why you want to find Liam?'

Valerie couldn't believe he'd actually asked her that. 'Ed, finding Liam could mean the answer to all our problems'.

'So you didn't tell her'.

'No I didn't tell her, Ed! And there's no reason for her to know'.

'I haven't seen this side of you for a long time, Val' said Ed in his usual quiet way that signalled disapproval. 'I thought all these games were well behind us'.

'Ed, I haven't been pushed into a corner like this for a long time and it's not a very comfortable place to be, let me tell you. But I'm doing this for the both of us, Ed. Don't you ever forget that'

'Oh I won't, Val, I won't. But that's what scares me the most. I know more than anybody what you're capable of'.